MIKE BRAVO OPS: ZEUS

EDEN FINLEY

TRIGGER WARNINGS_

While this is still the low-angst fun you can expect from an Eden Finley book, these guys have a lot of baggage. A lot, a lot. This book deals with recovery from domestic violence, sex trafficking/dub-con, torture, mentions of suicide and suicide ideation, and Mike Bravo's body count increases significantly without hesitation or guilt.

CHAPTER ONE_

ZEUS

THE MASSIVE SIGN OUTSIDE OF TRAV'S RANCH READS, "Welcome to the wedding of Andrew and Andrew."

The sign throws me. Atlas and Lemon, as we know them, both having the same first name is some weird twist of fate.

Trav's living-slash-dining room has been emptied of its furniture and replaced with large round reception tables and wedding decor. White ribbons drape from the ceiling, potted plants with fairy lights line a square big enough for a dance floor, and the whole place is decked out in white.

As I pass all of that and head for the wide-open glass doors leading to the backyard, there's an arrow to the left saying "Groom's side" and another pointing to the right, which also says "Groom's side."

I'd laugh if it wasn't so sickeningly cutesy.

Trust Atlas to go all out. His wedding is like a fairy tale and completely different to what you'd think he'd want if you didn't know him the way we do. But this actually screams Atlas.

He got his man.

And I'm happy for him. I really am.

But all this love is … catching. First, Iris fell—someone I never thought would—and then our boss, Trav. Now Atlas.

Though Atlas is the first one to make it down the aisle.

I spot Iris with his partner, Saint, and go sit in their row next to them, singing, "Another One Bites the Dust."

The sun is shining, though lowering toward the horizon. It's the perfect backdrop with sunset falling over the vast, empty planes of Palm Desert.

"You're next," Iris says, but it sounds more like a threat.

To me, it is.

There's a reason my name is Zeus, and it's not because I'm a god. Even if I tell people that's why. I'm not known for monogamy. Or relationships, really. Like everyone says, I fuck anyone who has a heartbeat. All consensually, of course. It's easy for me to find willing participants, and that's not being conceited. If anything, it's kind of sad. Sometimes it feels like how I look is my only personality trait. At least to other people.

Instead of denying that I, in any way, shape, or form, will be the next person to fall in love, I goad Iris. "Hell, at this rate, I'll be married before you two." I lean around him and say to Saint, "When *are* you tying the knot?"

They refuse to make eye contact with each other as a blanket of awkwardness passes over them.

My work here is done.

"I hear there's a new guy starting at Mike Bravo," Iris says.

"Nice subject change," I point out.

"I'm just saying, new gay guy on the team. Fresh blood. Someone who doesn't know you're a walking venereal disease."

"I'll have you know my last physical showed a perfect bill of health. So suck it. Also, you know it's against the rules. You found a loophole because you're in love or whatever, and that's something I'm not willing to do just so I can get some sex."

Saint leans in closer to his boyfriend. "Statistically, Zeus has probably already had sex with the new guy anyway."

I mock offense to that. "You've been with Iris for too long. You're starting to snark like him."

"Saint has always had snark," Iris says. "But he knew how to hold it in until me. You're welcome, world."

"On second thought, maybe you two shouldn't get married. You should break up instead. You won't be able to do as much damage that way."

"Damage to your ego? It could take a hit. Or ten." Iris smiles innocently, but Saint grabs his arm.

"Babe, I might have less of a filter, but I still know when to shut up."

"Eh, it's okay," I say. "My ego really could be taken down a peg. The only problem is with Iris. I know he's as full of shit as I am, so his words have no effect on me."

Iris and I love the fuck out of each other. Platonically.

"When does the open bar start?" I ask.

"After the ceremony," Saint says.

"And how long does that go for?" I shift in my seat.

"Scared you're going to combust?" Iris asks. "It's not like we're in a church."

"Scared I really am going to be next. Don't let me hook up tonight. Doing that at a wedding will bring you bad luck."

Saint frowns. "I don't think that's a thing. If anything, I've heard a lot of people meet the love of their life at weddings."

"Exactly. All the bad luck in the world."

"You know who you sound like?" Iris smirks, and I don't want to know, but he doesn't let me say that. "Me. Before this guy happened." He wraps his arm around Saint.

"And if I continue to avoid this supposed love of my life, I won't ever fall. See? Win-win."

"With how many hookups you have, statistically—"

I cut Saint off. "Nope. No more statistics. Shhh." I reach over and put my finger over his lips.

Music starts playing, and Iris stands, knocking my hand away. "That's my cue."

"His cue?" I ask.

Saint sighs as Iris walks away. "Iris insisted on letting Princess Smooshy Face be the ring bearer."

Iris disappears around the side of the house and comes back with his German shepherd ... wearing a white dress. The dog, not Iris. Though I wouldn't have put it past him.

"Do Atlas and Lemon know about that?" I ask Saint.

"Yes, but I think they thought he was joking."

Trust Iris to bring the entertainment, but not only has he made Princess the ring bearer, but he's assigned himself the role of flower person.

He walks down the aisle, throwing white flower petals above his head while Princess tries to catch them in her mouth.

Iris struts, and he spins, continuously reaching into a black fanny pack around his waist to pull out more petals.

Saint groans. "He's ridiculous."

"You're the one who fell in love with him."

"Just goes to prove you can't help who you fall in love with. Maybe one day, you'll learn that."

"And maybe one day, an asteroid might hit the earth and kill everyone. The chances of me falling are probably about the same."

He pats my arm, and I think it's supposed to be in sympathy. "I can't wait to see it."

"The asteroid?"

"You. Falling ass over tit in love."

Hope he's not holding his breath.

———

The best thing about weddings is the open bar. I'm happily tipsy before the grooms come back from having photos taken. And by tipsy, I mean delightfully Zeus-y.

But I'm still sober enough to remember I'm not allowed to hook up here. Even if Atlas's groom is a hot stripper with hot stripper friends.

Dick will remain in pants at all times.

In fact, as soon as anyone tempting approaches me, I walk away. Or hide behind Iris and Saint.

Atlas and Lemon are introduced as husbands—again. They already did that at the ceremony, so now it seems they're merely rubbing it in everyone's faces. After they make their rounds, greeting their guests while looking sickeningly in love, it's our turn to congratulate them.

My drunkenness is at that perfect level of happy where other people's views don't affect my own, and I can put on a smile and not ruin their day by holding back from rambling about how marriage is an outdated way of owning people. Lucky for them.

"I'm soooooo happy for you," I say to Atlas as I hug him.

He pats my back hesitantly. "Who are you, and where is the real Zeus?"

Iris steps in. "The real Zeus is being drowned by drunk Zeus."

"I'm not that drunk." My gaze focuses on a group of guys behind the grooms. "Oh no. Hot stripper friends coming this way."

I spin on my heel and walk away as fast as possible back outside to the ceremony area.

When footsteps sound behind me, I tense. I've been doing a really, really, really good job of avoiding the sexy people at this wedding, but if the opportunity presents itself, I'm going to be screwed. Literally.

I turn back and let out a relieved breath.

It's Atlas.

"Are you okay?"

"Yup. Just taking a vow of celibacy."

"You're *what*? Are you dying?"

I laugh. "It's only for tonight."

He relaxes again. "Oh, phew. I was really worried for a minute there."

"What's up? Shouldn't you be inside with all your guests?"

Atlas glances behind him and then steps closer to me. "I ... I need a favor."

"If it has anything to do with having sex with your husband because you can't satisfy him—"

"It's definitely *not* that."

"Then hit me."

"I need it to be off the books."

I cock a brow. "Intrigue."

"The thing is, you know how everything went down between Lemon and Callie ..."

Atlas's new husband got himself in some trouble about a year ago, thanks to his friend Callie. Callie's actions almost cost Atlas and Lemon their lives. But I could see what a lot of other people couldn't when it came to Callie. The dude was messed up after months of physical and psychological abuse by the hand of his boyfriend. His boyfriend was pulling the strings and made Callie spy on Lemon and everyone else at the strip club where they worked. Callie was a broken man who betrayed his friends because he felt like he had to.

"I ... I need you to locate him for me," Atlas says.

In our line of work, tracking down bad guys, killing bad guys, and even torturing them is in the job description, but I'm scared to ask if that's what he wants me to do here.

Atlas is the new second-in-command in Mike Bravo, and while I'm a good Marine and know how to follow orders, I do still have some morals. Granted, not a lot, but some. And taking someone out for revenge when Lemon didn't actually get hurt is a line I'm not willing to cross. For my superior or not.

"What am I supposed to do with him when I find him?" I wait with bated breath.

Atlas screws up his face. "Not take him out. Jesus. Lemon's been mentioning him, wondering how he is. He's still mad at him, but I think because we can't say for sure whether or not Callie made it out alive, I figure the least we can do is find out so we can give Lemon closure."

The strip club burned to the ground when everything came to a head, but there were only two bodies found in the rubble: Callie's boyfriend, Stephen, and David, the owner of the club.

"Callie got out." I'm almost sure of it. They would have found teeth or burnt remains. The fire moved quickly, but it was put out nearly as fast.

"Then I need to be able to tell Lemon that Callie is okay and that he's moved on now that he was able to escape his old life."

His old life of controlling ex-partners and abuse. Can anyone really move on from that?

"And if he hasn't?" I ask. "Moved on from it?"

"Then we keep our mouths shut, and I never ordered you to do this."

"Got it, boss. When do I start?"

"As soon as you're sober." He turns to go back inside.

"Wait, I don't even get to nurse my hangover first?"

"No. I need to know where he is by yesterday."

And now, the open bar has shut down for me.

I can't drink, I can't fuck …

I may as well get to work.

CHAPTER TWO_

CALLIE

THE MOVIES MAKE RUNNING FOR YOUR LIFE LOOK SO much more romantic and freeing. When I had to do it over a year ago, I had nowhere to go, no one to turn to, and absolutely no idea how I would escape my old ways.

All I knew was that I wanted to be in the middle of nowhere. Less chance of being found that way. Only, I think my subconscious took that literally because that's how I've ended up here, in Nevada, working at a cafe off Extraterrestrial Highway, telling tourists about *the aliens*. If only the aliens would come take me away, then maybe I wouldn't be constantly looking over my shoulder.

I've jumped from place to place. LA to Fresno, Fresno to Reno. I thought Reno would stick, but it didn't take long for some casino thugs to connect me to other casino thugs coming after me. From there, I went to Salt Lake City before coming back to Nevada. I figured only a stupid person would stick around Nevada after being caught in Reno, so they'd be looking for me in other states.

I'm either really smart or really dumb. I haven't decided yet.

My life in the last eighteen months could be summed up as simple as lonely boy meets handsome, rich man who promises to take care of him. Said rich man hits boy, conditions him to do whatever rich man wants, therefore losing autonomy and the ability to make good decisions, causing the boy to screw over one of the only people who had ever been there for him.

I blew my entire life up, and for what? Why? Because I was scared of what Stephen could've done to me? Even with the fuckface dead, I'm still not free of him. Of his shady business dealings and people who want him to pay up.

A little hard when he's charred remains.

And they're not the only ones I'm hiding from. My dear friend Lemon, the one I screwed over most, fell in love with some PI guy who has an entire team of other PI guys who are goddamn muscular soldier types. They gave me twenty grand to start fresh, but instead, I ran back to Stephen the first chance I got, and then Stephen went after them. So not only did I put their lives in danger, but I also took their twenty grand and ran off with it.

Even though I haven't heard boo from them in the last twelve months, I don't think I'll ever be confident enough to say they aren't looking.

I've just been good at hiding from them so far.

And I have to hide. Until the day I finally accept that my life is worthless and hand myself over to whoever will put me out of my misery the quickest, my only goal is to survive any way I can.

Honestly, some days, I don't even know why I fight to be here. What's the point?

Seriously, where are the aliens when you need them?

Yet, somewhere, deep down inside of me, there's that natural response. The self-preservation that has gotten me through the last eighteen months. I always used to say that if there were a zombie apocalypse, I'd walk into the horde and give myself up. I wouldn't want to deal with the constant jump scares, the paranoia, the *surviving*. But here I am, living my own apocalypse, and I keep going.

I keep pushing.

And I have no idea why.

The bell over the door jingles as someone enters the cafe. For a moment, I think my dreams have been answered.

Tentacles and rubber skin, tall, slim bodies, and huge almond-shaped eyes bore into me. Then I remember where I am, what I do for a living, and the fantasy comes crashing down.

"What can I get you?"

One of the aliens takes off his giant rubbery head. "Two coffees. Black."

The other one murmurs through her mask. "Cream and sugar for mine." She sounds mad, like her alien in crime should know her drink order.

"What makes you think either of my coffees were for you?" He laughs.

"Asshole." She takes her mask off, too, and turns to me. "Can you tell us where the best place to find extraterrestrials is?"

Time for my spiel while I pour them coffee from the percolated batch I made three hours ago. I'd make a new pot if the cheap-ass boss didn't have strict rules about that kind of thing. I get it. We don't have a lot of foot traffic out here, so it's a waste to make a new batch for every new patron, but still. We should be doing better than gross stale coffee. I won't fight him on it, though. I'm not here to ruffle feathers. Just make a wage and be ready to flee at a moment's notice.

And as I'm in the middle of my spiel—"Many people have come out here looking for signs of life outside this world and have failed, but if you ask me, the best place to look is—"—the bell jingles again.

Time stops.

My gut sinks.

Because seeing a familiar face fills me with dread. Especially a face so pretty. All golden hair, chiseled jaw, and a perfect complexion.

Zeus.

One of Lemon's soldier-type friends.

The time to flee has come, but I can't fucking move, too

entranced by his good looks to process that he's here to kill me, not take off his shirt like he did the first time I'd ever seen him. It was only within minutes of meeting him. I was joking when I'd asked him to do it, but he did it anyway. He made me laugh.

When Lemon "rescued" me from Stephen, Zeus was assigned to watch over me and my injuries that Stephen had given me.

Which I willingly took.

Like an idiot.

Zeus's lips quirk as he sees me, and as much as I'd like to say it's because he's happy to see me, it's probably more in a "Gotcha!" kind of way.

I'm too distracted by him that I don't notice the coffee cup in front of me is full, and I keep on pouring. "Fuck. So sorry." I reach for some napkins, but the dispenser is being a pain in the ass. "Let me duck out back and grab a towel." Or run like my ass is on fire. One or the other. Definitely the other.

I almost get away with it too, but at the very last second, I lose my focus. Maybe my survival instinct isn't so great after all because I can't resist one more look at the man who's been sent to kill me. I still think he's the most gorgeous man I've ever met.

His delicious features fall because, with that one look, he knows what I'm planning. I just need to get to my car faster than he can get to his.

I bolt through the kitchen doors, send up a silent apology to my boss for skipping out on him, and ignore the "Motherfucker" being hissed behind me.

The employee entrance is a fire door, so it can't be locked from the inside, and I'm smart enough to have parked right outside it.

It's impossible to tell if the footsteps echoing off the kitchen tiles are my own or Zeus's because the sound is competing with the erratic heartbeat in my ears.

I suppose it would've been too much to ask him if he could hold off on all the killing until I could fill the coffee orders and clear the register of cash to give me a leg up.

The money Lemon and the Mike Bravo guys gave me dried up really fucking quickly, even with scraping by on staying in low-budget motels the whole time. I'm talking Norman Bates–type motels where it was lucky I even made it out alive.

Now, I'm living out of my car—the biggest thing I spent my seed money on—and it's a good arrangement. There's a by-the-hour motel nearby where I'll pay to shower, but other than that and gas, my living expenses have become manageable. I eat from the horrible microwave meals at the cafe and use the bathrooms at work. I wish I'd developed this system earlier, while I still had some money behind me, because it's perfect.

Was perfect.

Now, I have to start over again.

That's if I can even get away.

I don't glance behind me again until I'm safely locked in my run-down Mazda CX5, and by that time, Zeus has caught up and thrown himself on the hood.

He's still got that smile—the one that says he's got me—and I know he's not going to let me get away. But he doesn't know what lengths I've gone to just to stay alive. Roughing up a pretty guy is low on the terrible things I've done.

I start the car and floor it, my tires flicking up dust behind me as I tear away from the cafe. Zeus manages to keep hold, and for a quick minute, I'm sure he'll be able to hold on forever. Or until I run out of gas.

But the corner is too much for him, and he flies off the side as I turn onto the interstate. I have two options from here.

Head south for Vegas and get lost in a crowd, or turn west and go back to California. The thought of returning home to where I got my nickname fills my gut with regret, guilt, and dread.

Vegas it is.

CHAPTER THREE_

ZEUS

I HIT THE DESERT GROUND AND SEND DUST FLYING AS I roll to try to protect all my vital organs from going splat.

That prick tried to kill me.

When I come to a stop, scraped to shit and breathing hard, I smile.

Callie's challenging me to chase him even harder. Not that it was difficult to find him in the first place. Through some undesirable contacts, I found out he'd been hiding out in Reno for a while. From there, it wasn't hard to follow his movements. Poor guy didn't even know how to register his car using a fake name.

Rookie move for someone on the run. Though, in his defense, he probably thought anyone looking for him would be searching for a stripper named California-slash-Callie, not Sam Eckles. Sweet summer child.

I slowly stand and check myself over while still trying to catch my breath, and other than some wicked road rash down my right side, I'm relatively unscathed; I've had worse injuries in my line of work. I take my phone out of my pocket and use the camera feature in selfie mode. At first, I think he broke my face, but it's okay. It's just my phone screen. I hold my chest and breathe in relief.

My phone still works, even with the crack, so I hit Atlas's number.

He answers with, "Hang on. Let me …" There's some shuffling around and the sound of a door closing. "What's the update?"

"Well, I found him."

"Alive?" Atlas croaks.

"And fiery as fuck. Asshole threw me off the hood of his car. While. It. Was. Moving."

Atlas tries to cover a chuckle but fails. "Is your face okay?"

"Luckily for him. Now hunting him down will be extra fun instead of a revenge plot for the sake of my ego. Unless, that's all you need from me? He's still got all four limbs, looked healthy, had a job. A shitty car, but I mean, how much money can he be making slinging stale coffee in the middle of alien central. Now that I've run him off, though, I don't think he has anywhere to go."

"Uh, let me talk to Lemon and get back to you on that. He doesn't know I'm looking for Callie, but I'll put it to him as a hypothetical."

"You know, I think this is the first time someone that hot has ever run away from me," I say. "Let me stay on it a while more. Maybe if I can pin him down—"

"Do not have sex with Callie," Atlas orders.

"I don't mean it in that way." Though, I wouldn't turn him down if he offered. We're similar in appearance, both of us with blond hair and blue eyes, but my features are often called pretty, whereas Callie has this thing about him. Not hardened or soft. Laid-back? If that's a thing. He really does look like a carefree Cali boy … you know, when he doesn't look terrified.

But thinking about how Callie is a good-looking guy is a waste of time. Considering he bolted the second he laid eyes on me, I'm guessing he doesn't want any other part of him to be laid on me.

Huh. So that's what rejection feels like.

Do I like it, or do I not like it? I'm not sure. But I do know after our interaction here, I'm looking forward to whatever he can throw at me next.

I should probably see a shrink about that, but meh. Why pay for therapy when C4, guns, and a good old game of cat and mouse can be as cathartic?

"Tell me when you have him," Atlas says. "I'll hold off a little longer before potentially upsetting Lemon."

"Aww, how sweet." I don't mean it to come out sarcastic, but it does. "I know that sounded insincere, but I really mean it." That came out sarcastically too. "I do! I mean it. Why does my voice sound like I don't? I'm trying to be nice!"

Atlas laughs again. "Just chase after him, okay? Trav's been asking what kind of job you're on, and I can't keep covering for you."

I snort. "You mean for *you*, right? Because I'm doing this for your husband."

"That too. But I don't want Trav to think I'm using my new position for personal gain. If it were up to me, we'd never utter Callie's name in our house again."

"Yet, you do. Because you're in love. Reason number five hundred and sixty-four of why I'll never fall."

"Yeah, yeah, you're aromantic and all that other jazz. We get it. Just do the job while keeping your dick in your pants. Think you can manage it?"

Aromantic? Atlas thinks I'm aromantic? Is that a thing I could be?

"Zeus?"

I snap out of a possible revelation and answer him. "I can manage it. Do dick, pants job."

Atlas sighs. "Close enough."

I have no idea which direction Callie went, and it takes me a day of driving in the wrong direction to get an alert on his car. He's in Vegas.

With a quick U-turn, I change my course, but an hour later, I get a phone call from Trav telling me to drop everything and come back to the office. There's a team meeting and what I'm assuming is some fuckery afoot.

Or Atlas broke and told Trav what I'm really doing out here, and he's pulling me off the personal job for a more important one.

I turn around yet again and make it to HQ in six hours. Navigating the halls of headquarters feels like coming home, and as I make my way to the war room where meetings take place, the sense of camaraderie and family is strong.

The majority of the team is here, and the meeting is underway already.

I hold my arms out. "Started without me?"

"Contrary to what you might believe, Zeus, not everything is about you," Trav says.

"Lies," I protest.

"Hurry up and sit. We've got some things to cover."

I take the available seat next to Decaf, right by the door, and lean in and whisper to him, "What things are we covering?"

"New guy," he whispers back. "And thank fuck because we need some help."

I want to argue with that because if Trav can call eight out of thirteen men back with only a few hours' notice, we're all probably not working very hard. Though everyone will be dispersing back to our current assignments after we're done here.

"What job you on?"

"Bounty hunt," Decaf says. "Have to stake out some house my mark is known to frequent, and I can't even sneak away for more coffee."

I mock gasp.

"Are you two done?" Trav barks.

Like scolded schoolkids, we both sit up straighter and pay attention.

"Now, as I was saying …" Trav waves a finger toward the doorway, and in walks a young guy who looks barely twenty. Did I pass him in the hall? Was he there the whole time? "Everyone, this is the new guy, Haz."

Decaf growls beside me. Almost imperceptible, but I hear it. He's probably pissed because breaking in new guys is a challenge, and this one … Seriously, is he even legal?

"Haz, as in *has* he even graduated high school?" I ask.

Iris smirks over at me. "Jealous you won't be the youngest anymore?"

"Youngest-looking," Scout says. "I'm a few months younger than Zeus."

I flip off my old Marine buddy. Iris, Saint, Scout, and I are all about to turn thirty, and the only reason we're the youngest in Mike Bravo is because we haven't recruited lately. We were a full team until Domino left.

If anything, the growl beside me only gets louder. "His name is Hazard. As in, hiring him is a fucking hazard."

"Dude, have you had enough caffeine today?" I ask Decaf.

Decaf stands. "This has nothing to do with coffee. Haz is too young, and this job is too dangerous."

My gaze flicks to Haz, who's standing defiantly, eyes narrowed toward Decaf.

"I'm guessing there's a history here?" I ask. "I know you like 'em young, Decaf, but—"

"No," Decaf barks.

"Someone get this guy an espresso, stat," I call out.

"Come on, old man," Haz says. "Why don't you tell them exactly how you know me?" The kid's blue eyes shine bright, and with only a few words, I've decided I like him.

He has spunk. Fire.

"It doesn't matter how we know each other because you're not working here," Decaf says.

Trav's frowning, flicking his attention back and forth like he's trying to figure out what's happening without asking. "Okay, we're going to have to talk about this." He turns to Haz. "Is there something you didn't tell me when you came to me looking for a job?"

"Nothing relevant," Haz says.

"Seems relevant to me. You, Decaf, in my office now." They exit the room together, leaving the rest of us to glance around, hoping one of us knows what's up.

We don't.

After fifteen minutes of speculating, Iris jumps out of his seat. "Meeting adjourned, then?"

"Stick close," Atlas says. "We'll probably call you back as soon as they get through whatever their issue is."

As we all stand, Atlas gives me the all-telling up-nod that says he wants to speak to me. We go into his office, and he closes the door behind us.

"Any update?"

"I got an alert on his plates. He's in Vegas."

"Keep tracking him."

"Yessir."

"And don't get distracted with slots and strip shows."

"Aww, where's the fun in that?"

There's a knock on Atlas's door, and Trav enters with the new kid. "Oh, good. You haven't run off yet. You know that mission Atlas has you on that you both claim is nothing but is totally something, but I trust you enough not to ask you about it?"

Can't get anything by our boss, I swear.

"Uhhh …"

Trav waves Atlas off. "That was rhetorical. New plan. Haz is going with you." He shoves Haz toward me. "Bye, have fun. Zeus, don't corrupt the new guy unless you want your balls chopped off."

"Did you and Rogue decide to have a young boy toy to share? Is that what's happening with the threats?"

Trav points at me. "And don't make jokes like that. Off-limits."

That's an interesting development. While hooking up with teammates is forbidden—or at least frowned upon—joking about it has never been an issue.

I turn my attention to Haz. "Okay, who *are* you?"

Haz's lips turn upward. "Hazard. Weren't you listening?"

To laugh or slap the shit out of him? It's a difficult choice. Trav doesn't know what he's getting into, hiring a guy like … well, me. "Okay, weirdo. Let's roll out. It's a long drive to Vegas."

CHAPTER FOUR_
CALLIE

I'M ALL OUT OF OPTIONS.

It's official. Nowhere is safe.

If Lemon's new muscled friends can find me, anyone can.

Which is why I'm standing outside the Ruby Resort and Casino, trying to get the courage to walk in there and ask Pierre Claremont to let me pay off Stephen and David's debt in exchange for protection. Even if Pierre is one of those people I need protection from. But I figure he might let me work for him. Sure, I'll probably be selling my body, my dignity, my soul, but I'll have a roof over my head and one less group of goons on my ass.

There's no other way to keep fighting. To keep running. There's no other way out other than ...

I don't let myself think about that. Not in depth. I'm worried I'd start to like the idea too much.

Hell, I have no idea why I haven't done it already.

I should give up. The world would be no different without me in it.

No one would care.

A car on the Strip backfires, and I jump a mile high.

Paranoid, I glance around at the millions of people walking by me. My hood is up, sunglasses on, but I'm sure I could still be recognized if I'm being followed ... If Zeus even got back up after I hit him with my car.

At what point did I stop being a victim and really become a bad guy? The first time I took Stephen back after he hurt me? The second? When he and David took me to secret meetings with assholes like the one I'm about to face and involved me in all their shit?

Or was it when I had no morals left, only fear, and the only thing getting me through was my survival instincts?

I chose my survival over people I care about. I'm selfish.

Stephen was right: I do deserve to be treated badly because it's not as if I'm any better than him.

It's those dark thoughts that get my feet moving toward the doors of the casino. Even if I only make it as far as the dingy back room where they take card counters, cheaters, and addicts who owe money before they put a bullet in my head, at least they'll do what I've been too scared to do. What that fucked-up survival instinct won't let me do.

The casino smells like smoke, sweat, and really bad decisions. If it also had the scent of dried cum, it could be mistaken for Peaches, the old strip joint I used to work at before it burned down.

I barely get through the door when two security guys approach me.

"Pierre's been looking for you," Goon One says, as if I didn't already know the guys after me in Reno were in the same ring.

"I tried to disappear, but it turns out, life will always catch up to me. I want to see him."

They look at each other with confused looks on their faces, mimicking that of dogs who cock their head when trying to work out what you're saying to them.

I get it. Me, voluntarily turning myself over to the fuckwits Stephen was involved with? No sane person would do it.

So, actually, yeah, checks out.

Because as much as I like to think I have a good head on my

shoulders, my life choices so far leave a lot to be desired.

I'm led—no more like escorted—to Pierre's office in the dim, darkened halls in the bowels of the casino, where "high rollers" take part in high-stakes games where they pay with their lives if they can't cough up what they lose. And by high rollers, I mean anyone stupid enough to trust Pierre's establishment and are willing to bet everything they have and more for a chance to win big.

Which is exactly the issue both David and Stephen got involved in.

What happens when a strip club owner becomes indebted to one of the biggest loan sharks in Vegas? Why, he brings in the heir of an entire bank fortune to gamble away even more than what David owed.

To try to pay back their debts, David started taking from the club. Stephen would make payments direct to Pierre. But now that they're dead, and I know their debts were nowhere near paid off, Pierre will be looking for his money.

Pierre knows me because I was always something shiny to distract the other players at games. David even offered me up to Pierre once. In exchange for a new line of credit, of all things. Could've at least bartered to have some of his debts wiped for my "services."

The worst part? When I protested, Stephen, my boyfriend, the person who was supposed to love me, agreed to it.

Yeah, Stephen was a real winner. Luckily for me, though, Pierre didn't want me. At least, not reluctantly.

So here I am, willingly offering myself up to pay off Stephen's debts. And for what? So I can live an extra day? A month? A year?

What am I doing? What is wrong with me?

Instead of learning lessons, I'm making it worse.

This was a mistake.

I stop walking, but the two big guys next to me box me in.

I snap my fingers. "Actually, you know what? I left something in my car. I might go and—"

They grab an arm each and start to drag me the last few steps to Pierre's office.

Honestly, I thought that plan was too dumb to work, but I was hoping these guys were even dumber. Apparently not.

Men with muscles and the tiniest bit of intelligence? If I wasn't so scared, I'd be turned on.

Someone inside opens the door for us as we get to it, no doubt having been watching us over security cameras.

I'm thrust inside Pierre's office, where he sits like a mob boss wannabe. The only thing missing from his evil Frenchness is the thin mustache he could twirl between his fingers.

"Aren't you a vision in my painful eyes," he says in his French accent, which I'm totally sure he emphasizes on purpose.

"That's ... not—" No, there's no point correcting the wrong turn of phrase.

"I was sorry to hear about your Stephen," he says. "Sort of. I like a good payday, but I can't say I'll miss that weasel."

You and me both.

Only, that's not entirely true. I don't miss Stephen per se, but I do miss that security and knowing that even though he treated me like shit, that I had someone. I had a home. Being alone this past year has made me ... well, lonely.

"I know he still owed you money," I say and swallow hard.

"And let me guess. You're here with a million dollars in your pocket and are willing to hand it all over."

"A mill ... he owes you a million—"

He waves me off. "I'm rounding up. Let's call it interest."

"I am here to make a deal, but I have no money to my name. I have nothing to give you, but I can work it off. In your casino, in your private poker nights. I'll ..." *It's this or death. It's this or death.* "I'll do anything you ask of me." I lower my head because even though I've stripped and Stephen made me do ... other things, it still feels shameful to sell my body.

When Pierre doesn't answer and I lift my head again, he's

staring at me, lips pursed.

"There's no way you can earn enough to pay back what was owed. No one would pay that much for a whore."

He's right about that. If I do this, I'm signing my life, my body, my time ... all for a dead guy.

You'll be dead if you don't.

I have one card to play. One card that could make the debt go away and where I could get Pierre's protection from anyone else on my tail.

"Not even you?" I ask.

I know he had a thing for me. Wants me. But he wanted it when I was a willing participant. Here I am, being willing.

His lips quirk. "I knew you'd come around one day, but no. I cannot wipe your debt—"

"Stephen's debt," I correct. "I have no debt."

"That's where you're wrong, mon cheri. You and Stephen came to my poker games together, so it is yours. I'm not willing to clear your slate for one night with you, and I get the feeling you're not here for only that. Tell me what it is you truly want."

A husband who takes care of me. A white picket fence. Children who have happy homes instead of the childhood I had. I want a lot of things that I can't have. Not if I'm constantly on the run. Not if I have people after me.

"You're not the only debt Stephen had, and you're not the only crime lord who wants me dead."

"Ah. You need my protection."

And as stupid as this makes me, as naïve as I've become, when he says the word *protection*, I feel safe.

Even though I know I'm not.

"That, I can work with," Pierre says.

I should have escaped while I had the chance because now? I owe my life to this man.

And he won't hesitate to take it if I screw up.

I would've been better on my own. It's not like Zeus could track me forever. I've probably already lost him. I'm sure of it.

CHAPTER FIVE_

ZEUS

"WHAT THE FUCK IS CALLIE DOING?" I MUTTER AS I watch Callie walk into the Ruby Casino. "He has to have a death wish."

"Who's doing what with the who now?" Haz asks, leaning forward in the passenger seat and staring out the windshield.

"That guy"—I point to where Callie disappeared inside—"was our mark."

"He was cute. Are we allowed to sleep with marks?"

I wish. "It's against the rules. Believe me, I've asked." Though, Atlas slept with a mark. Trav fell for his. Iris slept with someone else on the freaking team.

I'm beginning to think Trav's rules are all bullshit. Or that they only apply to me because ... okay, yeah, fair enough.

"Damn. What's his deal? Why is he our mark?"

Haz has been asking the whole damn drive to Vegas, but considering this is a top-secret mission—or supposed to be—I don't know how much I can actually tell him.

"Let's just say he screwed over one of our own, so we're keeping an eye on him, and by the looks of it, we won't have to look out for him much longer."

"What do you mean?"

"That casino? Imagine the kind of mobsters from back in the day who used to run this town."

"They still have those?"

"Sort of. They've gotten progressively worse and more hipster-y over the years. And the guy in charge of this one is one of the worst. He has a casino here and in Reno. Multiple body count, and I'm not talking about the fun kind of bedroom body count."

"Oh. Dang. So we need to get this Callie guy out of there?"

I bite my lip. Technically, our job is to make sure he's okay. And he's breathing. For now.

I can't help but blame myself for this. Callie ran terrified from me. So terrified he'd choose Pierre Claremont over Mike Bravo to face? I'm seriously not that scary.

Then I think about who Callie is really running from, and okay, on the outside, Atlas is intimidating as hell. I guess Callie didn't get to see how much of a marshmallow he is underneath. Atlas sent me on this wild goose chase to make sure Callie was okay and living his best life, for fuck's sake.

"Yeah, we do." Because I know this isn't what Atlas wants. It's not what Lemon would want, so therefore, Atlas would want us to protect Callie at all costs.

"How do we go about it?"

"If we go in there guns blazing, it's pretty much putting a target on all of Mike Bravo."

"So it has to be stealth attack?" Haz rubs his hands together. "Awesome. They're my specialty."

"I gathered with the way you stealth attacked your way onto the team when it's obvious you have beef with Decaf." Fishing? Me? Never.

"Don't know what you're talking about."

"You totally slept together, didn't you? You into the whole daddy kink?"

Haz laughs. "He's no daddy."

"I'll get the story out of you one day."

"Yeah, probably. But not now. We have a damsel in distress to save."

I want to argue with him, but from what I've seen and experienced so far, yeah, damsel in distress definitely describes Callie.

"We need to come up with a plan," I say.

Haz shrugs. "I'm more of a wing-it kind of guy." He opens the car door and leaves me in a flurry.

The new guy is fast, and it's possible he's going to get us both killed for it.

I fight with my seat belt and chase after him, worried he's gone in exactly how I told him not to—ready for a fight or to cause a scene—but when I get inside, he's … nowhere to be seen.

Where the fuck did he go?

I scour the casino for both Haz and Callie but come up empty. That is, until I turn back toward where we came in, and I find Haz at the check-in counter.

I catch up to him just as he asks for the biggest suite in the place. Why we need that, I have no idea, but I like the way he thinks. Trav will kill us, though. We haven't even got eyes on Callie.

"That would be our penthouse on the top floor, and it's five thousand a night."

Yup. Trav will definitely kill us.

"And that will get us certain … perks?" Hazard turns on his charms, which I would normally find attractive if he weren't so baby-faced.

Huh. Apparently, I've found a type I won't go for, and that's guys who look like teenagers. Good to know I have boundaries. Go me.

"What perks were you after, sir?" The clerk has an attractive smile, but it looks like she's forcing it. As if she's expecting the next thing to come out of Haz's mouth to be something about hookers.

"Me and Daddy over here want to get in on some of the more … private poker games. For high rollers."

Daddy? He can fuck right off with that shit. I don't have the patience to be a daddy. Being a brat, on the other hand? Well, I thought I was a pro, but it turns out the new kid might upstage me.

"I'm afraid we don't have those kinds of games here, sir. It would go against the regulations and laws set by the Nevada Gaming Commission." She says this yet takes one of the hotel's business cards off her desk and writes a number down, passing it to Haz. "Now, would you like to book that room?"

Haz smiles back. "Yes. Thank you." Then the asshole turns to me, grips my shirt, and bats his eyelashes at me. "You'll give me the room I want, right, Daddy?"

When on an assignment, improv rules apply. You always answer with "Yes."

"Of course. Anything for my sugar baby." I slap his ass. Hard. I just hope he doesn't like it too much. Then I take out my company credit card and slap it down on the counter. The account name is under Dushay Richard. As in Douchey Dick. It's a persona we've all played at one point or another, and I guess it's my turn again.

Once we're in the room, I'll give Trav the heads-up, but considering we're not on an official job, I still don't see him being okay with this.

"Thank you, Mr. Richard. Would you like help with your luggage?"

Haz's gaze shoots to mine. Amateur. This is why you don't barge in without a plan. I can be reckless and fun, but I'm not stupid.

"This was more of a spur-of-the-moment, spontaneous getaway. We'll be needing clothes sent to our room too."

"Right away, sir. What attire would you like?"

"Suits. I'm a thirty-two long, and my boo here is a kid's size large." I wrap my arm around Haz's shoulder, and he elbows me in the gut.

"Always teasing about my size. I'm a thirty, regular. Because unlike other people I know, I grew to a perfectly average-sized human and stopped growing."

She laughs at us. "You two are going to be fun."

I wonder if she realizes there's absolutely no emphasis or passion when she says it. Maybe "fun" is code word for "a pain in the ass."

Wouldn't be the first time I'd have been called that.

She taps away on her computer and places two key cards into her machine that codes it to the right room, and then we're sent on our way up to the penthouse.

When we get into the elevator, I turn to Haz. "How did you know she'd give you the high-roller number?"

"If you act like you have money, they assume you have money."

"Okay, but if Trav asks, you stole the credit card from me and did this all on your own."

He laughs. "You didn't put up much of a fight."

"Sure, I did. At least, in my version of the events, I did."

"Right. All the fighting. The loud protests."

"Trav will believe me. I'm a very responsible guy."

Haz scoffs. "Everything I've heard about you tells me the opposite."

"What have you heard? No, how could you have time to hear anything? You joined us today."

"And the twenty minutes I was in the office told me everything I needed to know. First, when Trav suggested I partner with you and *Decaf* immediately said no way because everyone knows you would try to hook up with me. Then Trav told me that if anything happened between us, I would be fired. Then Trav dropped me off with you and left the room muttering something about this being a horrible idea to leave you unsupervised with me."

"Hey, Iris is the one who needs supervising. Not me."

"If you say so."

"Besides. They're wrong. You're not my type."

Haz's lips curl upward. "Do you have a type?"

No. "Yes."

"Who?"

"Not you."

Haz full-on laughs now. "I thought you'd be more fun than this. I was promised a sexy time."

The elevator spits us out on the top floor into a private corridor that leads to two large black doors.

"You were promised you'd be hit on. Contrary to what Trav and Decaf believe, I can behave."

Do I behave? Not usually. But that doesn't mean I can't if I have to.

"Nah, this is much better because I wouldn't have had the heart to tell you the whole pretty-boy thing doesn't do it for me."

"You say that as if you're not pretty."

"But that's why. I know how high-maintenance I can be. Screw dealing with another me."

Truth. "Yeah, I can see your point there. So, what's the plan?"

We push through the doors, and Haz takes a moment to whistle at the expansive apartment.

"Good plan," I deadpan. "While you check out the view, I'm going to call Trav and explain why there's going to be a charge for a ridiculous amount of money on his—" My phone cuts in, the shrill ring echoing around the room. "And he's already been notified." I answer the call. "I can explain." But the words die on my lips. Because apparently, I do have a heart and can't throw the new kid under the bus after all.

"I'm waiting," Trav growls.

"Our target—"

"The one Atlas sent you after?"

"Yeah, that one. He, uh … is kind of involved with Pierre Claremont."

"What the fuck is Callie doing?" Trav asks.

"You know what my job has been this whole time?" I exclaim.

"Of course I knew. It's cute you and Atlas think I couldn't

work it out. You need to get Callie out of there."

"I know. That's why we got the room. We need to look like high rollers so we can get close to Pierre or one of his goons and try to find Callie so we can bring him back to, well, Cali. The state. Not some kind of healing his trauma and finding his true self kind of thing."

From the living room of the penthouse, Haz snorts, the little eavesdropper.

"Let me know if you need anything from us," Trav says. "Especially before you get in too deep with Pierre yourselves. You don't want to get mixed up with all that."

"I dunno. It kinda sounds fun," I taunt.

"Let me rephrase. You don't want to get mixed up with all that because *I* don't want to get mixed up with Pierre. And if you kill the new guy on his first week on the job, Decaf will kill you."

"Ooh, you know things. Tell me, tell me, tell me. What's their deal?"

Trav sighs. "I've gotta go. Get back to work. Oh, but before you go, how much can I expect to be out of pocket for this Vegas trip?"

"Umm, a lot. Pierre is expensive. And to get to him, we have to have money."

"Hmm. Pulling someone out of a casino sounds like it could be a stealth snatch-and-grab. Do you really need the front?"

"We don't even know where Callie is. Last we saw him, he headed inside the casino and was swallowed up by two security guards." I don't mention that we could technically stay somewhere else or in a cheaper room until we find Callie. "Besides, it was the new guy's idea. You don't want him to feel unwelcome, do you?"

Trav groans. "Just get the job done as fast as you can, and don't die."

"Aww, you love—"

He ends the call.

Sounds about right.

CHAPTER SIX_

CALLIE

It's only been a day, and I'm already trying to figure out a way to get out of this situation with Pierre.

I was stupid to think he would actually protect me or treat me decently. It was naïve of me to think he'd keep me as some side toy he got to play with and put me up in a hotel room with food and clothing and anything else I might need.

When I offered him my body, he took it to another place. I'm not his toy but anyone's who wants me.

There's a high-stakes game tonight, and I'm going to be there. Flirting. Serving drinks. Wearing nothing but a bow tie and underwear that's two sizes too small.

Flashbacks to working at the club try to take over. Stephen coming to see me—only me. Him tempting me with big offers to make my life better.

I thought I was getting the world, and now I'm here, doing more than just taking my clothes off so I can survive.

The door into the bedroom I was shoved through earlier opens, and the Gaston-looking bodyguard who put me in here deposits another person. She's in a bra and panties, though that might be overdescribing the thin material she wears. I can't tell her age because her face is caked on with so much makeup I have no idea what she really looks like underneath, and her doe-eyed expression tells me she's either strung out or nervous.

"Hi," I say. "I'm Sam, but everyone calls me Callie."

Suddenly, her whole demeanor changes. She loses the doe-eyed nervousness, and her shoulders sag. "You're new here. Never give your real name, sweets. They'll use it against you."

"I was trying to make you more comfortable. You looked terrified."

"That's how they want me to look. I'm Arabella." She winks.

Arabella. Pretty. Innocent. Looks like she could be really young. I don't want to know the kind of man who pays Pierre to be with her.

She crosses the large bedroom, looking at home as she glides past the king bed and to the closet on the other side. She slips on a sheer robe to cover up, but I don't have the heart to tell her that it really doesn't cover anything.

"How long have you worked for Pierre?" I ask.

"Work for. Good one."

"How long have you been trapped here?" I rephrase, but the words taste bitter on my tongue.

I knew what I was getting into when I turned to Pierre, but now it's real. Too real. I shouldn't have come here, but I did. And now I'm unable to leave. Unable to say no.

"Forever," she whispers before turning to me. "Let me guess. Gambling addict? Got in way over your head?"

Isn't that the kicker? I'm here because that was my boyfriend. "I was collateral in my boyfriend's addiction."

"Oh, honey. That's even worse."

I look around the room, anywhere but at her, because I don't think I can stand the pity in her pretty eyes.

"Few things you should know. There are cameras everywhere, so don't even try to leave. You can't reject anyone. You can't lie and say you followed through when you didn't, because again, cameras."

"Wait. They even film ... in here?" I wave toward the bed.

"I'm sure Pierre has a collection worthy of some kind of porn awards. There's no audio, though, or if there is, it's inaudible."

My skin crawls. "Are they ... I mean, is that why you and I are in here together? Because you're gorgeous, you really are, but—"

"If they want you to bed someone, you do it."

Pierre knows I'm gay. Not everyone can be as fluid as he is. I wouldn't even know how to—

"But I'm not here for you," she adds.

I relax. A little.

"And tonight, there's only men invited."

I relax some more.

"But next time, you might not be so lucky."

My shoulders tense. My gut drops.

Because *next time.*

That's when it really dawns on me.

Just like when I was with Stephen, every hit, every punishment, every outburst ... No matter how many times he said it would never happen again, I knew he was lying.

There will always be a next time.

With no escape, there isn't even the option of begging for death. Because Pierre has me now. Why would he grant me mercy when I can make him money?

Okay, Callie. Get it together. Do not freak out. Do not break down.

"You look like you're going to pass out," Arabella says. "Here. Take one of these." She goes to the nightstand and pulls out a small tin. When she opens it to me, there's an array of pills all different colors and sizes.

"Is it a lucky dip?" I ask.

"Pretty much, but this one will help. It's an upper. I've also got this little blue one if you think you won't be able to perform." She points to what is clearly Viagra.

I'm tempted to take the upper because at least then I'll be buzzing, but this whole thing makes me feel sick. "Is there anything that will prevent me from throwing up?"

"Unfortunately, that's a skill you're going to need to learn all on your own."

Cue panic attack.

⸻

The night is slow to start. Men trickle in and take their seats. Arabella and I serve drinks, and she plays up the innocent act while I try to smile and speak as little as possible.

There's one guy who takes a shine to me, and even though he's older, at least he doesn't look slimy like the men interested in Arabella.

There are two more empty seats remaining, but the men have started playing, so I don't know if they'll be filled or not. I hope they stay empty. The one guy who's interested in me here doesn't seem too scary, and I'm confident I could handle him. The not knowing who could show up is making me more nervous than it would to see exactly who else I have to deal with. If at all.

At least if I knew what I was getting into, I could prepare myself mentally.

Only, as the door to the enormous suite opens, nothing could've prepared me for who steps through.

I'm fucked. More than fucked.

Because he found me.

Again.

Fucking Zeus.

He has another man on his arm, similar build but shorter, and young. Hot.

I automatically don't like him, but I can't pinpoint why.

They're both in suits that are too tight for their wide bodies, and they look like they could be in a catalogue for hottest men who could kill you with very minimal effort. If there was a subscription for that magazine, I'd throw all my money at it. If I had any. Which I don't.

"Oh, they gave us two seats. We'll only be needing one." The young guy pushes Zeus down on the chair and then sits on his lap.

When Zeus wraps his arm around the other guy, it's tender. When he rests his chin on his shoulder, it's gentle. And I find myself staring at them with longing.

That's what I want. What I miss.

The only thing I've ever craved from a partner. To be choked in bed but loved outside of it. Is that so much to ask?

I'm caught staring when Zeus's eyes land on mine, and I flinch.

He kisses his partner's cheek. "As much as I love being close to you, boo, I need to concentrate on my cards."

The other guy dramatically flops into the spare seat.

I follow Arabella's lead, walking around the table and asking if we can get the players anything, but I purposefully avoid Zeus and his ... toy.

Arabella is flirty and giggly with everyone, and she's an amazing actress, considering I saw the real her.

And maybe this is why I didn't immediately tell security that Zeus is here for me, that he's not really a high roller, and it's his job to kill me. Because staring at Arabella, I'm seeing my future, and I hate it.

I'd rather be dead.

So maybe I should let Zeus take me. Maybe this is rock bottom.

The moment of defeat.

Hey, if I struggle hard enough and make a huge scene, it's possible Zeus could take out Pierre's guys, and then ... Hmm, no. Pierre would still be alive. He'd find other minions to come find me.

There's a point in the game, where Arabella and I are standing back, that I catch a glimpse of Zeus's cards. He's one card off a flush, but instead of betting, he folds.

Did I not see the cards right or—

"I'm getting the worst cards ever," he complains. "Come on, dealer, give me some magic next time."

Is he bluffing, or is this part of his game to get to me?

The next hand, he bets big on a pair of twos and obviously loses.

"Damn it. It's the first pair I had all night."

Maybe Zeus doesn't understand how poker works.

I almost want to facepalm when he goes all in on three of a kind. It's a decent hand but not the best. I wouldn't risk everything—and he's out.

"I don't know why you drag me to these games," he says to his partner and kisses him on the head. "But while you play, I'm going to have some fun of my own." He stands and approaches Arabella and me.

And that's when it clicks. The real reason he threw that game.

I suck in a sharp breath because he's not going to take me into the bedroom and kill me right here and now, is he? He wouldn't do that. How would he get out?

Right?

Right?

Just like any other time I've resigned myself to giving up, to getting it over with, that thing inside me that won't let go takes hold again, and I want to run. I want to scream that he's going to kill me so Pierre's men will kick him out. This is the whole reason I came to Pierre in the first place. For his protection.

Then why when I open my mouth does nothing come out?

Zeus lifts Arabella's hand and kisses her skin. My own hand tingles with warmth, like it wants his lips too. Traitorous hand.

I still don't know how I can be attracted to someone who wants to kill me—oh, wait. Been there, done that with Stephen. Though I don't think he wanted to end my life so much as to simply hurt me.

Zeus says to Arabella, "You're absolutely stunning."

Either Arabella is a better actress than I thought and can make her cheeks pinken on cue, or even she can't resist Zeus.

See, it's not only me who finds him attractive. It must be a universal thing. No one real should be that hot.

Those stunning blue eyes land on me, but he keeps talking to Arabella. "But I have a craving for something else tonight."

Zeus takes my upper arm and drags me toward the bedroom one of Pierre's guys points him to.

"Have fun," Zeus's partner sings from where he's still playing poker.

"He's not really your boyfriend, is he?" I ask in a low tone.

"Nope."

Once inside the bedroom and the door's closed, I remember Arabella's warning about the cameras.

So, instead of standing here, waiting for Zeus to do or say something that could get us both killed, I move toward him, press against his insane body, and before I can think, before I can anticipate what I'm going to do, I practically maul his face in what's supposed to be a searing kiss. Only, it doesn't pan out that way because the minute our lips touch, he grips my hips hard and tries to push me away. For both our sakes, I hold firm.

"There are cameras," I murmur against his mouth. "And there's probably someone watching, so you can't kill me here." Even though Arabella says there's no audio, I can't be sure, so I make sure to speak in low tones.

Zeus doesn't miss a beat, and when he pulls his head back, he orders me to "Get on the bed."

My eyes widen. "W-why?"

"So it looks like I'm taking advantage of you when I'm not going to," he whispers.

"Because you're going to kill me instead?"

He laughs, but he must see the fear in my eyes because he says, "I'm not here to kill you." For show, he cups my cheek like he's admiring his merchandise, and I hate that I have the urge to lean into it.

I don't for one second believe he's not going to kill me.

"Now, get on the bed before I make it look like I'm forcing you to."

"The sick fucks in this place will probably get off on that, so do whatever you need to," I blurt.

Zeus's eyes flutter closed, and his body gives an almost imperceptible shiver.

Hey, it's not the first time someone's been turned off by me. By what I used to do for a living.

In the next second, Zeus is on me, his big hand around my throat, pushing me toward the bed.

God damn my cock for responding.

With a swift-looking but gentle shove, he forces me onto the bed and nods for me to wriggle up so my head is on the pillow.

The literal Greek god physique of his is revealed little by little as he slowly takes off his suit jacket and tie and then unbuttons his shirt.

My mouth waters, and he can tell the effect he has on me. Zeus licks his lips while staring at my cock trying to break free of the tight underwear.

I lie still, my hands fidgeting at my side from nerves.

Is he … is he actually going to go through with this? Am I … Are we …? Why do I hope the answer to that is yes?

He finally loses the shirt, and I get it now. He hasn't been sent here to straight up kill me. He needs to torture me first.

I bite my bottom lip, and something like heat fills his eyes.

Zeus's knees hit the bed, then his hands, as he crawls on top of me and lowers his body weight to press against mine.

He leans in, talking into my neck and sending his warm breath all over my skin. "Is there any audio I need to be aware of?" His voice is raspy and so damn sexy.

"I was told no, but I can't be sure."

"Okay. Noted." Zeus's hand goes back to my throat, and my hips involuntarily thrust upward.

Fuck.

He chuckles.

Of course he'd be entertained by his target being unable to control himself. He's probably used to having anyone and everyone throwing themselves at him.

"So, what's the plan here?" I croak.

Zeus's hand is relaxed at my throat, and even I know not to ask him to tighten his grip. Even if I want him to.

"Where are the cameras?"

"I have no clue. I was just told there were some."

"Got it. Let me think about how to get you out of here without alerting them to it." His brow scrunches.

"Why? So you can move me from one trapped situation to another? So Lemon's boyfriend has the chance to kill me himself?"

"Husband," he says.

"What?"

"They're married now."

Fuck. I mean, I'm happy for Lemon. Truly. He got a chance at a real knight in shining armor, and he deserves all the happiness in the world. What I did to them—setting them up to be killed by Stephen and David—I'm the reason he almost didn't get to have that.

"Am I their wedding present?" I ask.

"Nah, they don't share. I've tried."

I want to laugh. Really, I do. "I mean giving me to them. My head on a silver platter."

Zeus lifts up on his forearms to meet my eyes. "I'm not going to hurt you."

There's a stupid, naïve part of me that believes him, but I can't let myself think like that. So for now, I'll do what I have to. And if that includes going with Zeus, letting him get me out of here and trying to ditch him later, then that's what I have to do.

"I'm sorry I hit you with my car," I say softly, and he laughs.

"Hey, it was fun."

"And as much as I appreciate you not taking advantage of this

CHAPTER SIX / 41

situation, I don't think they're going to believe you're getting off."

"Isn't this what most johns do? Lie on top of you, wriggle around a bit, and then come their brains out because their unused dicks can only take so much friction before they give in?"

"I ... I wouldn't know. You're my first."

"First ... john?"

It's a weird thing to be ashamed of, but for some reason, that's all I feel. "Yeah."

"In that case, let's hope we can make me your last too. I'm going to get you out of here."

And I've decided that I'm going to let him. I shouldn't have tuned to Pierre. I should've kept running.

But I'm so tired.

I'm also not convinced that Zeus isn't here to kill me, but I can deal with that later. If I have to choose between selling myself for Pierre or death, I'm ready to accept my fate.

I am.

I think.

CHAPTER SEVEN_

ZEUS

I'M HOLDING ON BY A SINGLE THREAD.

I haven't had sex since I can't remember when, and one of the sexiest men I've ever seen is splayed out for me. I have to remind myself that his hard cock pressed against me doesn't mean shit.

He's not here because he wants to be. He's here because he's got himself into a tangled mess, and just because his body is reacting, that doesn't mean he wants it. It's biological. Hell, he's probably force-fed pills so he's constantly hard.

"You're going to have to do something soon," he says, low. "Kiss me or … I dunno. Slap me. Do something."

I don't play this way.

I like my participants willing.

I close my eyes and whisper, "*Think, think, think, think.*"

"Want me to suck you off while you try to think?"

Why is he doing this to me? "I'm not going to force you into anything you don't want to do. I need a way to get my supplies in here—"

"There are supplies in the drawer if you wanted to fuck me."

I pull up and hover over him. "I mean to get you out of here. I just said I won't make you do anything you didn't want to."

The corners of Callie's lips turn upward. "Cute you think I wouldn't want you inside me. Have you seen you?"

While that makes me feel fractionally better, I'm still not going to go there. As much as I really, really, really want to.

I'm hard as steel. At this point, I'd fuck Haz if he offered.

Haz.

He's what we need.

I roll off Callie and onto my back. "Get on top of me."

He does so immediately.

His ass against my groin is warm, and he swivels his hips.

I throw my head back because I'm about to become one of those old men I was mocking him about.

I take a deep breath, put my hands behind my head, but sneakily press the receiver in my ear.

"Play with yourself for a while," I say to Callie and then immediately wince because—

"Whoa," Haz says in my ear. "I, like, need the bathroom, like, right now." He sounds like a damn Valley girl, but I can already hear him shuffling to the powder room near the front door.

"Not you," I growl at him.

Callie freezes on top of me. "Not you, who?"

"Not you."

"Who's you?" they both ask at the same time.

This plan is already getting too complicated.

"Haz—"

"You're not actually hooking up with Callie in there, are you?"

"No."

Callie looks confused. "What's going—"

I slap my hand over his mouth and raise my hips so it looks like we're doing something, even if the friction is going to short-circuit my brain.

"I need you to lose as much money as you have and more," I say to Haz.

"What? But I'm up ten thousand."

"There are cameras in here. The only way to get out is the

need to go get more cash and smuggle in our equipment to scale the building."

"Equipment to what?" Callie yells, his voice luckily muffled behind my hand.

"It's the only way," I say and remove my hand. "I haven't checked out the bathroom in here yet, but I'm hoping the sick fucks running this operation at least give their moneymakers the decency to clean up alone. We'll need to work fast just in case. Lose quickly, Haz. There's only so much foreplay I can pretend to enjoy."

"Mr. Player doesn't take his time with foreplay. Shocking," Haz says dryly. "I got you. I'll bet big and lose even bigger."

"Good."

"Give me twenty."

I groan. Twenty minutes? No way am I going to last that long.

I stare up at Callie. "Now, we just have to wait."

He leans over me, and I give in to the urge to grip his ass cheeks and squeeze. For show, of course.

"You know," he says lowly. "If we're going to be waiting a while, we're going to have to do something."

I know. And I feel like a complete creep for it.

Angel would always complain about being the honey trap, but I never understood it until now. Though it's a bit different here. The men Angel seduces are usually dumbass criminals who want to get their dick wet. They're not prisoners being passed from person to person like a possession.

"What are you comfortable with?" I ask.

"You're really not good at playing the john, are you? It doesn't matter what I want."

"You know I'm not a john, and I'm not going to do anything you don't want to. We'll have to do *something*, but you get to tell me what that is."

The fact we're having this conversation, no longer really talking in hushed tones, and no one has come in yet, it's pretty safe to say there's no audio recording too. Either that or no one's actively keeping an eye on the live feed. I hope it's that because that will give us more time to get Callie out of here, but either way, there's some solace in knowing we can talk freely. For now.

"Please can I suck your cock?" Callie begs, shocking the hell out of me.

"Are you saying that because you think there's a listening device in here or because you actually want to?"

Please be the latter. Please be the latter. I'm so desperate.

"After rubbing all over it for the last ten minutes, I'm dying for a taste." Callie's face is so bright. So eager. It still doesn't sit completely right with me, but had I known I'd be making a sex tape, I wouldn't have dragged him in here.

But we are in here now, and other than faking a premature incident or limp dick, both of which would end our reason to be in here, we have to make it look like we're actually hooking up.

And to make it look like that, we're going to actually have to do it.

I've never been so reluctant to have sex before, but it has nothing to do with Callie and everything to do with having a conscience.

Man, the guys would get a kick out of the thoughts running through my head.

I actually feel sorry for Callie. He's been through so much, and most of that is only what I've seen from the sidelines. I'd hate to see what's underneath that kind of trauma.

Having been in the military, I've seen my fair share of trauma stacked on top of trauma, stacked on top of trauma. It's not healthy, and I have to hope I'm not adding more layers to his.

I slowly sit up, still gripping Callie's throat. His hard cock is against my stomach, his legs straddled each side of mine.

"I promise I'll go easy on you," I say.

The heated stare he gives me makes my cock throb, but it's followed up by a whole lot of guilt.

Then he says the one thing that has the power to make me

snap, to make me get out of my head and let my instincts take over. That primal need. "Please don't."

Two simple words giving me permission to do whatever I want, however hard I want to do it.

My eyes flutter closed, and I take in a deep breath.

I'm not strong enough for this. I'm not strong enough to resist Callie.

"Fuck, do it."

He pulls away from me, shuffling backward and sinking to the floor at the end of the bed.

With surprising strength, he grips my thighs and pulls me down so my ass sits at the edge of the mattress. I'm stretched out more now, leaning back on my elbows.

My cock strains against my fly, but that last teeny-tiny thread of control has my hands rooted in place, gripping the comforter for dear life.

Callie's long fingers undo my belt and then pop the button on my suit pants.

God damn, I know strippers are good at the tease, but I'm practically panting already.

The sound of my fly going lower and lower echoes in my ears, drawing it out. It probably takes him less than a second to do it, but it's as if time slows.

Minutes tick by.

And he still hasn't even touched my cock.

My aching, leaking cock.

Callie grips the sides of my pants and underwear, pulling them down my legs and letting them drop to my ankles.

I'm bare, my cock so hard against my stomach, my balls tight.

A warm breath ghosts along my shaft, but he doesn't lay his mouth on me. Not yet.

"You might want to look like you're forcing me to do this."

I glance down at him, my lips parting to tell him I don't want to do that, but he cuts me off.

"I know you're not, but this is for show, isn't it?"

He is right. It's just sex. For show.

I'm amazing at sex. They should be so lucky to see me get blown.

I grip his blond hair, making a fist at the roots but not pulling tight.

Apparently, that's not good enough for Callie because he still doesn't lower his head.

His mouth is so close, teasing the fuck out of me, so instead of forcing his head down, I lift my hips off the bed.

The first touch sends a shiver up my spine. He mouths my cock softly, only parting his lips slightly to let his tongue peek out and taste.

It's warm but not wet, and I want to force my cock inside his mouth, but I stay strong.

I thrust upward again but still don't get the full effect, the satisfaction I'm craving.

"Fucking hell," I breathe.

As much as I try to let him lead this, he's driving me too crazy. Too wild.

I've never been in this position before where I know I shouldn't take the thing I want. Sex has never been so conflicting for me before. It's always been an exchange. A promise.

And I don't want to promise Callie safety and then take advantage of him like the assholes in his past or even the ones in his present.

Finally, on the third thrust of my hips, he closes his mouth around me and sucks me deep.

Oh, holy mother of blowjobs. I now have regrets of the other kind.

The regret of wanting more. Of getting frustrated at the teasing. Because then I could've complained and grumbled about it.

Now … Now it's like a point of no return. I need to come, and I really want it to be soon.

I pull out of his mouth to catch my breath and take a break, but he bobs his head and follows my cock with his tongue.

He takes me into the back of his mouth, his throat contracting around me as he swallows, and then he pulls up to the tip and repeats it over and over again.

I've never …

This is …

Fuck, no BJ has ever made me so speechless before.

I worry I'm going to blow this whole thing by, well, *blowing*.

I need to last. Haz hasn't come back online yet, so I have no idea where he is with losing the money, but you can bet your ass the second he lets me know he's ready that I'll be unleashing the orgasm that's simmering in my gut.

My balls feel ready to explode. Callie's mouth is perfection, and the way his eyes are rolled back in his head … He's either a good actor, or he's enjoying sucking my cock as much as I am watching him do it.

His tongue does this swirly thing around the head of my dick after every upstroke, and I almost want to hold him there so he can do that over and over.

I go from being strong in holding my orgasm back to being certain I'm going to lose it before I'm ready within the blink of an eye.

Chanting *stay strong* in my head over and over is no longer working, and when I mutter aloud, "Don't come, don't come, not yet, not yet," Callie hums around me.

I'm so close. "I can't … I can't—fuck."

Callie either doesn't have time or doesn't want to move away, and when that wave finally hits me, I briefly forget where I am.

I grunt through my release, and sweat rolls down my forehead from pure exertion of trying to hold it all in, and Callie … Fucking Callie …

Just when I think my orgasm begins to ebb, he swirls his tongue around me again, and I come some more.

I swear it will never end, but when it eventually does, I collapse backward, sated. Happy. If somewhat feeling a little guilty.

I think it's the first time I've ever had sex where I've felt something other than the need to get off. It was more than that. Probably because I knew what I was doing was wrong on so many levels, yet I wanted it anyway.

There's a weird protectiveness I have over Callie after everything he's been through.

The others might see him as a traitor or someone who should suffer, but hasn't he suffered enough?

For him to run to someone like Pierre for help ... He's lost, and I'm scared what we did will only lead him further into the darkness instead of into the light he deserves. The poor guy has earned a break.

A gruff voice fills my ear. "I hope you can pay up."

"Dushay can. Let me get him."

"Sit down. I'll get him."

I grip Callie's hair and lean in to say quietly, "We've got company incoming."

The door bursts open, and I shove Callie off me and stand, pulling up my pants and underwear.

"Knock much?" I complain.

The beefy private security guy folds his arms. "While you've been having your own kind of fun, your boy has been out here spending more than you came with."

"Fuck." I act like this is all brand-new information. "How much?"

"A hundred Gs."

What the fuck, Haz? I said lose, not lose that fucking much.

I whistle. "That's going to come out of his allowance. I'm guessing you won't take a bank transfer."

He blinks at me.

"Right. Cash it is. We'll go down to our room and—"

"Just you. He stays here."

Makes sense.

"Fair enough, but he better still be here when I get back." Not that Haz wouldn't be able to handle himself. "Can I take my snack with me?" I point to Callie.

Another glare.

"Fine." I turn to Callie, who's still on his knees on the floor. "But I'm not done with you. When I get back, I want to see you and my man together. It'll be so hot."

"Go get the money," the security guy barks.

"Tell you what, big guy. I'll even bring back extra if you make sure no one touches him until I get back." I thumb behind me.

I get affirmation in the form of a simple nod.

"Okay then. I'll be back shortly." I pick up my shirt from the floor and slip it on.

When I get back into the main room, where they're still playing, Haz has been moved to a seat in the corner and is surrounded by other big guys.

He has his head downcast, but I can see the small smile on his lips.

"You're in so much trouble," I grumble as I pass him.

And both of us are screwed.

If I were them, I'd escort me to my room, but they let me go on my own. I guess they figure Haz would be worth more than a hundred grand if I don't return, and hey, that might be the only option for him if Trav won't pay for it.

I don't dare call him until I'm off that floor and on my own. I hit his number as I key into the suite Haz got us.

"Update?" he answers.

"So, umm, funny story …"

Trav sighs. "How much now?"

"A hundred large."

"What the fuck are you doing out there? Have you even found Callie?"

"We have."

"Are you buying out his debt or—"

"Umm, Haz's debt," I say quietly.

"Jesus H. Christ, you're all going to put me into an early

grave." He must move the receiver away from his mouth because when he calls out, "Atlas," it's muffled.

"Yeah, boss?" Atlas says from even farther away.

"Your job is FUBAR."

"It's not FUBAR," I say. "Yet."

"I'm switching you over to speaker." The phone clicks over to an open line.

"What's happening?" Atlas asks.

"Okay, so to find Callie, we had to pretend to be high rollers, which is all good and well, but you know, we actually had to buy suits and play the part and then play real poker. With real money. And then I took Callie into a bedroom, but we were being filmed, and the only way I thought to get out of it was to make Haz lose all his money so we had an excuse to leave, get said money, and come back with equipment so we can get Callie out of here without … you know, killing people."

"I'll pay," Atlas says. "Whatever it takes."

"Will this work?" Trav asks. "Or would you be better off cutting your losses and stealth kidnapping him like I said in the first place?"

"I think this will work," I say. "And I'm worried …" I bite my lip.

"What? What is it?" Atlas asks.

"I'm worried if we don't get him out tonight, they're going to force him to pay off his debt with other men who aren't as nice as I am."

There's silence.

"Hello? Did the line cut out?"

"What did you do?" Atlas's words come out real slow. Real accusingly.

"Nothing!" My voice cracks.

"When you say you were filmed …" Trav matches Atlas's tone.

"He's being sold to the highest bidder, okay? He's one of the high rollers' treats, and we had to play the part. It was … you know … the job."

"I can't believe you," Atlas hisses. "I'll wire the money to the casino downstairs so you can pick it up in cash."

"It's not like that," I say. "He encouraged me to!"

"He's gone." Even Trav sounds disappointed.

And now the guilts are back even more.

Like, I get it. I'm known for this kind of thing. But it irks me that they are assuming I took advantage of the situation. Of him.

"Don't screw this up, Zeus," Trav says.

"I won't. At least, I'll try not to. The new kid doesn't seem to care about consequences. You'll have to train that out of him."

He scoffs. "Like I've trained you? Do what you gotta do to get out of there."

"Yes, sir."

We end the call, and I go downstairs to collect the money with a duffle bag that has a hidden compartment at the bottom with ropes, harnesses, and everything else we'll need to scale the side of the building.

Let's fucking hope we don't get caught before our feet touch the ground.

CHAPTER EIGHT_

CALLIE

I'M STRUGGLING TO CATCH MY BREATH, AND MY HEART pounds so hard I swear I can hear it. I'm still on the floor, though I've at least shuffled so I'm resting against the bed instead of on my knees.

The guy Zeus left to guard me stands by the door with his arms folded, but it's not like I'm going to try to get past him. Out there, I'll still be under Pierre's thumb.

But in here, I'm throwing all my faith at Zeus.

Zeus. I'm still at attention after sucking his phenomenal cock.

I want to trust him, and I think I do—at least to get me out of here—but what then?

He keeps saying he's not going to kill me or he's not here to kill me, but why is he so adamant about chasing me down if it's not to drag me back to Lemon and Atlas?

Atlas is scary as fuck, but if I'm honest, I'm more terrified about coming face-to-face with Lemon again.

My betrayal hurt him, but it probably hurt me more.

Fear of the unknown is what kept me going back to Stephen time and time again, and even though Pierre wants to sell me to his friends to earn money off my body, I know what I'm in for with him.

I have no idea what I'll endure with Zeus.

Other than possibly being hard twenty-four seven.

I've given a lot of blowjobs over my life, but none of them were like ... that.

I shake my head. Just because I've drunk his cum, that doesn't mean he's not as dangerous as Pierre.

Do I take this chance and go with Zeus, or do I wait for another? I've only been with Pierre for twenty-four hours, and he's already put me to work, but at the same time, I've already stumbled across an out.

Surely, there'll be more opportunities for me to skip out. Even though I'm the stupid one who got myself locked into this situation to begin with.

I should've kept running.

Yet, that thought alone makes me bone-tired.

What's my plan? Run for the rest of my life?

"We squared away now?" Zeus's deep voice travels in from the other room.

He's back.

"We're square," one of Pierre's men out there says.

"Good. I brought extra in case my boo wants to play some more, but I'd rather he play with me first and have some fun with the talented mouth I experienced earlier." Zeus's voice gets louder as he comes closer and appears in the doorway to the room. "We'll be back soon."

The mere sight of him makes my cock harden again. Not that I ever got fully soft to begin with, but I'm back to full mast as easy as that.

Zeus has these broad shoulders and a swimmer's waist. Golden hair that is somehow messy yet looks perfectly styled. Blue eyes, strong jaw ...

I'm blond-haired and blue-eyed, too, but in that California boy kind of way. Hence the nickname. I'm all-American. He's a literal Greek god.

The dude he came with follows him in, and while he's just as physically fit and has a nice face, next to Zeus, he's like any other generically attractive man.

"Thanks for keeping an eye out for him." Zeus reaches into his duffle bag and pulls out a wad of cash, thrusting it at the security guy. "Now, if you could give us some alone time and make sure no one comes through this door, that'll be amazing." He claps the guy's shoulder and guides him out of the room, closing the door behind him and flicking a lock.

"Do I get an in-life porno now?" Zeus's partner asks. "The soundtrack was hot."

"Haz," Zeus snaps. "We need to get out of here. While I find a way, why don't you play with our mark?"

"I have a name." It shouldn't make me snippy, but it does.

And it has nothing to do with him being able to forget the unforgettable blowjob a lot faster than I can.

"Sorry. Can you please maul Callie while I find a way to save his ungrateful ass?"

"You sure you don't want another go at him?" Haz asks, suddenly looking uncomfortable.

I love how they're talking as if I'm not even here. Not even human. Though, I guess doing what I do, I'm going to have to get used to that.

Unless they can get me out.

I stand from the floor and approach *Haz*. "You don't want a turn?" I pout and grip his shirt.

"Don't want to come in between whatever you two have going on."

I get the impression that's not the reason at all.

"We're still being filmed," Zeus says. "It might not be a live feed or being watched constantly, but the more time we play the role, the longer we give ourselves to set up."

"Okay." Haz shrugs. "Just don't punch me in the face for kissing your man."

"Not my man." Zeus's nonchalant and dismissive tone cuts deep, which is stupid.

What am I expecting?

I take it all back because he is good at playing a john. He *is* a john.

Pretends to care until he gets off, and then it's the cold shoulder.

The "I'm better than you because you're cheap and have no respect for yourself" kind of attitude.

This is my life now.

Haz's touch doesn't make me come alive like when Zeus did it.

I feel Zeus's stare on me as Haz kisses me, but in the next second, it's gone, and Zeus mutters something about "going to the bathroom to find a way out that won't get caught by the cameras."

I open my eyes and watch him disappear into the bathroom with the duffle bag.

Haz moves his hands down the middle of my bare back and grips my ass cheeks. "Jump," he mumbles against my lips.

I do and wrap my legs around his waist while he supports me and carries me over to the wall right next to the bathroom.

Even though his hands are firm, his mouth is passionate, and he might be putting in the same amount of effort as Zeus, it's not the same. The heat is missing. The tension. While both were for show, this kind of feels like filming a porno, not a sex tape. And yes, there's a difference.

Zeus comes back out of the bathroom and wraps his arms around both of us.

I break my lips from Haz's and turn my head so fast Zeus can't get a word in because I want his mouth.

The expectation of him pulling back like he did earlier makes me hesitant, but when he pushes his tongue in my mouth, I relax into it and return as much as he gives.

When I moan, Haz asks, "Are we really doing this?"

Zeus pulls away from me and sucks his bottom lip into his sexy mouth. "Bathroom has no recording devices."

"Are you sure?" I ask. "They could be hidden."

"I have a scanner that can check for that kind of thing. We're good."

"Is there a window in there?" Haz asks.

Zeus hesitates. "Yes."

"One that will fit us?" Haz adds.

"Umm, sure. Maybe. But at this point, we don't have much of a choice because they'll see us escaping if we do it from that balcony." Zeus points across the room.

"I have a question." My voice cracks. "Once we get out the window, how exactly are we supposed to get down?"

"Fly," Haz says, and I immediately feel sorry I asked.

"He's joking. We're not high up enough for the parachutes."

That doesn't make me feel any better.

"So whenever you're ready to put Callie down, I'll lead you two into the bathroom to make it look like we want to get it on in the shower."

Haz sniggers. "After what I heard earlier, I'm surprised you don't actually want to have shower sex before we jump out the window."

"That was the job."

"Nice perks."

They bicker between each other until I can't take it anymore.

Maybe this is my issue. A guy pays attention to me or comes down my throat or takes my ass, and I think it's more than what it is.

I'm a trick, I'll always be a trick, and even if I'm not selling myself, I'll still want more than anyone is willing or able to give me.

Sex doesn't equal romance. When I learn that, I'll stop making shitty decisions.

Hopefully.

"Let's go."

Haz lets me down, and Zeus takes our hands.

Once we're in the bathroom and the door's shut, there's

barely any room for the three of us to move, let alone do anything else.

"I couldn't fit clothes in with our gear, but here ..." Zeus takes off his shirt and hands it to me. "You can cover up with that."

He's shirtless again, and I want to lick his abs. I regret not having more time earlier to taste more of him, but it's done now.

The two of them pull out ropes, harnesses, and a whole stack of equipment I never would've guessed could fit in one bag, but I guess he wasn't lying when he said he didn't have room to stash some clothes for me.

No one will notice a guy barefoot in a shirt that's way too big and long on him and nothing else. We're in Vegas. People will assume I did it on purpose. Or am drunk. One or the other.

The no-shoes thing will make it harder for me to get away from these two.

If we go near a crowd, I could sneak through and lose them. I'm small and agile. Their big bodies will hold them back.

As I try to think through a plan, I'm distracted by Haz trying to squeeze through the small window that I don't even think I could fit through.

He gets his head and one shoulder out, but there's no way he's getting his second shoulder free.

Haz climbs back inside. "There's no use. It won't happen."

"Fuck." Zeus turns. "Okay, we're going to have use the balcony out there."

He says balcony like it has any right to be called that. It's more like a window with a railing two feet in front of it.

"We'll strap in here and then go as fast as we can. Hopefully, we'll at least make it to the street before they're alerted to anything wrong."

Zeus grips the collar of his shirt that I'm wearing and tugs me close to him. "Step in."

He holds a thong-looking harness out for me to get into and pulls it up my legs. My traitorous cock must think he's doing the reverse and taking things off my body instead because even the slight brush of his hands along my skin makes me hard.

I swear I see his lips twitch as his gaze drifts over my hard dick tenting the oversized shirt, but he doesn't acknowledge it to my face.

Once I'm in the harness, he fastens the loop at the front to the loop in his, and now we're tethered together. Which I'm thankful for because I don't think there's any world where I go out of a window and down fifteen stories willingly.

"Did you see anything we can anchor ourselves with out there?" Haz asks.

"No, but I do have this." Zeus pulls out a cordless drill. "Worst case, we drill into the building."

"With someone strapped to your front?" Haz reaches for the drill. "I'll do that. You just get ready to move." He leaves Zeus and me alone in the bathroom.

I can't swallow as my throat clogs with anxiety.

Forcing myself to take deep breaths, I try to convince myself it'll be okay. "Worst-case scenario, I fall to my death. Worst-case scenario, this all ends."

Zeus laughs. "I won't let you fall."

That cynical, ready-to-give-up-on-life voice in the back of my head suggests that maybe he should. It would be a lot easier than this.

Doing … whatever the fuck I'm doing with these guys. Fighting for a life I'm not so sure I want or can handle. I hated being on the run, but here I am, doing it again.

Do all normal adults know how hard it is to be responsible for yourself, or is that just me?

"I've got you," Zeus says, trying to reassure me some more. "You don't have to worry about me breaking you."

"I already know you won't do that."

He frowns. "You do?"

"You can't break a man who's already broken."

Zeus pins me with his blue stare, his pretty lips pursed. His mouth opens as he goes to say something, but whatever it is dies as Haz knocks on the doorjamb.

"We're ready. Let's go and get out of here before they notice."

I want to say I'm prepared and can handle myself, but I think all three of us would know I'm lying.

"As soon as we get to the window, you wrap yourself around me, okay? I'll be going out backward, so if you're scared of heights, close your eyes."

Immediately, the world goes black as I wrench my eyes closed.

"Once we get out there," he clarifies. "You kinda need to see where you're going right now."

On second thought, maybe the best thing that could happen would be falling to my death. It would be less embarrassing.

CHAPTER NINE_
ZEUS

CALLIE CLINGS TO ME AS WE CLIMB THROUGH THE window, and I lean back, checking we're secure before letting go of the window frame.

At least if these harnesses do fail, my hard dick could support Callie and keep him from falling.

I hated seeing him and Haz make out, and I have no idea why. It doesn't make sense when it was so fucking hot.

It has to be sympathy. Right? The last thing he should be doing is sucking my dick and putting his tongue down Haz's throat.

Callie puts on a front, but I can see it. The fear, his uncertainty, but most of all, the desperation to escape his life. Or maybe all of that is because we're about to rappel down this building.

"You're good," Haz says below us.

Callie tenses more.

"I got you," I murmur.

"Weird how that doesn't ease my worries when these ropes could break and send us hurtling to the ground."

Behind him, the door to the bedroom opens with angry-looking men rushing through it.

Guess the cat's out of the bag, and now the real fun begins.

"If it makes you feel any better, the ground is less scary than the men with guns chasing us."

He squirms, trying to turn to look, but I let go and pray Haz rigged us up correctly. The first jump is a big one, and I push my legs out to protect Callie from hitting the wall when we come back in.

Callie's screams get drowned out by the gunshots, and fuck, maybe I should've put Callie on my back instead, but I needed his weight on top of me instead of pulling me down faster than I was ready for. Ideally, he would've scaled the building himself, but I could tell he wouldn't do it, or if he did, we would've spent time we don't have trying to coax him to let go.

And I was right because they're shooting at us. Already. I was hoping to have more time than this.

"Go, go, go, go," Haz yells.

We rappel quickly, bouncing off the side of the building lower and lower, but it's possibly not quick enough. At least they're terrible shots and miss us. Unless …

When the gunfire stops, I get suspicious. It's like when my niblings were younger and they'd go quiet. Silence only occurred when something bad happened.

I glance up at the window, and yep. A flash of metal. They probably weren't aiming for us but the ropes. And now they've got knives.

"How close are we to the ground?" I ask Callie.

"You think I have my eyes open?" he yells.

I'd laugh if I wasn't too busy trying to problem solve here. I look over my shoulder. If the rope severs, I'm at a minimum breaking my back, if not going splat completely.

I have to keep going and hope the rope holds out. Trav only buys the best equipment, so it should be high enough quality to take longer than a second to cut through.

I force my legs to keep going, not give up, and get us down as safely as we can.

"You're almost there," Haz calls out. "Keep going. I got you covered."

More gunshots ring out, but from Haz this time, which sets off the crowd below us, screaming and trying to get away from the dude with a gun.

When my feet hit the ground, I don't waste time. I undo the carabiners connecting our harnesses to the ropes and to each other.

"I'm taking him to our prearranged meeting point," I say to Haz.

We agreed beforehand where to meet if we got separated or shit went to hell. And this is the definition of shit going to hell.

"I'll hold these guys off and meet you there." While Haz continues to point his gun up at the fifteenth floor and people on the street around us run screaming, I take Callie and disappear into the convenient manic crowd.

That could've gone smoother, but we're out now. We did it.

Trav is going to be pissed when I update him, though.

I'd take out my phone and call him, but *oh no, people are probably after us. I need to be alert and ready for anything and not be distracted by my phone. What a terrible shame it'll have to wait.*

Knowing Callie and I will stick out like a sore thumb, considering he's only in a shirt and I'm only in pants, I pull him along with me, moving at a fast clip.

The motel we're meeting at is at least fifteen blocks away, but finding a ride share or a taxi will take up too much time. Not to mention, that's probably the first place I'd look if I was trying to find someone fleeing.

So walking it is. Callie doesn't talk, and I can't find any words to say to him. I'm not good at reassuring people.

In stressful situations, in sad moments, I can't think to do anything but offer terrible jokes that make things worse. I also need to focus on making sure we're not being followed.

The adrenaline doesn't die down for the whole rush to get off the main strip and only kicks in more when we get to the side streets where we'd be easier to spot because there aren't the same crowds.

"Are you okay?" I finally ask Callie when we get to where I think is a safe enough distance away—for now.

"I have no idea how to answer that question."

"Maybe try honestly?"

"I am being honest. I have no idea how I am because I don't know what I'm doing."

Amen.

"Welcome to adulthood. I think ninety-five percent of it is faking it."

"I don't ... I still don't know ..."

"Still don't know what?"

"Why?"

"Why, what?"

"Why are you going to so much trouble for me? Were you at the club last year when it burned down? I put everyone's life in danger all because I was too scared to walk away. I had the opportunity, and I still couldn't do it. And I ... I—"

"Fuck." I turn to him and put my hands on his shoulders. "People make mistakes. It doesn't mean there's no redemption for them."

Callie lowers his head. "I don't deserve redemption. I deserve to be punished and pay for what I did."

This is such a heavy conversation to get into here. My gaze ping-pongs around the quieter streets, but there's no one running toward us with guns, no cars going at a snail's pace to try to see us.

I crook my finger under Callie's chin so he has to look me in the eyes when I ask, "Is that why you turned yourself over to Pierre? Because you believe you deserve to be treated like that?"

"No. I did that because I knew what I would be walking into with him. With you ... with Lemon's boyfriend—sorry, *husband*—I have no idea what you want with me."

"I can tell you now, it's not … that. What you and I …"

"It could be worse."

Worse than that? I don't think so. "I would rather face death than have people force themselves upon me."

"Really? You?"

Ouch. I step away from him. "Ah. I see my reputation precedes me. Let's keep walking. We still have a ways to go, and I don't want anyone catching up to us." I turn on my heel, back to the mission at hand.

He follows. "Did I say something wrong?"

"Apparently, I'm such a man-ho, why would I care about consent?"

"That's not what I meant. I meant—"

"That I have no standards, so I'd let anyone play with me?"

"Okay, when you put it that way."

What is this rage building within me, and why can't I stop it?

I whirl on him again. "I didn't even want you to suck my cock in the beginning, or are you forgetting that bit? Trust me, it wasn't because I didn't want your gorgeous mouth all over me. It was because I don't believe anyone should be forced into anything they don't want to do. Respect is a big thing to me, and yeah, I have the reputation of someone who sleeps around a lot, and I do, but everyone I hook up with knows the score. I don't do relationships. I do mutual orgasms, and that's it."

Callie just stands there, listening to my rant, but as I keep going and become more animated, hands flying everywhere, he shrinks in on himself.

Little by little, and then all at once until he's cowering away from me, and I want to slap myself across the face.

He's a victim of abuse, and here I am, yelling at him on a street corner.

"Fuck, I'm sorry." I try to reach out my hand for him.

He flinches.

I'm officially a horrible person.

"I'm not going to hurt you." I step closer tentatively, and he doesn't back off. "I'm sorry for getting heated. I'm frustrated at everyone who makes assumptions about me, and you don't deserve to take the brunt of it. Not here. Not now. Not ever."

Callie's bottom lip trembles, and I want to take him in my arms and tell him everything will be okay, but I have to be careful with him.

Behind him, headlights glow from a car headed our way. It could be a random car, but it's going too slow for my liking.

"We've gotta move." I pull Callie into an alleyway and crouch down behind a dumpster.

Callie lets me pull him along with me, but before I let go of him, I give him a reassuring squeeze on his forearm. Nothing hard, just a soft, supportive grip to let him know I'm here.

The car passes, still too slow for my liking, but I can't see anyone through the darkened windows, so it could be Pierre's guys, or it could be someone looking to buy drugs and keeping an eye out for someone on the street who's selling.

"I think it's safe to go back out there," I say and turn back to Callie, who's staring at me.

His lips are parted, his eyes soft. And when he slowly leans in and touches his lips to mine, I let him.

I have no idea what's going on in his head—maybe it's a psychological break—but I remain stock-still and let him kiss me.

It's soft. And weird.

It's not sexual. It's … something else. Something I can't define or pinpoint.

When he pulls back, he says, "I just wanted to do that so you know that you didn't force me to do anything back there. I did what I wanted to under the ruse of having to put on a show. And I'm sorry if I came across as judging you. I, of all people, should know what that feels like."

I lower my head. "Thank you."

"No, I guess I should be thanking you."

"Don't thank me yet. We still have to get to the meeting point and get you back to LA."

"L ... LA? You're taking me back?"

And now he looks like he's going to try to run from me again.

I have my work cut out for me.

CHAPTER TEN_

CALLIE

ZEUS SAYS HE HAS TO MAKE SOME CALLS AND TELLS ME to shower as soon as we make it to the cheap motel, and even though he saved my life, I'm still plotting ways to get myself out of here.

I go into the bathroom and turn the water on but leave the door ajar and put my ear up against it.

He has spent the last however many hours trying to get me to safety, but what kind of safety is it? He's taking me back to LA, which means he's going to force me to see Lemon again. Face Atlas.

I'm not ready for that because I have nothing to offer them. Just empty apologies.

Don't get me wrong, I'm so fucking sorry for what I did, for every single one of my past actions, but if someone betrayed me that way, all the sorries in the world wouldn't be enough for me to forgive.

There are muffled voices coming from the other side of the door, but I can't hear the exact words.

Something about someone being burned? And being fired? Or on fire?

Logically, I try to tell myself that he wouldn't have rescued me only to set me on fire, but with where I'm at, it's not like I can afford to take that chance.

Then again, I can't afford to do anything because I have no money. I don't even have any clothes.

The window in this bathroom is even smaller than the one in the last hotel, so I won't be able to escape through there, and even though my urge to flee is high, I need to be smart about it this time.

Zeus tracked me down so easily. First at the cafe in the middle of nowhere, then to Vegas. If I didn't know any better, I'd wonder if he put a tracker on me, but as it stands, everything I own is on my body, and even the shirt isn't mine.

Just my underwear.

I left my car at a park and ride, so maybe he could've somehow tracked me with that, but how did he know I was with Pierre?

These guys are professionals, and I don't think running without any sort of plan is smart. I've already fucked up so much because I'm not thinking clearly.

Running to Pierre was the dumbest decision I could have made, but obviously, my worst-case scenarios were not, in fact, worst case.

So I do what Zeus told me to do. I get undressed and slip under the hot water, washing away the ball of Pierre-induced tension in my gut.

Sure, the Mike Bravo tension is still there, the guilt from screwing over everyone in my past life and that all-round sense of dread that constantly lingers, but tomorrow, I'll be out of Nevada again, and Pierre will be behind me.

So long as he doesn't follow.

Because I don't have any clothes with me, I wrap myself in the bath towel when I'm done and go out into the small room with two double beds to ask Zeus for something to wear.

Only, he's not there. The other one is.

"Where's Zeus?"

Haz, who's on one of the beds, scrolling through his phone, points to the door. "Went to get you some clothes and supplies."

"So I'm supposed to wear a towel until then?"

He turns his head and eyes me from head to toe. "I'm not complaining."

"Sorry, you already had your freebie. If you want more, it'll cost you." Maybe he has a lot of cash on him, and I could steal it and get away.

Sure, I'd be naked, but it could work.

"I'll pass. You're not my type."

I want to take offense, but at the same time, I'm relieved. I wasn't lying when I said to Zeus that what I did with him was what I wanted, but if I were to go there with Haz, it really would be forcing myself to go through with it.

I would, though, if it gave me a chance at freedom.

To go where, I don't know.

To do what? I'm not qualified for anything other than taking my clothes off.

Maybe I'd try to make it to the East Coast and become a New Englander. Or Floridian. From what I hear, Florida is about as fucked-up as I am, so it could be fun.

I sit on the opposite bed and stare at Haz. "So, what is your type, then? Zeus?"

"Hell no. I need to be the pretty one in the relationship."

I laugh. "Fair enough. I usually have that rule too."

"I like older guys," he says.

"Oooh, kinky."

He waves me off. "Nah. I mean more the lifestyle than the kink. You know, someone to actually show they care for me. Run my life for me. That kind of thing."

"Daddy issues?"

"Understatement."

I'm about to ask why when the door opens, and Zeus comes back in.

"Here." He throws a plastic bag at me, and I pull out an "I heart LV" T-shirt and Vegas hockey sweats. "It's all I could find around here."

"At least it's better than the towel."

I stand and pull on the shorts under my towel and throw the shirt over my head. "No shoes?"

"In the bottom of the bag. I wasn't sure of size, so—"

There's a pair of flip-flops that are about two sizes too big. I won't be able to run in them, but like the clothes, they're better than nothing.

"Thank you. When are we heading to LA?"

"First thing," Zeus says. "We could head out tonight, but I get the feeling there'll be eyes everywhere for the next few hours."

My gut does a tumble because even though he's probably right about that, I don't want to think about it.

Just because we made it out of that hotel, away from Pierre's overbearing babysitters, that doesn't mean they'll let us go. And if Pierre wants to find someone in this city, he'll easily be able to achieve that.

"What about CCTV? It's practically impossible to disappear in Vegas."

"I asked a friend to work on scrambling the footage from the last couple of hours," Zeus says as if it's not a big deal. "Right after my boss tried to fire me for spending so much of his money and causing a scene in the heart of the Strip. Gunfire in the middle of a crowded place causes issues. Who knew?"

"That was me, though," Haz says.

Zeus glares at him. "I know. Yet, somehow, I keep taking the fall for you."

"Aww, is this where you confess your undying love for me and take a bullet to save my life?"

"Fuck no, and I would never take a bullet for anyone."

"Then why did you take the fall?" I can't help asking.

Zeus is not like the guy I first met over a year ago.

Back then, he was the clown, always joking around, acting like he didn't have a care in the world. This Zeus is ... He's the same but also not the same.

There are glimpses where this serious side comes out, a caring side. Passionate. Considerate.

When I met him a year ago, I thought he was conceited and in love with himself. To be fair, if I looked like him, I would be too, but he's right when he said I made assumptions about him. Manwhore-y assumptions.

And I was wrong.

He's still a manwhore, but he's not the type that leads people on.

I get the impression that with Zeus, what you see is what you get, but you have to see past the bullshit that surrounds him first. The superficial stuff.

I want more of what's underneath because even though he scared me when he went off on his tangent, the message was clear. People misunderstand him, and he lets them.

Though, he didn't let me.

"Is that why you said something about being burned earlier?" I ask.

"What?"

"On the phone. You said something about fire and being burned."

His lips turn upward. "Were you listening to my very private phone call?"

"I was curious. You two say you're not going to kill me, but you have said you're taking me back to LA. You haven't said what you'll do with me once we're there."

"Atlas sent me, but he told me under no circumstances am I to kill you or hurt you or whatever. Because even though you did something horrible, Lemon still asks about you. Cares about you.

Atlas wanted me to make sure you were okay, but the second you saw me, you ran and got yourself into an even bigger mess than you were in before. That's talent, by the way."

Haz is now staring at me, eyes narrowed. "What exactly did you do? All I was briefed on was that we need to get you back to LA."

It hurts to admit it out loud, but I need to own my shit. "I spied on my friend and his boyfriend and then set them up to be killed by my boyfriend and his best friend."

"Only, the best friend's business partner set the whole place on fire. Callie, along with Atlas and Lemon, were lucky to escape with their lives," Zeus adds.

"Damn," Haz says. "Tell me you're attracted to toxic people without telling me."

"I made a mistake," I admit.

Zeus shakes his head. "You did what you thought you had to so you could survive because in your brain, you had that asshole's voice reminding you that you would never be able to escape him."

How does he do that? Like, how does he know? It feels like he's in my head.

"Are you sure we're not taking him back so Atlas can take his time setting him on fire?" Haz asks.

My gaze flits between them.

Zeus takes off his shoe and throws it at Haz. "If you scare him off and he runs again, you're the one chasing him this time."

"I-I've noticed you didn't answer the question, though," I say.

Zeus holds up his right hand. "I, Oren Owens, solemnly swear that I will not kill nor let anyone else kill Sam Eckles."

Haz snickers. "Your real name is Oren Owens?"

"What's yours? Spawn of Satan?" Zeus throws back.

Okay, it's time I accept that I can trust Zeus.

I think.

I really want to, but what if Atlas just hasn't told him what he actually has planned for me?

Or what if Zeus's charisma is pulling me under? I'm falling for an act again. The savior complex.

His promise to keep me safe.

How long will it be until he turns on me like Stephen did?

Would he wait until I trust him completely, or will I be blind-sided tomorrow when I come face-to-face with my old friend's husband and a 22 pistol?

The truth is, no matter how much I want to trust, and no matter how much faith I put in my gut ... I'll never be sure if I can trust someone completely ever again.

CHAPTER ELEVEN_

ZEUS

"Let's try to get some sleep," I say. "Haz, move your ass over."

"What, so he can suck your dick, but sharing a bed with him is too much?" Haz snarks.

It's too personal, too clingy, and way too dangerous. My cock hasn't had enough of him, and because of some fucked-up, deep-seated protectiveness over him, I don't want to play with fire.

I'm already on thin ice with Trav. I usually am, but this time, it's more.

Probably because nothing about this mission has gone to plan, we're not getting paid for it, and I've already eaten into a huge chunk of Trav's budget. And by me, I mean Haz.

I really want to like the guy, especially because he's another smartass like Iris and me, but dear God, I need the strength to deal with him. I'm suddenly seeing what it was like for any of my commanding officers to put up with me, and if this is some kind of karmic justice, I've well and truly learned my lesson.

Callie looks up at me with his dark blue eyes. "I ... I'd probably feel safer if you were next to me."

Fucking hell.

"So it's settled, then." Haz shuffles so he's completely in the middle of his bed and then spreads his legs so I wouldn't be able to fit if I tried.

"Settled," I say through gritted teeth. "I'll set an alarm for four in the morning." That's three hours from now.

Fuck my life.

And fuck this job.

The reason I love Mike Bravo so much is because I can mentally detach myself from the mission. Killing people I don't know? Scarily easy to disassociate. Saving people from bad situations? As soon as they're in safe hands, I don't think about them again. Job done.

Callie, though. It was supposed to be an easy check-in to see how he was doing and report back. Now we're on the run, and I'm finding it harder and harder to disconnect from Callie because I know what he's going through. I've witnessed it firsthand.

I've seen the kind of toll abuse has on a person, so from the beginning, I've been too close to this case. Had I known this is what it would've turned into, I never would've accepted it.

Then again, maybe I would have because I wouldn't want anyone else to do it. The last thing Callie needs is for anyone to make him feel like this was all his fault, and after the fire, after almost losing one of our own, I know a lot of my teammates wouldn't be able to see Callie any other way.

I'm definitely the right person for the job, but not for the reason anyone would suspect. It's not because of my detached nature.

It's because I will do anything I can to make sure another person isn't lost to the fallout of domestic violence.

So I swallow the lump in my throat, take a deep breath, and climb into bed next to Callie.

And my dick is immediately hard.

I think it's about time I acknowledge that I'm in trouble.

I'm startled awake by the sound of a loud engine rumbling like an angry thunderstorm rolling in. When it comes to a stop and the world is quiet again, I don't immediately go back to sleep.

Sure, it's probably someone returning to their room for the night, but I can't be too careful.

It took me a while to get to sleep, and I have no idea what time it is now, but from what I can tell, it's still dark outside.

I slip out of bed as quietly as I can so I don't disturb Callie or Haz and make my way over to the window to pull back the curtain.

The old-style radio clock in between the beds reads three in the morning, and considering how long it took me to fall asleep while hard as a fucking rock, I've had maybe an hour. Tops.

When I pull back the curtain slightly, just enough I can peek outside, my gut is on high alert.

Being in Mike Bravo, having served as a Marine, a lot of it has to do with gut instincts. I always trust my gut. And as I stare at two men who look like they're casing the joint, I can't help thinking they're not here to rob us.

"Haz," I hiss.

He doesn't wake.

A third man joins the two guys outside and points toward our room.

I should've gotten Trav to send a team to get us out of here, but I thought we weren't going to be traceable.

If Saint was able to scramble random CCTV cameras around the place, they wouldn't have been able to track where we went.

But they somehow were, and they did.

"We need to get out of here," I say as calmly as I can.

Haz moans and grumbles, "What's happening?"

"We have company."

The three men reach into their pockets, and I don't even need to see the guns to know they're there.

"Get down now."

Haz rolls off his bed, pulling the mattress off and up for

protection. Minimal protection, but it will still slow down the bullets.

I duck down and crawl to the other bed, where Callie still sleeps.

There's no real graceful or respectful way to wake him up without startling him, so I cover his mouth to try to muffle any screams he lets out.

Surprising me, he doesn't scream, but his eyes do widen. One of his knees connects with my balls, and I grunt in pain before doubling over.

My balls are in my throat, and it takes all of my energy not to yell out in pain.

Sure, I probably deserved it, but fucking hell.

"I'm sor—"

I put my finger up to my mouth and then point outside.

It's impossible to know for sure, but I swear his skin pales.

"We're going to get you out of here," I whisper. "But first, we're going to put up a barricade to slow them down. Got it?"

He nods.

"Get behind the bed and stay there."

He does as I say, moving quickly, and then I turn back to Haz.

"Let's do this."

Each of us gets a side of his flipped mattress, keeping ourselves behind it as we place it against the door.

Just as we manage to do this, there's a knock.

Haz and I stop breathing.

And when a deep voice says, "Open up. It's the manager," Haz rolls his eyes.

How dumb do these guys think we are?

I point toward the small dining table to our left, and Haz moves first.

The curtains are drawn, so they won't be able to see what we're doing in here, but our main objective is to put as much between us and them as we can.

This will hopefully buy us enough time to figure out how to get out of here.

We manage to lift the table and turn it on its side without a single sound, but when we go to lower it to the floor, there's a thud, followed by a scraping sound as we push it up against the mattress.

Time stops, and the silence is deafening.

Like a calm before a storm, it's eerily still.

Quiet.

And then all hell breaks loose.

The gunshots ring out, and as if time is still catching up, it's like watching us move in slow motion. Haz dives behind the base of his bed, using it as an extra shield. I drop to the floor and commando crawl across the room to get to Callie.

I find him with his hands over his head in the fetal position, and I want to reassure him everything's going to be okay, but I can't promise that. Especially with bullets flying at our heads. Instinctively, I cover his body with my own while I try to think of a way out of here.

The constant echoing of rapid fire is so loud it's hard to organize my thoughts. I try to find one of my duffle bags that has some weapons in it, but it's difficult to see when everything around you is exploding because of flying bullets.

"Stay down," I say to Callie. "I'll be right back."

He reaches for me, not letting me up. "Please don't leave me."

My heart breaks for him. "If I'm going to keep you safe, I need to arm myself."

"Here," Haz yells over the noise, and then something bounces on the bed beside me.

I lift my head. It's a semiautomatic loaded and ready to go. At least one of us managed to get to the bag.

I don't leave Callie, but I do position myself so I can fire from where I am. "I got you covered," I call out to Haz.

He stays low to the ground and comes around our side,

bringing the bag with him. From here, we can both let loose without worrying about friendly fire.

We fight back, letting round after round fire in the direction of the bad guys. When I'm out, I turn back around, release the magazine, and reach into our bag for another one.

Haz is out too, but while he stops to reload, the noise stops everywhere. The only sounds to fill the air are those of our heavy breathing and Callie's soft sobs.

"Is it over?" he asks softly.

Haz and I share a glance, because who knows if it's over.

Reloaded and ready for more, we position our guns back over the mattress, staying as low as we can, and then we wait.

Seconds tick by.

Nothing changes.

And then, when our ears finally readjust to the quiet, we hear it.

The reason they would flee if we haven't killed them.

Police sirens.

CHAPTER TWELVE_

CALLIE

ZEUS AND HAZ LEAVE HALF OF THEIR STUFF BEHIND AS we rush outside and jump into their car. There's blood on the sidewalk but no bodies, so whoever was shooting at us must have run off when they heard the sirens.

Zeus is frantic but confident behind the wheel, and I'd be lying if I said I didn't find his competence hot.

I do worry, though. I worry that I'm getting used to him saving me. Twice in one night might have ruined me.

One day, he won't be there, and then what am I going to do?

I would never have thought to barricade the door with furniture. Or jump through the smashed window to get out faster.

"Call Trav," Zeus rumbles.

"At this time of night?" Haz asks but takes out his phone.

"He'll want in on this, and we need more hands on deck. They're not only after Callie now. They're after us too."

My stomach churns. If it wasn't for me, Zeus and Haz wouldn't be in danger.

I'm doing it again. Being that selfish person and dragging others into my mess. You would think I'd learn my lesson, but clearly, I'm doomed to repeat the same mistakes over and over again.

I can't have more blood on my hands. "Maybe you should take me back to Pierre."

The car swerves, and Zeus levels me with a look in the rearview mirror. "My brain must be scrambled from all the gunfire because I swear I heard you say we should take you back."

"I did. You shouldn't have gotten involved. It would be easier for everyone if I disappeared again."

Neither of them says anything, and the car doesn't change direction.

"Did you hear me?"

"I heard you," Zeus says. "I'm just ignoring you because that's the worst idea in the history of ideas."

"He's finally picked up." Haz puts his phone on speaker.

"This better not be you asking for more money," Trav says through a yawn. "It's going to take a while to set up a new identity, seeing as you burned Dushay Richard's name to the ground."

"Good news," Zeus says in a cheerful voice. "We don't need more money."

"Then what's so goddamn important in the middle of the night?"

"It's practically morning, boss. Early worm and all that."

"It's early bird," Haz mutters.

"Yeah, that phrase."

"Zeus," Trav barks.

"Well …"

"For fuck's sake, what have you got yourself into?"

"Nothing biiiiig, but …"

This hesitant side to Zeus is new. He still has his bubbly persona going on, but he's positively nervous about telling his boss what's happened.

So I do it for him. "Pierre's men found us in the motel we were staying at and shot up the place. The cops were on their way when we got out, but there's a good chance we're being followed, and your men refuse to hand me back over to Pierre."

"Callie?" Trav asks.

"That's me."

"Do you want to go back to Pierre?" he asks next.

"No, but I also don't want to put anyone else's life in danger, and all Zeus and Haz have done tonight is fight off bullets and jump down buildings to try to save me. It's too much effort. Too much risk. And I don't want—"

"We're not taking him back to Pierre," Zeus says. "End of story."

"Agreed," Trav adds.

I throw my hands up in defeat.

"We might need more of us on this," Zeus says. "I know Dushay Richard isn't traceable back to us, but they've seen our faces, and with the type of connections you've had over the years with people from Vegas, it won't be hard for them to figure out who we are, and then—"

"There isn't going to be long before they work out who we all are and will want to take us down for screwing over Pierre," Trav finishes for him.

"Exactly."

"Okay, take Callie out to the ranch, and I'll put a team together and meet you out there in the morning."

"See you in a few hours, boss."

They end the call, and now I really do feel like a selfish jackass.

I think back to how close all the strippers were at Peaches before it burned down. We were supposed to be like family, but the moment I left to be with Stephen, I didn't hear from any of them. Not even Lemon. But I also never tried to reach out to them.

Stephen would tell me to forget about my old life and to start a new one with him, but it had nothing to do with being ashamed I was a stripper and everything to do with separating me from those who would have my back.

They still looked out for me when I resurfaced, and how did I repay them? By setting them up, knowing they'd be killed.

They say nothing will change until a person hits rock bottom, and I was hoping to have already reached that, but no matter how much I wish that were true, all I manage to do is sink lower and lower.

Will I ever feel hope again? Is it even possible, or am I too far gone?

━━

I fall asleep in the back seat somewhere along the way, the soft voices of Zeus and Haz lulling me like a fucking lullaby.

I wake when the car stops and a door slams, and when I sit up, I find myself outside of what looks like a five-star resort in the middle of … "Where are we?"

"Palm Desert. You're at a safe house … of sorts," Zeus says from where he's still in the driver's seat. Haz has disappeared.

"Of sorts?"

"It's Trav's house." Zeus bites his lip.

My heart thuds to a stop. "Lemon's here, isn't he?"

"I don't know yet. But that—" He points out the windshield. "—is Atlas's car, so I'm assuming he's brought his husband with him, considering it was Lemon who wanted to find you in the first place. He's been worried for you. Hoping you were okay."

Of course. That's so Lemon. If someone ever screwed over one of us dancers, he was always there to pick up the pieces. If we had money troubles, boyfriend troubles, or we were plain old lost, he always found a way to make us feel better.

But what I did to him is unforgivable, and I don't want to face him.

I can't face him. "I can't go in there."

"I promise no one will hurt you."

"I'm not scared to see Lemon because I think he'll hurt me or get his husband to do it." At least, physically.

Seeing his disappointment or my betrayal reflected back at me? That's what I'm terrified of.

"Then what is it?"

"It's … It doesn't make any sense."

"What doesn't make any sense?"

"You're going to think I'm fucked-up—"

"Oh, that ship has already sailed."

I want to be offended, but I'm really not in the position to be. "I mean even more so."

"Try me."

"If I don't ask for forgiveness, I know I will never get it, but if I ask and he can't bring himself to give it, I'll be heartbroken."

"So you'd rather go through life pretending like forgiveness is out of reach because you're too scared to put yourself out there to ask for it?"

"Yup." But it sounds even worse when he puts it like that, so my voice comes out way too high-pitched.

"You're right. That is fucked-up."

"I know it might not make sense—"

"No, it does. It's putting yourself out there. No one can hurt you if you're already hurting type thing. Before I take you in there, what if we go somewhere, just you and me? There's something I want to share with you."

That little self-sabotaging voice in the back of my mind tells me to run. Because whatever he has to show me, it's not going to change my mind.

My stubborn streak wants me to dig my heels in and refuse. My beaten-down and abused side tells me that whatever he's going to say to me will only draw me deeper into his orbit.

Trust no one, I tell myself. But on the other hand, if I don't follow him, I'll have to face Lemon sooner than I'm ready to.

"Okay. Where are you taking me?"

Something tells me that the way he smiles should scare me, but it doesn't. Neither does the gleam in his eyes. If anything, the way his eyes shine only makes me more intrigued.

CHAPTER THIRTEEN_
ZEUS

I DRIVE US OUT TO THE BACK OF TRAV'S RANCH. IT'S ON acres of dry land that he has sectioned off into training areas.

There's a paintball field and two different shooting ranges, but everyone's favorite is a special place in the middle of the property, far, far away from where anyone can hear it.

"Are you driving me out to the middle of the desert and telling me to find my own way back, or are you going to end it all for me and put me in a ditch?"

I don't like the way he says "end it all for me" like it's something he wants to do but either can't or won't for whatever reason.

"I brought you out here because whenever one of us in Mike Bravo is struggling, whenever we're trying to make a tough decision or need to blow off steam, we'll come out here."

"And where is here?"

I grin. "Somewhere you get to put all your feelings inside a box and then blow it up. *Literally*."

"Wait, what?"

"Follow me." I pull to a stop and get out of the car, waiting for Callie to climb out too.

He does, but hesitantly.

We go through the scrap yard first, and I pick up things I know will make the C4 really shine. And by shine, I mean make the explosions go higher.

"Pick anything you want to blow up."

"You keep saying *blow up*. And I know you said literally, but you know how people say literally when they don't actually mean literally? Like, 'If I don't get to eat chocolate ice cream, I will literally die!' Is it one of those situations, or do you mean literal literally?"

My smile doesn't fade. "Literal literally. Part of our job is knowing how to get in and out of places. If we're prepared, we can blast our way out of anything."

"That would've come in handy a few hours ago."

"Sure would have. But it wasn't our fault we had no idea how much shit you'd gotten yourself into."

Callie looks away. "If I'm honest, I don't think I realized either. I knew Stephen and David had debts and that Pierre and anyone else they owed would look to me to pay them off. What Pierre wanted me to do, though ..." He shakes his head. "I thought I had worst-case scenarios worked out. I had not."

"It wasn't even your debt?"

"Nope."

My eyes close because I'm so disgusted at his situation. I brought him out here to blow up his feelings and whatever is scaring him, but the more I listen to him, the more I learn, the deeper I get, and the more I can't hold back my own issues.

I don't want to face my baggage because it will turn me into someone I don't want to be.

I'm fun. I'm flakey. I'm not serious.

Because if I dealt with everything serious in my life, I'd never see light again. I'd be cloaked in darkness.

"Are you okay?" Callie asks, and I snap out of it.

"Yeah. You remind me of someone, is all."

"Who?"

I take a deep breath and hold it, hoping I can find the words when I let it out. "My sister." As if the pure mention of her stabs me in the heart, my chest aches.

"How do I remind you of her?"

I lift my head and look over the field of debris from past excursions out here. "Let's get this set up, and then I'll make you a deal. I'll tell you something about my sister for every bad thought or feeling you dump into the pile."

Callie turns and looks around the heap of trash. "Nope. There's no way you have enough here to cover every bad thought running through my head."

"I can't tell if you're serious or joking."

Callie sighs. "If I'm honest, neither can I." He picks up a literal kitchen sink. "Can I just put all my thoughts and feelings in this?"

"Let's see if we can get them all to fit."

"I doubt it, but it should get some of the big ones away at least."

We pile all of our things up in the middle, and I duck behind the safety barricade and unlock the storage unit that contains the C4.

When I bring the brick back to Callie, he looks confused.

"What? Never played with explosives before?"

"You really did bring me out here to kill me!"

I think he's joking. I hope he is. Because if he still doesn't understand that I will protect him from anything bad coming his way, I have a long way to go to earn his trust.

It makes sense. That he'd be so hesitant to believe anything anyone ever says. I wish there was a way for him to know how serious I am about protecting him.

Maybe he could be my do-over.

My redemption.

Maybe both of our souls won't be lost forever.

I take out my pocketknife and cut a chunk off the C4 block, passing it to Callie.

"What is this?"

"Just some C4."

He drops it like it could explode at any minute.

"It won't kill you. I mean, it will if you stand near it when we detonate it, but we're not going to do that until we've filled the entire area with secrets."

That intrigues him. "Secrets?"

"Yep. I'll go first." I cut another chunk of C4 and mold it into the drain of the sink he picked and fit it with a shock tube so it'll detonate when we want it to. "My sister was in an abusive relationship."

I don't have to look at Callie to know he's surprised. His gasp echoes in my ears.

"Did … did she get out?"

"She did. But it's your turn."

He thinks about it for a moment before confessing, "I've never thought I was good enough for anyone. Didn't think I deserved love. So, when I found it—or what I thought was love—I did everything I could to hold on to it."

"Even screw over those who were truly there for you."

"Yup," he whispers.

I cut some more C4 and approach him. "I'm not saying that you don't owe people an explanation or that you don't need to ask for forgiveness, but I am going to tell you that none of it was your fault, and you need to let go of that burden. All of your guilt. You need to forgive yourself first and foremost, or you're never going to move on and heal."

His glassy eyes make my heart hurt, but not as much as when he says, "Maybe I don't deserve to heal."

"And that right there is the reason we're here. You need to put all of that in the literal kitchen sink and watch it explode into nothingness."

Callie's shoulders sag. "I don't understand."

"Understand what?"

"Why you even care. Why you're doing this."

"Atlas asked me to find you. To check in on you. And seeing

you, what you were willing to go through because you're scared to face the consequences of what you did, I'm glad he asked me."

"Again, why?"

"Because my sister? She didn't let that guilt go. She felt like her kids were better off without her because she wasn't strong enough for them. She didn't fight for herself or my niece or nephew. She gave in to those intrusive thoughts, never forgave herself, and I wasn't there to pull her out of the darkness."

"Where were you?"

"Serving my country."

"What happened to her?"

This is where I'm not sure if I should tell him the truth or not. The truth is she never recovered. She dropped my niece and nephew off with my parents, told them she loved them, and then drove head-on into a tree. No brake marks. No hesitation.

"She gave up. And that's exactly why I was the right person to find you. Because even if you're willing to give up, I'm not. In moments where you can't fight for yourself, I'll fight for you. I wasn't able to save her, but maybe I can save you."

"That's a lot of pressure to put on me. What if you can't make it better?"

"I hope to fuck I can because I can't lose someone else like that. Someone I should have been able to protect."

"This isn't because ... you know, you think you owe me now because I sucked you off?"

"Hell no. That was ..." I want to say it was nothing, and I mean, it was. At least, I think it was. It was ... weird. "We did what we had to so we could have a chance to get out. It was nothing. If anything, having done that with you should make me want to drop you at Atlas's feet and leave."

"Why's that?"

"When we first met, I'm sure you were briefed about how unattached I am. By choice. After I get off with someone, that's it. I'm done."

"Is that because of what happened to your sister?"

"No," I say quickly. Perhaps too quickly. "It's because relationships are so much work. Why put yourselves through that when you can have fun?"

"Ah. Why be serious and deal with your issues when you can pretend everything is fine?"

Exactly. "If you don't get in too deep with anyone, you can't be hurt to the point you don't want to live anymore."

"Definitely sounds like you've healthily dealt with all your feelings over your sister's death. Why am I taking advice from you again?"

Ugh. He makes a point, but I hate that he does, so I throw it back at him. "Because right now, I'm the only person you have. Are you ready to blow your shitty mood away or not?" I hold up the remaining C4.

"We can try. I still don't think it'll work, though. Especially considering your situation."

I shrug. "Hey, whenever I start to think about Olive, I come out here and blow more stuff up."

"I think if I were to do that for every issue I have, I'd probably blow a hole in the world."

"Baby steps. First, let's blow up your emotional baggage, and then we can work on world domination."

Callie manages a smile. "You're not what I expected."

I wish I could say the same, but I can't because Callie's exactly what I was expecting. He has the ability to bring me back down to earth, to care again. And even if that might be seen as a good thing, for me, it can only mean one thing:

Callie has the potential to break me. He's already seen me pull down my fun façade. He's seen my protective side. My vulnerable side. And now, he knows my deepest secret.

Even some others in Mike Bravo don't know about my sister, and the ones who do, all they know is she died in a car accident. Scout's the only one who knows the full truth. He served with me. He was there when I got the call.

I've confided in Callie, something I haven't done with people for a really long time because I've been too afraid of showing my hand. Too scared that they'd see right through the cracks and find the helpless soul I am underneath.

"Are we going to blow this up or what?" Callie asks, bringing me back from the edge of having an existential crisis.

My reputation wants me to reply with something like "Oh, you sure know how to blow all right" or some other innuendo about blowjobs, but the truth is, it's not just C4 we're blowing up. It's my entire motto when it comes to living my life.

No being serious.

No getting close.

No getting too deep.

I'm worried I've already done all three with Callie.

CHAPTER FOURTEEN_

CALLIE

OKAY, NOT GOING TO LIE. BLOWING UP MY FEELINGS works. Even with earplugs, the blast is deafening. Debris shoots into the sky, small pieces hitting the protective Perspex between us and the explosion area.

There's no fire, though, no plume of smoke or anything like that, which is surprising. It's almost as though everything blasts outward.

Even though I think Zeus's form of therapy is another version of pushing it all down and pretending it doesn't exist, it does make me feel better.

That is, until we drive back to the massive mansion, and I know I'm about to come face-to-face with Lemon again.

I'm not ready for it, but I doubt I'll ever be ready, so there's no time like the present. Because Lemon deserves at least an apology. It will never be enough, but at the moment, he doesn't even have that.

Zeus opens my car door for me but lowers his head so I can see his face. "Keep reminding those flight instincts of yours that you're safe, and you'll be fine."

I climb out of the car, shaky on my legs.

"I've got you," he says.

I'm not scared of Lemon or his boyfriend hurting me anymore. Well, that fear is still there, but the biggest fear of all is … abandonment. For Lemon to see me, not forgive me, and then tell me to get out. If he doesn't accept my apology or at least want to work through what I did to him, I'd rather he get his boyfriend to kill me.

It doesn't have to be right away. I'm not expecting him to throw himself into my arms and offer forgiveness, but all I want is a chance.

My heart is in my throat as Zeus leads me inside. Or maybe it's a pile of vomit waiting to come up.

Thud, thud, thud. My heart beats so hard I swear Zeus can hear it.

When we push through the front door, the loud, boisterous, and deep voices stop. There's a kitchen to our right, where there are two guys milling about, but they stop moving and stare. Behind them, in a dining area, are more of the Mike Bravo guys, some of whom I recognize from my short stay in their care last year.

They might be familiar faces, but their stares are cold, and none of them are the one I'm here to see.

I'm not ready, I'm not ready, I'm not ready. My mind gets stuck on the loop.

But then … Then Lemon turns the corner, staring up at his new husband, and he looks … so fucking happy.

The relief is sweet, though also bitter. Not because he was able to move on from what I did—I'm thankful for that—but because he has what I've always wanted. What I've desperately searched for but can't seem to find.

I fall for empty promises too easily, and my standards are basically nonexistent.

Atlas nods in my direction, and Lemon's gaze follows.

We're both frozen in time, unsure of what to do or where to go from here.

"Callie?" he squeaks. "You … you're alive?"

Panic sets in, and I turn to Zeus. "He didn't know I was coming?"

"Uh, that's on me," Atlas says. "I didn't want to tell him anything until we knew for sure you'd get here. Apparently, you've been a bit ..." He glances at Zeus. "Slippery."

"Callie," Lemon says again. "I ... you ..."

I stand stock-still, willing myself to apologize, to fall to my knees and beg for forgiveness, but I'm too scared. Scared that he'll say no. Terrified he'll tell Atlas to make me leave.

Then I'll be back on the street, my car abandoned in Vegas. No money. Only the clothes on my back, which are still the cheap souvenir clothes Zeus bought me.

Everyone is staring at us, and the large open-plan space suddenly feels too small.

Claustrophobic.

So instead of doing the right thing, I do what I do best. I cower.

My feet stumble backward. "I can't. I don't ..." Something stabs me in the lungs. Panic, guilt, fear, maybe all of them. I can't breathe. "I need to get out of here."

Zeus's supportive "Callie" sounds like it's coming from underwater.

I turn and continue to stumble outside, gasping hard when the desert air hits me. I bend at the waist, hands on knees, trying to swallow as much oxygen as I can. It doesn't work.

My cheeks are wet, my vision blurry.

A gentle hand lands on my shoulder. "Cal?" Lemon's soft tone makes me break even more. "You're okay," he soothes in that way he has about him.

I manage to straighten up, even if my breathing isn't back to normal. "I don't ... I don't deserve nice. Please don't be nice to me." My voice is croaky, laced with the sob that's stuck in the back of my throat.

And there's the real reason why I couldn't bring myself to be here. To see him. Because even though I want his forgiveness, I don't believe I'll ever deserve it.

Instead of listening to me, though, he wraps his arms around me.

I hold on to him and dip my head on his shoulder, burying my face into his neck.

"While I don't agree with the choices you made, I do know you felt like you had no other way out."

"I couldn't … I couldn't see myself surviving on my own. He … he always told me that. That I was useless, that no one else would have me, that I couldn't live without him."

Lemon's arms squeeze me tighter. "I know. That's abusive relationships 101. They cut you off from the world and then make you believe that the only reason you have purpose is them."

Logically, I know this, but no matter how many times I tell myself it's not my fault, I can't help feeling stupid for believing him for so long.

I lift my head to look at him. "I did so many things I'm not proud of. So many things I didn't want to do—"

"You're safe now," he whispers. "I promise."

It might be the first time I've heard those words where I actually believe them. As much as I wanted to trust Zeus, I couldn't be sure.

With Lemon, there is no doubt.

"I'm so sorry," I say. "I'll spend the rest of my life making it up to you. I don't know how, but I'll find a way."

He hugs me again. "You can make it up to me by finding your old self. I know he's in there somewhere. You need to get better so you can move on from what you've been through."

My head throbs as I frown. "I thought you'd be angrier than this."

"Let's go inside and talk." Lemon tries to pull away, but I grip his wrist so he can't.

"I can't go back in there yet. Too many people staring at me. Too much judgment."

"The only person judging you here is you, but I get it. You're self-conscious and insecure. We'll go around the side of the house and go to my room, where we can talk."

"I can do that. There are so many things I want to say. So much I don't know how to let out."

"That all sounds good and well, but can I go first?"

"Having you yell at me first seems fitting." I prepare for it. Wait for it. But I should've known it wouldn't come.

Lemon smiles. "I won't be yelling, but we do have some things to deal with."

That's an understatement.

We go around the side of the house and through a sliding door that leads to a pristine bedroom with a four-post bed and fireplace.

"Nice place," I say.

"These guys are loaded. You should see Atlas's house. Uh, my house, I guess. Now we're married."

I swallow hard. "Congratulations, by the way. I'm really happy for you." Even if my tone comes out like I'm speaking at a funeral.

I'm not jealous. I'm not.

Lemon really does deserve the world. He deserves the best. I just wish ... I wish I had a shot at happiness too.

"You can be happy too, you know." He's always been able to see right through me. Well, except that one time when he couldn't.

I was terrified the whole time I was deceiving him that he could tell, but he either didn't want to see it or chalked up my weird behavior to the abuse Stephen had laid upon me.

"I'm a mess," I say.

"Come here." Lemon pulls me down onto a small couch by the fireplace and holds my hand. "I'm not going to lie, I was so angry and hurt when everything happened. So were the other guys at the club."

"I had no idea it was all going to go down the way it did. And when the fire started—"

"I know. It took a while for me to realize you were just as trapped there as the rest of us, and I can't say that I'm not still hurt, but I can acknowledge that you need support. It can't have been easy."

I shake my head. "It wasn't. And the shitty thing about it all is that these Mike Bravo guys gave me the means to get away. Money, a bus ticket, everything. I could have left, but …"

"But you were convinced you wouldn't survive. That you needed Stephen."

"I made the wrong choice, and I've regretted it ever since. You were right about Stephen. I never should've gone home with a client or trusted that he was there to 'save' me when all he wanted to do was manipulate me to do his bidding."

"He's gone now," he reminds me.

"He might be dead, but he still haunts me. Zeus came after me, and I immediately didn't trust that he was there for me. I ran, and I ran to the wrong person, and Zeus had to save me. I'm so sick of putting my trust in the wrong people."

"Trust is a fucking crapshoot."

I huff a sad laugh. "You don't need to worry about that now, though. You have a husband—"

"I do, but even in the beginning of our relationship, learning to trust him was difficult. He worked for David's business partner. Undercover. I found out before anything happened between us, but it made me question all the flirting beforehand. Like, he was only doing it to get information from me, not because he wanted to. That situation has nothing on what you've been through. I need you to promise that you won't be too hard on yourself."

Relief sweeps over me, but I don't for one second think our issues will be forgotten.

No one gets over a betrayal like that. I know I wouldn't.

I'm still nursing scars from my past, and I don't expect anyone else to help me heal. It's something I'm going to have to learn to do on my own, even if it seems impossible.

"Do you think you'll want to come to the club and see the others?"

I cock my head. "What do you mean? The club burned down."

Lemon's face breaks into a wide smile. "Uh, Atlas rebuilt it for me. He bought the land, had everyone pitch in, and yeah, Peaches is back up and running. Though he renamed it Juicy."

"Fitting," I say but can't muster any enthusiasm. "I ... I don't think I'm ready to face the others we used to work with. I can barely face you without breaking down."

"What about the Mike Bravo guys?"

I glance at the closed door leading back toward the end of the house where all the big, daunting men were hanging out.

"They all looked like they wanted to kill me. Atlas nearly died because of me. You nearly ..." I get choked up again because if Lemon had been killed because of my actions, I know I would've given up on life a lot earlier than I have.

"Their brotherhood is intense. There's only one woman on the team. How sexist is that? But anyway, if I can forgive you for almost killing my husband, the rest of them will come around. Even if I have to put my hands on my hips, stomp my foot, and demand Atlas tell them all to forgive you. He's their boss now, so they'll have to do it."

There's the Lemon I know. The protector. The amazing man I've always looked up to. Uh, metaphorically. Physically, he's a tiny thing.

"You're too good for your own good," I say.

He slaps my chest in a playful way—it's not even hard—but when I flinch, his hand goes to his mouth. "Oh my God, I'm sorry. I didn't mean to—"

"It's fine. It's just something I do now. Fun times."

"I only did it because Atlas says that to me all the time. Like when I said I wanted to find you and make sure you're okay."

"I thought you didn't know I was coming. Or that I was alive."

"I'd said it to Atlas in passing. That I'd hoped you were okay, and I wanted to know you were safe, and he sent Zeus as a gift to me. Which I'm thankful for because you obviously weren't okay."

"I'm fine, but normal human interactions are difficult for me to read now. Eighteen months ago, you playfully slapping me would've made me tackle you and try to tickle you or mess up your hair. Now ..."

"A lot has happened."

"Maybe too much."

"You'll get there. I promise."

I hate that word. Promise. Because even if you say it, it doesn't mean it's true.

It won't happen again, Sam. I promise.

I was drunk, but I've given up drinking now. I promise.

Everything will get better. I promise.

I promise.

I promise.

I promise.

It actually has no meaning.

But instead of arguing that point, I reluctantly nod. Because even if he is making an empty promise, I want it to be true.

I hate feeling like this. Hate the person I've become. But most of all, I hate that I still want a man to promise me the world.

What the hell is wrong with me?

CHAPTER FIFTEEN_
ZEUS

Iris puts a beer in front of my face. Literally. I take it off him just so I can keep staring outside where I saw Callie and Lemon walk by the window not too long ago.

"We're day drinking now?" I ask but sip my drink anyway.

"You looked like you needed it. Haz tells us you jumped out a fifteen-story window and have been shot at multiple times in the last eighteen hours or so. Why do you get to be so lucky?"

I should've known that would be his response because on any other job, it would've been my kind of excitement too.

But with Callie, it's different. He's my … project. My retribution. I can do for him what I didn't do for Olive.

"Speaking of Haz." I change the subject. "He's fucking reckless. Trav thinks you and I were hard to tame? He should see this guy."

"Mm, says the person who got a blowie from his mark." Haz is behind me. Great.

I glare at Iris. "Thanks for the heads-up."

"Callie blew you?" Iris asks, his face lighting up. "No way. I'm not all that surprised because you are you, but—"

"It was part of our cover. I had to."

"Uh-huh. 'Had to.' Got it." Iris winks. "Just like I 'had to' climb in the shower with Saint this morning."

I give up because no matter what I say, they're not going to believe me. I'm a shallow man-slut and obviously let Callie blow me because any hole's a goal and all that shit.

I turn to Haz. "Shouldn't you be off hassling Decaf? He's the entire reason you joined Mike Bravo, isn't it?"

Iris practically vibrates out of his skin. "You and Decaf? No way. This is amazing." He addresses me. "Did we know Decaf dates? Like, hook up, yeah. And he can pass for someone in his late thirties, so he always goes for guys in their twenties, but—"

Haz screws up his face. "I am not here for Decaf for … that."

"Are you sure?" I could've sworn he had a thing for him. "How do you even know him?"

"I'll tell you, but then I'll have to kill you." Haz walks off on us.

"Please tell me we aren't that annoying," Iris says.

"Right?"

Scout passes us at that moment. "You are."

We both flip him off.

"Seriously, though," Iris says to me.

"You? Want to be serious? Does not compute."

"No, I was seriously asking if you really got a BJ from Callie. He's hot. He's, like, a younger version of Saint. All sunshine hair with the all-American vibe."

"Heard that," Saint calls out from the kitchen. "And if you think you can trade up to a newer model, you're mistaken."

"Pfft. I've already broken you in and trained you. No way I'm going through that nightmare again." Iris isn't fooling anyone.

We all know if anyone's breaking in anyone else, it would be Saint training Iris on how to be a grown-up.

Lemon appears in the hallway that leads to Trav's guest rooms and a side door from the backyard.

He's alone, though.

I abandon Iris and go straight over to him. "Where's Callie?"

"He, uh, didn't feel up to facing the whole group of you, and in his defense, you're all a little ... intimidating."

"Yeah. That's fair enough." I stare down the hall. "Is he okay?"

"He is. We found an empty room for him to crash in for a few hours. He said you didn't get much sleep last night."

I've had practically no sleep, but if I nap now, I won't sleep tonight.

Callie, though, he's been through a lot. He deserves some rest.

"He's okay," Lemon says again. "We had a good talk."

Good. That's really good. That means that they can repair their friendship, and Callie will have someone else on his side.

"He was really freaking out about seeing you," I say.

"I know. And I feel terrible."

Of course he does. That's the most Lemony thing to ever Lemon. Atlas is always going on and on about how caring his husband is, always putting everyone else first.

"You have nothing to feel terrible about," I say and mean it. I don't believe either of them do.

"I can't help it. I knew him before all of this happened, and you should've seen him. He danced to the Beach Boys, had this carefree smile, and was so goddamn optimistic. Now, he's a shell of that person. It makes me ragey. If Stephen wasn't already dead, I could kill him with my bare hands."

I cock an eyebrow at him.

"Okay, I'd get Atlas and you guys to do it."

I laugh. "It's good that you know your place here."

"Don't get me wrong. I'd want to do it myself, but I can't pull off murder."

"You'd probably try to strangle someone but keep asking if they're okay while you do it."

He waves me off. "Then it would turn into this whole 'choke

me harder' sex thing. I'll leave the killing up to you guys. I'm only here to look pretty."

Atlas appears out of nowhere. "Aww, you're so much more than a pretty face to me." He kisses his husband's cheek.

"I know, but in general. Around your people. I mean, you wouldn't want your guys to see me as more than something pretty to look at, right?"

"Hell no," Atlas growls.

Unlike at their wedding, where their cutesy love schtick made me want to gag, it makes me want to go and make sure Callie is okay. I don't know why. Probably because it's Lemon. And Lemon and Callie are tangled up in the same world in my head.

"I'll leave you two to be gross all over each other." I abandon the drink I only had one sip of and sneak down the hall to try to find which room Callie is in.

I open doors as I go, but they're all empty, which means he's in the room at the very end. It's the one that no one generally wants because there are no windows, and it's small. It only has enough room for a double bed and one nightstand.

Being as quiet as I can, I open the door and find him facing me, but his eyes are closed. When he realizes he's no longer alone, he flinches awake.

"It's only me," I say.

"I wasn't really sleeping."

"Just resting your eyes? My parents used to say that one all the time. They still do. Especially at Thanksgiving dinner after they've eaten a huge meal and the kids are hyped up on sugar from all the pie they ate."

"Kids?"

I glance away. "My sister's kids. My parents took custody after everything went down."

Callie pats the bed next to him. "Come tell me more because I want to focus on something that's not my fucked-up life."

Even though I'm in real danger of getting too close and I know

I should turn around and walk back down the hall to where the other guys are, I can't help but do as he asks.

Being around other fucked-upness cancels out your own. Why else are reality shows so popular? The screwed-up people who go on there make you feel better about your own sad life.

I shut the door behind me and then lie down next to him but lie on my back so I don't have to look at his face. I also make sure I keep a foot or two distance between us.

"My sister left the kids to me. She wanted me to be their guardian."

"What stopped you?"

Okay, I have to turn my head now to see if he's even serious. "Are you suddenly forgetting my reputation? No responsibilities. Nothing to tie me down."

"That's to do with finding a partner, though. Not kids."

"Kids are an even bigger responsibility than a relationship. No way was I ready for that a few years ago. Hell, I'm not ready for that now. My parents had already done the parenting thing, and they love those kids."

"Why do I sense some bitterness, then?" Callie asks.

Damn it. This is why I don't let people in. Why I don't let them see the real me. Living the fast life, having numerous people warming my bed, there isn't the chance to fall for anyone when you don't share anything real.

"I would've taken them," I mumble. "Mom and Dad are old. They're going to be in their seventies when the kids are teenagers, and I often think I'll end up with them anyway, but ..."

"You're hurt they didn't let you take them when your sister died."

"I get it. I really do. I'm reckless, I'm never home, and I'm not exactly the best role model. But for them? I would've changed. I would've grown up. Because they need protecting and nurturing, and they deserve all the love my sister had for them. Instead, when my parents asked if I really thought I was mature enough to take them, I sank into my irresponsible persona even more. Psychologically, it doesn't make sense. I should have wanted to prove them wrong."

"Sometimes we know a lost cause when we see one."

"Are you saying I was a lost cause?" That pisses me off.

His warm hand touches my forearm, sending tingles all over my skin. "No. I didn't mean that at all. I mean that sometimes, no matter what we do, no matter what we show or prove to others, sometimes we know that they will never see us as anything else. Like when my parents hated that I wanted to do ballet and wanted me to play football instead. I did as they asked, tried to be the jock they wanted me to be, but all I wanted to do was dance. No matter how hard I tried to be the person they wanted and hid that side away, they never looked at me the way I thought they would."

"What made you become a stripper?"

"Me realizing I would never be good enough for my parents. I came out, they expectedly kicked me out because of it, and by that time, I was twenty-one and could get into bars. I couch surfed for a while with some of my high school friends, but it was when I first went to Peaches and met Lemon that he saw me and gave me a shot. He chose my name, my persona, my everything."

I hold my heart. "You mean to tell me you're not really a surfer dude from California? I am so shocked. Are all strippers liars?"

At first, I worry my joke might offend him, but it doesn't.

He laughs. "All of us are. It's for our safety more than anything."

"Well, that's depressing. Do you think … do you think you'll go back to stripping? I'm sure they'll have you at Juicy if you wanted to."

He really thinks about it. "What kind of a life can I have when Pierre's going to come after me? After you for helping me? I keep getting myself into these messes, and I just …" He buries his face in his hands. "I don't know what to do anymore."

I grip his wrist to pull a hand off his face. "We can help you."

"How?"

"We'll get you somewhere safe."

He drops his voice low. "I don't want to run anymore. I'm sick of looking over my shoulder. Of living out of a car and moving from place to place just to survive. I ... I don't think I'll be able to survive it much longer."

"Fucking hell," I say under my breath. "Can I please hug you? You can say no. I will never tell you to do something you're not comfortable with."

He licks his sexy lips. "Please hug me. I need it. I need affection that isn't bought or traded."

I roll onto my side and slip my arm under his pillow, pressing myself against him and cupping his cheek with my other hand. "I'm so sorry for what we did last night. Maybe Trav was right, and we should've just tried to kidnap you while Pierre or his men weren't on top of you, but—"

"I would've been stuck there a hell of a lot longer if you'd waited to be able to do that. And I know you're sorry about the blowjob, but I'm not. It might have been a necessity, but I'm glad it was you and not some random man who wouldn't have treated me as nicely as you."

"I promise I will never have transactional sex with you again, and I will never make you feel like you're being used."

Callie blinks up at me, and I realize what I've said. My actual words should have been I will never have sex with you again, period. End of sentence.

"I mean—"

"You want a repeat?"

I shouldn't want one, but I do. I want to make him feel as good as he did for me. No, I want to make him feel better than that because my orgasm came with a side of guilt. "It would only be fair to return the favor." I roll us so I'm on top of him. "Or you can tell me to back off, and I'll get up and walk out of here. Or stay and cuddle you some more. You've been through so much trauma in such a short time. You deserve a break. You deserve—"

"I want you to make me feel not so alone." His voice cracks.

"You're not." I lean in, my lips inching closer to his, but I'm not going to be the one to take it from him. He's going to have to make the next move.

It doesn't take Callie long to catch on, and he lifts his head.

The first connection, his mouth on mine, it's explosive. He pushes his tongue inside and teases mine. Licks, caresses.

Callie whimpers at my groan, and the sound drives me wild.

This is a mistake. I already know that. But I can't help myself. I've never had much self-restraint when it comes to sex—with anyone—but I've always been strong enough to say no or pull away if something didn't feel right.

This feels so wrong but so fucking right. That's what's messing with my head. It's the reason I can't bring myself to stop, even though I should.

I might not be able to make myself stop, but I can force myself to slow down.

Only he doesn't like that. His hips buck, and he writhes beneath me, his desperation making his skin practically vibrate.

Callie's hard cock slides against mine, and even through layers of clothing, I love it. But I let him do the work. I hold stock-still on top of him and let him thrust upward to get what he needs, all the while fucking his mouth with my tongue.

He reaches between us, wrapping his fingers around my clothed cock, but I grip his wrist.

"This is going to be about you," I say and break free of his lips. I lay kisses along his jaw, down his neck.

"A-about me?" The uncertainty in his voice makes me angry. Not at him, but at every asshole who's ever treated him like their own personal sex doll. Anyone who hasn't cared about his needs. His wants.

I mask my anger with a half-smile. "I already told you. I need to return the favor."

I slink down his body, kissing my way down his chest and the god-awful I heart LV T-shirt. My fingers dip under the hem and draw it up, revealing Callie's toned abs, which only become more defined as he breathes hard.

Callie runs his hand through the top of my hair, gripping it tightly. "You don't have to," he says.

I lift my gaze while tonguing his belly button. "I know I don't. But you deserve to be worshipped. You deserve pleasure and not to just be an afterthought. You made me come so hard—so fucking hard—and now I want to make you do the same."

He shudders and releases my hair, but his hand falls to the side of him and fidgets, like he's uncomfortable about being the only focus of attention.

I pull up. "What's wrong?"

"I ... I don't know what to do with my hands."

I chuckle, but it's not really funny. "Not used to having sex be all about you?"

He avoids eye contact as he admits, "No."

"Let's fix that, then." I shuffle onto my knees and tap his leg. "Sit up for me."

He does.

"Lift your arms."

He does that too.

I strip him out of his shirt and then follow suit to make it an even playing field. His skin is already flushed, breaking out in goose bumps.

"Hips," I order and take down his sweats when he lifts up.

His cock is long and thin, and I can't wait to have it in my mouth. It points straight up, resting against his stomach, and the urge to dive in is almost too overwhelming, but Callie still fidgets with the bedsheet beneath his fingers.

"Roll over," I say.

"I don't get to see your cock?"

"Will that make you more comfortable? You've already seen it. It's been in your mouth."

"I want to see it."

"I did say this will be all about you and what you want, so ..."
I pull down my pants slowly, slipping them down my legs until I
can kick them off.

Then I straighten up and stroke myself, loving the way Callie's
eyes focus on what I'm doing.

"Got your fill yet?"

He shakes his head. "I don't think I will until that thing's
inside me."

I throw my head back because that's not going to happen. "I
don't have supplies with me, and this is supposed to be about
you. Roll over and let me do my thing."

He doesn't move, just keeps watching as I tease myself, slowly
tugging on my cock, even though I want to speed up and come all
over his skin.

To save us both the torture, I release myself and grip Callie's
hips, fully prepared to flip him over myself if I have to.

His hands cover mine, though, and I pause. "Just please
promise me you'll get off too."

I lean down and kiss the tip of his nose. "I will, but I don't
want you to have to worry about that. Just relax and feel."

He licks his lips. "Okay."

"Roll over," I order him again.

When he does, he gets up on all fours.

I push him down by the shoulder blades, but not hard. Just
enough to get him to lay his arms flat, his chest on the mattress,
while his knees are bent with his pretty hole right there for me to
play with.

His balls are tight, his cock rock hard, so I reach between his
legs and hold him tight. I give a few strokes before pulling it
backward toward me.

I stroke him enough to make him crazy but not enough to
actually get him anywhere. There's a delicate balance in bringing
someone pleasure and just wanting them to hurry up and get off.

I want to show Callie that he's worth more than a rush job.

He deserves someone who'll take their time with him. Who'll make sure he's flying high through the whole thing and not just at the end.

And when I do finally let him come, I want it to be so powerful that it fucking breaks him.

CHAPTER SIXTEEN_

CALLIE

Zᴇᴜs ɪs ꜰᴜᴄᴋɪɴɢ ʙʀᴇᴀᴋɪɴɢ ᴍᴇ, ᴀɴᴅ ʜᴇ ᴅᴏᴇsɴ'ᴛ ᴇᴠᴇɴ know it. Or maybe he does. I can't really tell.

With my ass in the air, my arms stuck under me, it's easy for me to do as he says and just feel him, but a part of me still won't relax. In this position, I'm bare, I'm open to him—physically and mentally—and I'm exposed.

It's hard to push away intrusive thoughts of him sliding his dick inside me without lube, of taking advantage of me when it would be so easy to.

Even though it would make no sense for him to reassure me and then break that trust, it's happened before.

He's still stroking my cock at an agonizingly slow pace. One of his hands bites into my ass cheek, gripping so hard it might leave bruises where his fingers are. It's a mix of pleasure with a tiny bit of pain, and it makes my mind fuzzy.

Slowly, with every stroke, I'm able to push my hesitance to the side, to sink into it and relax.

He's pulling all my strings and playing me like an instrument. And when I think I can't take any more and am about to beg for him to go faster, do more, do … something, his wet mouth licks over the head of my dick.

I curse under my breath and feel his silent laugh as his breath hits my sensitive skin.

That's when he sucks me in deep, all the way he can. His mouth is warm and wet, and then the hand gripping my ass lets go, only to move to my lower back, right above my ass crack.

At some point, I don't know when, he covered his fingers in spit.

They slip into my crease, traveling down, down ... I shiver when they brush over my hole, but they don't stop. He cups my balls, squeezes, and then moves his hand back up so he can push a finger inside me. It's teasing and only gentle.

My entire body lights up. My nipples are hard, fucking aching. I'm flushed with want and need.

But I get the impression he's still only playing with me. He slowly works me open with his fingers while sucking on my cock. And he's doing exactly what he said he would. He focuses on me and only me, drawing it out.

His fingers brush over my prostate but then retreat. He does this over and over again until, finally, he presses against it. My feet tingle, my gut warms, and that need for more only intensifies.

Zeus pushes me to the edge and then pulls it back.

I'm desperately whining, letting out my frustrations the whole time, but I can't deny how amazing this is.

I'm helpless but in a powerful way. He's not restricting me so he can get what he wants. He's restricting me because if he didn't, I would be distracted with what I could do for him. How I could get him off. How *he* feels.

Zeus is giving me something that I've never had before. It's dangerous because the more I get used to being treated not only like a human but something that should be goddamn cherished, the worse off I'm going to be when it's done.

When I have to face the consequences of my actions. When I have to run again just to survive.

Zeus says he can help, but there's no way it'll be easy. I don't think there's enough money in the world for Pierre to forgive what I did to him, let alone what Zeus did.

Zeus, Haz, and, by extension, the rest of Mike Bravo has just been added to Pierre's shit list.

Zeus pulls off my cock. "Stop thinking. You're in your head."

How the fuck can he tell that?

Also, I kind of have to be. "If I stop thinking, I'm going to come."

"You can let go," he murmurs. "At any time."

As if giving me permission, I release that tension, the thing holding me back, and it only takes his mouth on my cock for a few more seconds for me to fall.

All I can get out in warning is "Oh, fuck."

Zeus pulls off me, replacing his mouth with his hand as he strokes me through the waves that keep coming.

I'm so sated that I want to cry. It doesn't make sense, but somehow, that was more than getting off. That wasn't about the end result, though it was explosive.

I can't move. My knees are locked in, my ass still in the air, and my chest pressed against the mattress.

Zeus's strokes slow down as I become empty, and when I'm done, he removes his fingers from my ass.

Then, his front covers my back as he lies on top of me. His hard cock digs into my ass cheek, and if I had any energy at all, I'd push backward to give him friction. To encourage him to rut against me.

"You did so good," he says in my ear and then kisses my neck softly. "So fucking good."

"Your turn," I rasp, but my voice goes up at the end as if I'm asking a question. I'm not. I want to make him feel as good as I do.

"Nope." He lifts off me. "I told you, that was about you, not me."

His protest finally gets my body moving. I roll to my side and then inch my way onto my back. "But this almost looks painful."

I grip the base of his cock with one hand while cupping his balls in the other.

The growl that comes out of his mouth is feral and so fucking hot, but his big hands wrap around mine, and in the next instant, my arms are suddenly above my head, being pinned to the pillow.

"I'm going to get off, but you're not going to do a thing to get me there except look like you do right now. Like I fucking wrecked you."

He did. And I don't want him to stop.

Zeus rises up, straddling my legs but keeping my hands pinned above my head. He's so big and domineering on top of me, and considering my past, I should be scared. This guy could kill me six different ways with his bare hands, but one thing I don't feel when I look at him is scared.

Not anymore.

Those fingers that drove me so wild not five minutes ago wrap around his cock, his strokes slow but firm. His blue eyes pierce mine, staring down at me with unrestrained lust shining through.

I want to touch him. I want to help. But the second I move my hands, they're pinned again but in only one of his.

He continues to jerk himself, faster now, but he sticks by his word. I don't have to do anything. I want to, but he won't let me. Which is oddly freeing.

With him pinning my hands, he's leaning over me now, and we're face-to-face. I can feel his hot breath on my skin, see the pleasure across his face.

He's no longer holding back, his hand frantically trying to get him across the finish line. We're so close his hand moves against my lower stomach, and my cock tries to get back in on the action but is too spent.

Zeus stiffens, and his warm cum hits my abs. His grip on my wrists tightens as he closes his eyes and rides out his orgasm.

His O face is something worthy of a goddamn porn award. He could make so much money putting that all over the internet.

Zeus's muscles begin to shake, as if tired of holding his weight up, and in the next second, he collapses on top of me.

I jokingly grunt, and he laughs.

"Sorry. Couldn't hold myself up any longer."

"Being crushed by a superhot naked guy isn't the worst way to die."

Zeus tenses and rolls off me, releasing my hands as he does.

I turn to my side to find him staring at me with a concentration line in his brow.

"You didn't actually hurt me," I say.

His gaze narrows, but he nods. "We should get cleaned up." He rolls out of bed, and my gut sinks.

He just spent that whole time making sure I knew that this was all about me, about what I want, what I need, and the second it's over, he just gets up and leaves?

He uses his discarded shirt to wipe himself off, and for a second, I think he's going to throw it to me for me to do the same, but he hesitates. His hardened features soften, and then his knees hit the mattress.

Zeus leans over me, cleaning me up with his shirt, and when he's done, he leans down and kisses my mouth.

It's soft. It's … caring. Whatever I saw a second ago is gone, or maybe I imagined it in the first place. I was sure he was going to get up and leave me here, but he didn't.

And even as he tosses his shirt to the ground and settles beside me, there's a part of me that reminds me that it's temporary.

I wish I could drown that voice. Literally. I don't want to be this pessimistic guy, but it's really hard not to be with the way I've been treated for years. Not just by Stephen but by any man.

Clients at the strip club, all the boyfriends I've ever had, no one has ever treated me right. No one's ever looked at me the way Zeus does.

Zeus pulls the covers up that got all tangled and kicked to the bottom of the bed during our tryst and covers us both.

"Turn over." He already sounds half-asleep.

I put my back to him, and his beefy arm comes across my midsection.

Who would've thought the notorious manwhore was a *cuddler*?

CHAPTER SEVENTEEN_
ZEUS

NOT GOING TO LIE, WAKING UP WRAPPED AROUND someone is unusual for me. It gives people the wrong impression. With Callie, though, I couldn't bring myself to walk out that door.

I wanted to. Everything in my being told me to, but when he joked that being crushed under my weight wouldn't be the worst way to die, all I could think was that he'd actually contemplated how many different ways he could die.

I was hit with panic, rage, and then an all-encompassing surge of sympathy. It wasn't pity, though. He would hate that, and so would I.

With the way we're positioned, though, I should tell him that it can't happen again. Remind him that I'm a temporary person.

Yet, I can't bring myself to do it.

We have other things to focus on. Like a ranch full of immature gun nuts, Callie's ex-best friend, and both my bosses, who will need to be briefed on the situation with Pierre.

Which I should go do as soon as possible. Depending on what the time is. We fell asleep during the middle of the day, and there's no window in here.

I could've been asleep for twenty minutes or six hours, for all I know.

I slink out of bed, cautiously trying to detangle my limbs from Callie's so I don't wake him.

He notices, though, and rolls over to face me just as I sit up.

"I'm just checking the time." I pull my phone out of my pants on the floor. "Fuck, we slept the afternoon away. It's nine."

"PM?" he shrieks.

"Yep. Way to screw with our sleep patterns." I run my hand over my hair. "Want some dinner?"

Callie stretches, his long, lean body catching my attention. "I could go for some breakfast."

My gaze drifts up to his face, where he's already smiling at me.

Right. Food. Feed the man. Don't fuck the man.

"You ready to face anyone out there yet, or do you want me to bring stuff back in here to eat?"

He bites his lip.

"They're probably all drunk at this time, and when they're drunk, they don't see far past their noses. They shouldn't even notice you."

Callie is about to give in. I can feel it.

"I'll stay by your side the whole time."

That's what he was wanting. "Promise?"

Again, this is where I should be saying no, but because of my past trauma over my sister, I don't want to say no to Callie. I don't want him to feel alone.

"Always. Unless you tell me it's okay. You never know, you might get out there and be all, 'Geez, Zeus, leave me alone already. You're so suffocating.'"

"Hmm, that sounds like something you would more likely say. That's in the manwhore's rule book, isn't it? Thou shalt always feel suffocated."

He's not wrong.

"Yeah, yeah, yeah. Let's throw some clothes on and see what

we can raid from the kitchen." That's when I remember my shirt and all the dried cum that will be on it.

Guess I'm going shirtless, then.

Callie puts the I heart LV shirt back on and the sweats I bought him.

"We need to get new clothes," I say.

"Yes, please. I don't love Las Vegas this much."

"Does anyone?"

Callie thinks about that. "Gamblers?"

"True. Though that's probably more a love/hate thing. Ready to get out there?"

"Yes? Uh, no?"

"Food. Let's just concentrate on getting food."

Callie holds his stomach. "That works. Let's go."

I fight the urge to hold his hand, to show him that I'm here for him, but if we walked out there hand in hand, I would never hear the end of it. Ever. Like, the guys would write it on my tombstone. "Here lies Zeus. He liked to pretend he was a fuck-boy, but let it be said, he once held a boy's hand."

Luckily, with how drunk everyone is when we get out there, there wouldn't be any issue. Because I wasn't lying. All the Mike Bravo guys are messy as fuck when drinking.

We're able to breeze past Iris and Saint, fussing over their dog lapping at some spilled beer one of the others must've dropped and trying to get her to stop drinking. Iris is wailing about his daughter being an alcoholic, and Saint is telling him he's being dramatic while saying he should be more worried about the broken glass.

Haz is playing poker at the coffee table with Angel, Alphabet, Scout, and Rogue.

"Didn't lose enough in Vegas?" I ask Haz.

Somewhere behind me, there's a loud growl, and I turn to find Decaf leaning against the wall and glaring at me. Oh, wait—I follow his gaze, and he's glaring at Haz.

I call bullshit on them never hooking up.

We get to the kitchen without incident, and Callie relaxes a little.

"You were right," he whispers.

"Can't see past their own noses on a good day, let alone after a few drinks."

And just when we both think we're safe, Trav rounds the corner. He leans his hip against the island and folds his arms, eyeing my shirtless body before flicking his gaze over to Callie, who looks like he's about to shit himself.

"What's up, boss?" I don't stop what I'm doing because I have no reason to be scared. Other than, you know, costing Trav over a hundred thousand dollars in one night, but really, that's like spare change to him.

"Sorry I missed you earlier," Trav says, and I sense a trap. "I went to go find you both, but ..." He pauses, and I have no doubt he either overheard us messing around or just has a hunch we did.

"We were sleeping. We were up all night after, you know, being shot at."

"And before the sleeping? I swear I could hear ... explosions."

Callie pales as if he's forgotten how to breathe.

"Oh, you mean the C4. Right. Um, so I was showing Callie how to deal with all that emotional stuff by blowing up our feelings."

"That's going to bite you in the ass one day," Trav says. "You know that, right?"

"Like you're the pillar of mental health? You played playground bully to Rogue for years before you finally admitted you liked him. Like, *like liked* him."

Would I say I'm an expert at turning any conversation around so the focus is no longer on me? No, but it usually works. Apparently not this time, though.

"We need a debrief," Trav says. "Or have you already been debriefed tonight?"

Okay, that all but confirms it. He came to find me, only to hear me messing around with Callie.

But like I'm so good at, I deflect. "You know I'm all for cloth-ing-optional opportunities."

"Yet, you don't deny being naked tonight?"

I tap my chin. "Define naked. In the great words of RuPaul, we're all born naked, and the rest is drag. So, was I naked, or was I just not in drag?"

Trav's last nerve snaps. "Okay, enough bullshit. You, me, and Atlas. Meeting in five?"

"Callie will be there too," I say.

Trav narrows his gaze.

"I promised I wouldn't feed him to the rest of the wolves. He's stuck to me like glue until he believes none of our guys will hurt him."

Callie lowers his head. "Now it seems like I asked you to be my bodyguard. I can go back to my room and hide."

"Nope. I promised. I don't break promises." Mainly because I don't make them, but that's beside the point.

Trav folds his arms. "I can respect that, but—"

"It's fine," Callie says but then glances around the room at everyone with a terrified look in his eyes.

"Is Lemon around?" I ask Trav. "Callie feels safe with him."

"He and Atlas went to bed not too long ago, but I'm assuming it wasn't to sleep." He takes out his phone to text Atlas, and he gets an immediate response. "Lemon will be available in a couple of minutes."

"Is that all Atlas takes?" I know I've fucked up the second I've said something.

"Do we really want to get into how long people last while doing things with others?" Trav asks.

"You talking in circles, boss? Have no idea what you're saying. So, meeting, then? Yes, let's get to work. I'm just going to go drop Callie with Lemon, so, uh, bye."

I grab Callie's wrist and pull him back through the house,

only realizing once we're at the 2IC's closed bedroom door that we didn't end up eating.

"Shit. Food. You were starving."

"It's okay. I don't think I could eat now anyway. Not while worrying about what's going on with you and your boss."

"You can sit in on the meeting. It is about you."

He shakes his head. "It's about what I've dragged other people into. Again."

"That was our choice. We could've left you as soon as I saw you in that dive of an alien cafe. I could have noped out when I saw you go into Pierre's casino. I've had plenty of chances to run away, and I haven't. I also haven't been ordered to abandon the mission of finding you, so it's obvious Trav and Atlas are fine with stepping in too."

"You shouldn't have to, though."

I grip his shoulders. "This is what we do for a living. It's our job to get involved in corruption like this. And with what Pierre did to you ... what he's doing to that woman who was with you? This is the exact type of drama Trav loves to stick his nose in. And hey, his DEA boyfriend will probably love to get insight on who's supplying Pierre with all the party drugs that were lying around that hotel room. It's a win-win, really."

"You're not just saying that, are you?"

At that precise moment, Atlas opens the bedroom door. "He's not just saying it."

"Eavesdrop much?"

Atlas stares at my hands gripping Callie's shoulders, and I drop them so fast it's as if merely touching Callie burned me.

"I couldn't help it," Atlas says. "I heard your voice and that you were being dead serious, and my mind was completely blown. You didn't mention sex once in that whole spiel, and I was impressed."

I roll my eyes. "Oh, fuck you."

Now, Lemon appears behind him. "Nope, sorry. That's my job." He takes Callie's hand. "Apparently, we're hanging out while these guys plot how to take down all the bad guys with their pew pews."

"I already told you," Atlas complains. "Calling guns pew pews diminishes how lethal they are."

"Sorry. Pointy bang bangs. Is that better?" Lemon looks up at Atlas, but when he glares back, Lemon says, "Love you. Okay, bye." He pulls Callie down the hall. "We could hang out in our room, but it smells like sex" is the last thing I hear as they round the corner, no doubt going back to the room Callie and I were in.

Yeah, it's going to smell like sex too.

I don't care if everyone knows Callie and I hooked up. Except they all know I had to for the job too, and if any of them find out I had a repeat with someone, they're going to do that annoying, immature thing that I would normally do, which is sing the wedding march whenever we enter a room.

I'm fucked.

CHAPTER EIGHTEEN_
CALLIE

"Huh. It smells like sex in here too." Lemon lifts his arm and sniffs his pit. "Is it me? Am I so full of Atlas's cum that I'm sweating it now?"

"I've totally heard that's a thing." Yup. Definitely. Nothing sexual happened in this room. Not. Even. A. Little.

Lemon spins on me. "You had sex with Zeus!"

"Shh." I close the gap between us and put my hand over his mouth. "Say it louder, why don't you?"

Muffled, he gets out, "Moo mab mex miff Meus."

I throw myself on the bed. "It was nothing."

"Nothing? His reputation implies the moves he has are not nothing. Is he too overhyped?" He screws up his face. "All talk and poor execution."

"What? No. The sex was fine. Amazing even. It just didn't mean anything."

Lemon joins me but sits on the side of the mattress with his feet dangling to the floor. "It never does with Zeus. Or so I've heard."

Even though he's made it clear he was only blowing me to repay what I had to do to him in Vegas, it stings to hear Lemon say that. Sure, he might've told me about his sister and wants to look out for me because of that, but that still doesn't mean the blowjob meant anything.

"So, what was it like?" Lemon asks.

"I'm not telling you."

"Please? You don't think I had wicked fantasies of what he could do from the moment I met the guy? Even Atlas knew I was checking him out."

"He didn't care you were checking out someone else?"

"That's the best part. Atlas knows how good-looking Zeus is. It was impossible to fault me. That, and I'm pretty sure by that point, he knew I was his." He lifts one shoulder. "Let me live vicariously through you."

"Mm, and who doesn't love a good story of pity sex?"

"It was pity sex?"

"When he was getting me out of Vegas, we had to keep his cover of being a john. I blew him, and it made him feel guilty. Like he was pressuring me into it. He wanted me to have an experience that was all about me because I'm a lonely, used, broken person. Sounds like pity sex to me."

"I dunno about that. Seems like he actually cares about you."

And maybe that's true to some extent, but it's probably in a "you deserve better, and here's a taste of what it can be like" thing instead of a "I can be that man for you."

"Doubt it. Everyone knows he's not the serious or caring type. I'm just another notch on his bedpost or whatever that saying is. And I'm okay with that. At least he didn't make me feel used. That was a first."

"Is it weird that the one guy who uses everyone for sex made you feel the least used?" Lemon asks.

"Probably not. If everyone wants to sleep with him so badly and he's had countless partners, it would make sense that he'd be good at it."

He turns toward me, bending one leg out in front of him.

"You know what we should do? This place has amazing facilities—"

"Zeus already took me to blow shit up using C4. It cheered me up for about five seconds."

Lemon's mouth drops. "He took you to the C4 field? Even I'm not allowed there. I've begged Atlas, and he keeps saying 'one day' and then never takes me. Oh, he's in so much trouble."

Oops. "I'm sure he just wants to make sure you're safe."

"I want to play with explosives," he whines.

I laugh. "Yeah, I can see why he's reluctant."

Lemon goes to shove me, but he pauses when I suck in a sharp breath. "Shit. I almost did it again. It's like second nature with you."

I cover his hand with mine. "I hate that I'm making you feel bad."

His eyes turn down. "I hate that you even have to think about it. I'm sorry. I'm going to try to do better."

"Hey. You forgave me. That's more than I ever could have asked for."

"I wish I could fix you."

I smile because I know what he's saying is the truth, but even I know it's only something that will come with time, therapy, self-acceptance, and whatever other bullshit all the health professionals say. Or would say if I could afford to see a professional.

"What are your plans now?" Lemon asks.

I huff. "Good question. It's up to your husband, Zeus, and Trav to decide that."

"Why?"

"They're having a meeting about it as we speak. Pierre will be looking for me. And Zeus. Haz. Anyone else who aided in our escape."

"How would they even find you?"

"They found us at the motel we were staying in, didn't they? It's like Pierre has eyes everywhere. I stayed in Reno briefly before someone ratted me out to Pierre."

"Okay, so after the Mike Bravo guys take out Pierre, what will you do then?"

Ergh. I don't want to talk about this. Mainly because I don't know. When I see my future, all I see is darkness. It's a black hole of thoughts, and every time I dare dream of a real life, it gets sucked into the vortex, never to resurface again.

"If I get that privilege, I'll give it a think then. Right now, I just hope to see tomorrow. Then, when tomorrow comes, I'll hope for the same. A string of tomorrows is really all I can hope for."

"That's dark."

At first, I think Lemon is being snarky, but when I glance up and see the worry in his eyes shining back at me, I can tell he's worried. Maybe he has a right to be.

"I thought you said you had an idea? Let's get away from this depressing stuff. There's a reason I didn't want to be in that meeting with Atlas and Zeus."

"Because you don't want to face the future?"

I nod. "That, and Trav scares me."

Lemon laughs. "He did to me too, but then I saw him with his partner, and there's no way Trav is as hard and stern as he acts."

"Zeus said Pierre's guys took a shot at Trav's men, and therefore, Trav will take revenge."

"Oh, that's true."

"Lemon, I took a shot at his men. Sure, it was a different situation, and I didn't use an actual gun, but I trapped Atlas, and—"

"You're going to need to forgive yourself when it comes to that. Trav understands. Was he pissed in the beginning and gunning for your blood? Yes. But Atlas could see your deeper issues. He witnessed what you'd been through. He might not have agreed with what you did or accepted it, but he understood it."

"I guess I owe your husband my life, then. And you. And now Zeus." My eyes tear up. "Will I ever get to a position where I don't owe anyone anything and I can just fucking live?"

Lemon shuffles to hug me. "We'll find a way."

And even though I believe he wants to, I can't believe it'll happen.

I've gotten my hopes up one too many times for my heart to believe in anything.

CHAPTER NINETEEN_
ZEUS

"It had to be Pierre Claremont, didn't it?" Rogue mutters.

Trav side-eyes him. "Babe, I thought you'd be pleased. An excuse to take out an organized crime head? I think the words you're looking for are 'Thank you.' You're welcome. Anything for my boo."

Rogue crosses his arms. "Yeah, when you say take someone out, you mean end their existence. Not taking them out to dinner before collaring them and charging them with all their crimes."

"Hey, we do what our justice system can't." Trav smiles at his partner.

Rogue sighs. "If this is what this conversation is going to be about, I'm going to need to leave so I can have plausible deniability. I'm still a DEA agent." He moves toward the door, and Trav calls after him.

"Not for long."

"Whoa. You're trying to recruit Rogue?" I ask.

"Nah. We're going to adopt, and he's going to be my stay-at-home baby daddy."

Atlas and I share a *what the fuck* glance before turning back to our boss. Our big, hard-ass boss who looks like he eats children for breakfast.

"Of course I'm trying to recruit him," Trav says. "It was my plan from the start, but he's even more stubborn than I am. It took me years to wear him down to even date me. Joining the dark side? Hell, I think there really is more chance of us having kids than him actually becoming an official Mike Bravo member."

Atlas releases a subtle but relieved breath, his reaction hidden well behind his manners.

I'm not so polite. "Thank fuck. No offense, boss, but you are not the child type."

"No shit. Okay, now that the narc … I mean, the love of my life has gone, how are we really going to deal with Pierre?"

I rub my chin. "Blow up his whole casino and burn it to the ground?"

Atlas glowers at me. "That better have been a joke, considering Lemon and I were almost collateral damage in a similar plan last year."

"If there was a way to make sure everyone else was safely out of the building and only bad guys were left in there, it wouldn't be a joke."

"Wouldn't work anyway," Trav says. "That much demolition in tight spaces like the Strip in Vegas, debris would go for blocks. Not exactly subtle."

"I know that. But still. It's nice to imagine Pierre's tiny head going *boom*."

Trav and Atlas both stare at me as if they're trying to work something out.

"What?" I ask.

"I've never seen you so …" Trav's brow is scrunched, his lips turned up, like he's trying to think of the right word.

"Trigger-happy," Atlas finishes for him.

"What do you mean? I'm always itching to get in on the action."

"Not like this," Trav says. "I haven't seen you *care* so much."

He's right about that, but no way am I admitting to caring about anything. "I don't care about Pierre or whether he lives or dies. I just want something in Callie's life to go right for once."

As soon as I say those words, I know I've made a colossal mistake.

Trav gasps. "You don't care about killing Pierre. You care about what killing Pierre will do for Callie." He wipes a fake tear. "My little manwhore is all grown up."

Atlas chuckles.

I throw up double fingers. "Fuck off. That's not true. And if you so much as utter any of that to the other guys, I will end both of you. Got it?"

Now they break down in hysterics. "Zeus cares about someone," Trav says.

"Do not. You take it back!"

"I guess monogamy really is catching, hey, Zeus?" Atlas asks. "You caught it at my wedding after you were adamant you weren't going to sleep with any of Lemon's stripper friends. Guess you didn't consider that when I asked you to tail Callie."

I try to center myself and be my usual carefree self, but I can't bring myself to do it. "Okay, I know I'm known as the manwhore and that jokes always land on me about being a slut and everything being about sex, blah, blah, blah"—I used to share the burden with Iris until he fell ill to the monogamy curse. It's doubly as much since he shacked up with Saint—"but I'd like to think you all at least know I can be a decent person, especially to someone so goddamn broken he thinks he doesn't belong in this world anymore, and I wouldn't use that vulnerability to my advantage just to get my rocks off."

That shuts them up.

Finally.

Or so I think.

"Nah," Trav says. "You can be a decent person and still find a way to get your rocks off."

I'm almost at the point of yelling that wasn't the point of

hooking up with Callie earlier today, but that will prove their point even more.

Prove their point that Callie must mean something to me, that is. Not that I'm a decent person but still a manwhore. Which I am, but they say it in such a way that it makes me feel bad about it when I really shouldn't. No one should feel shame for enjoying sex and wanting it as often as possible.

Society for years has been so buttoned-up and conservative, more worried about a teenager's virtue than being emotionally well-adjusted. People's priorities are screwed up, and purity culture is toxic.

But just because I'm freely open about that, it doesn't mean I don't respect the people I'm with. I sometimes think the team actually believes the jokes about me. That I use people or only see others as a hole, a mouth, a warm body to get off to, when I don't.

You better believe I'm respectful to everyone I've ever been with, but look what happens when I try to say that out loud. They jump on the *ooh, he's catching feelings* train, when I'm not.

I never will.

Do I care slightly more for Callie than I do for anyone else I've had sex with? Of course. But that has nothing to do with love or what-the-fuck-ever. It's about a connection we have over bonded trauma. He's the sister I couldn't save ... and ... who I have sex with? Okay, that analogy is bad, but my point remains.

I'm more protective over him, am willing to break rules for him and help him move on from his past because he is my do-over.

I wasn't there for Olive, but I can do everything in my power to get him through this.

Hopefully without the rest of my team being assholes about it.

"Okay, real plan time," Atlas says and turns to me. "You said Dushay Richard was burned, didn't you?"

"Yep. They know me as Dushay and that I kidnapped their boy toy."

"So we send Zeus back in but with the whole team behind him."

Trav balks at Atlas. "You want to take the fight to Vegas, where he has all his manpower?"

"The alternative is having Zeus lead Pierre's men back here or somewhere else where we'll be waiting, but he won't come in blindly. He'll send proxies first."

We need to get Pierre. "Callie's debt—which isn't really his debt, by the way—is with Pierre. If we don't cut off the head of the snake, Callie will never be free of him."

"Whose debt is it, then?" Trav asks.

"That fucknugget of an ex-boyfriend who beat him. Apparently, he took Callie on gambling trips. When he died, the debt was put on Callie's head."

Trav says something under his breath while Atlas's mouth turns down at the corners.

"I know he's not everyone's favorite person here," I say, "but he's been through a lot. I'm not excusing his behavior or what he did, but don't we all know what it's like to try and survive out there? What about all those threats you had against you when you served, Trav? When Don't Ask, Don't Tell was repealed, and you were still targeted for your orientation? You created a new life for you and for all of us here at Mike Bravo. Now, picture not being able to do that. Being trapped in your old life. What would you have done to survive it?"

I glance at Atlas, and he puts his hands up.

"Hey, I worked through my issues with Callie when Lemon told me he wanted to make sure he was okay. Do I hate that his actions almost killed my husband? Of course. But I can also recognize that he wasn't in complete control of that situation."

"I have no issues with Callie as a person," Trav adds. But then he levels me with his hard, cold eyes. "My worry is that Callie has done everything he can to survive the last twelve months. What's to say he won't screw us over or do what it takes to survive again?"

"Easy. He won't be there for it. He and Lemon can stay back. We go in, we take out Pierre, free some trafficked people, and come back and tell Callie that he never has to look over his shoulder ever again."

"You think your husband can stay behind and not invite himself along for the fight?" Trav asks Atlas.

"You say that like I wouldn't put my foot down. Lemon is going nowhere near organized crime again."

Trav says something under his breath about needing to hand-cuff him to the ranch in order to get Lemon to stay.

Lemon likes to think he's an attack dog. Poor Chihuahua is all bark, no bite. He's more likely to get himself killed than to kill anyone.

"I'd prefer not to fuck up the Vegas Strip," Trav says. "But the desert will work. If we can lure Pierre there, we have a chance."

"Who've we got on hand?" I ask.

Atlas picks up a tablet from Trav's desk. "Iris, Saint, Decaf, Haz—"

"No," Trav interrupts. "One or the other. We're not taking Decaf and Haz together."

"Please tell me what their deal is," I whine.

"That's Decaf's mess to deal with," Trav says.

"That gives me nothing."

"Exactly."

"Haz was also there, so if we really want to get Pierre's atten-tion, I say we send them both back in," Atlas says, getting back to work.

"Then it's settled. Lemon and Callie stay here, and Decaf can babysit them. Oh, and get Angel on the phone. We're going to need her to pry herself away from her girlfriend for this job."

"Are we really doing this?" Atlas asks. "Taking down the head of a crime syndicate in the middle of Sin City?"

"You're making it sound like it's impossible," I say. "Like those *National Treasure* movies."

"Nah, what he's saying is it's a hell of a lot riskier than those movies. Hell, at this point, sign me up for stealing the Declaration of Independence or kidnapping the president because I could do those things in my sleep." Trav looks smug.

"Didn't take you for a Nic Cage fan, boss. He seems too normal for you."

Trav laughs, but I was being serious.

"Let's go brief everyone else." Trav stands, and we follow him out to where everyone is drunk, getting drunk, or, in Iris's case, cuddling his furbaby and crying about more upcoming vet bills.

Here's the thing about everyone in Mike Bravo. We love the adrenaline. We love the chase. We love being motherfucking badasses. But every job has a risk rating. Everyone has their limits.

A lot of these guys are still single, don't have much in the way of family or partners, so they have nothing to lose.

But those like Atlas, Trav, Iris, and Saint, there are other people to think about when it comes to accepting a job. And with this particular job, I can't see too many volunteers to risk their lives for essentially someone who tried to kill one of our own.

Mike Bravo is a family in its own right. Hurt one of us, you're hurting all of us.

I'm nervous as I ask them all to join us in our crusade against Pierre Claremont, but as soon as those hands go up with volunteers, I'm reminded of the other great thing about this family.

We have each other's backs. No matter what.

CHAPTER TWENTY_

CALLIE

WHILE ZEUS HAS HIS MEETING, LEMON WON'T SHUT UP about me hooking up with the one who's named after a sex god. No matter how many times I tell him Zeus was the god of the sky, he doesn't believe me.

"If he wasn't the god of sex, why did he have so many kids to a billion different people?"

"I'm not getting into Greek mythology with you," I say. He goes to open his mouth to ask something else, but I know what it is and cut him off. "Or talking about the sex between Zeus and me."

Lemon whines, but I ignore him.

"I'm actually really tired. I think I'll be fine to be left alone."

Lemon looks at me with concern in his bright eyes. "Are you sure?"

"After everything I've seen here, I don't believe any of your muscled friends will come in here and hurt me."

Lemon leans over me and kisses the top of my head. "Good. Because they won't. They'd have to answer to me if they did."

"You mean Atlas?" I smile.

"Same thing. We're married now. I am him, and he is me."

"That sounds kind of delusional, but sure. Let's go with that."

"Are you sure you're going to be okay on your own?" he asks again. I love him for it but also kind of hate it because he can't be sure if I'm telling the truth.

Which I am. Mostly.

I am tired. I do want to be alone. But I'm not sure I'll be able to sleep. Not until I know what's happening with Pierre. Not until I know I'm actually free.

I've been offered a chance, and I'm terrified I'm going to blow it. Just like I did last time.

"I'll let you sleep," Lemon says and stands. "You're probably going to need the rest for when Zeus comes back." He waits by the door to see if I'm willing to give him something. *Anything.*

"Still not talking about it. And it's not going to happen again." Even if I've never felt more alive than when he was blowing me. Making sure I was okay. Doing it all for me.

I've never experienced that kind of high. Not even while I used to shake my ass on a stage where people would be screaming my name and paying me money to see my body. That felt good. But Zeus?

He knows how to make me feel more than that.

Important.

Cherished.

Fuck. I'm already getting in my head and thinking Zeus could give me more than what he's promised. Which is absolutely nothing.

And now that I've realized that all he gave me earlier was pity sex, my stomach churns.

I want to be mad at him for giving me false hope. Not for something real between us but something real with anyone. He says things like I deserve better but then makes it clear that he's not the one who can give it to me.

"You're disappearing into yourself," Lemon says.

I frown. "What do you mean?"

"You're in your head. I can see it. It's why I'm so reluctant to leave you in here by yourself."

"I'm not going to hurt myself if that's what you're worried about." I just want to wallow.

"Not that. But ... you're not thinking of running again, are you?"

"Wouldn't it be better for everyone if I did?" Everyone but me.

"No. It wouldn't be better for anyone. Where would you go?"

"Back to the middle of nowhere? Back to where I was fine before Zeus showed up, spooked me, and made me make terrible decisions like going to Pierre for help?"

"Maybe you should've heard Zeus out first before trying to run him over."

My eyes widen. "He told you about that?"

"Atlas did."

"I didn't try to run him over. I had to shake him because I thought he was there to kill me."

"You know what's crazy? You hit him with your car, and now you're having sex. Most adorable meet-cute ever."

"Not a meet-cute. I'd met him before, remember?"

"But it was the beginning of your love story."

"Dear God no. And since when did you become a romantic?"

"Ever since I lap danced my way into Atlas's heart. Maybe that's what you should do! Dance all up on Zeus's lap."

Zeus's voice startles us from the doorway. "He doesn't need to do that to get my attention."

I have no idea how long he's been standing there, looking sexy leaned against the doorjamb, but I hope he didn't hear Lemon talking about love stories and meet-cutes.

"Meeting over already?" I ask.

"Meeting over."

Lemon stands. "I'll leave you two to it."

Zeus steps aside to let him pass.

Once Lemon's gone, Zeus goes back to his position, leaning against the entry to the room.

"You okay?" he asks.

Not really, so I don't answer him. "Did you come up with a plan?"

"We did. Sort of."

"Sort of?"

"We haven't nailed down all the details. We'll do that in the morning before heading out tomorrow evening."

"Heading out?"

Zeus leans back, checking the hall before sneakily slipping inside and closing the door behind him. I can't tell if he doesn't want to be seen in here with me or if he's not supposed to tell me anything but is going to anyway.

I hope it's the latter, but I can't be sure.

"We're going back into the lion's den."

"We are?"

Zeus joins me on the bed. "No, we as in Mike Bravo. You're going to stay here with Lemon and Decaf for protection. If we can take Pierre out, we're going to. And then you'll be free."

Free to do what?

Stop running?

Create an actual life?

Why is that more daunting than what I've been doing for the past year? I haven't allowed myself to see a future because I've been adamant I can't have one.

And this is why I stayed with Stephen for so long. I was miserable, hurting, and terrified of him, but ... I was more terrified of what being on my own looked like.

"Did you hear me?" Zeus rolls on his side to face me.

"I did."

"Why do you look like you're going to throw up?"

"I can't let myself get my hopes up yet," I lie.

"No matter how it all plays out, we're not going to dump you back into the wild. Especially if we don't bring him down."

Ergh, that somehow makes me feel worse. "I've already taken so much from you guys. At what point do I stop relying on others and fight my own battles?"

Zeus's arm envelops my waist as he pulls me closer. "How about when you don't have a crime lord after you?"

"But that's what I mean. Thanks to me, you and Haz now have Pierre after you too."

"We can handle it. Well, I can. I still don't know Haz well enough to know for sure with him, but from what I've seen, he can handle himself."

"He shouldn't have to. I hate feeling this way. So ... so ..." I can't even think of a word that means so riddled with guilt that I question why I don't do everyone a favor and—

Before I can finish that thought, Zeus's lips are on mine.

Whether he's doing this to distract me or shut me up, I don't care. I let it happen. Because even though he's clear about where he stands about love, sex, and relationships, I'm going to take every second of him making me feel cherished.

He pulls back before I'm ready, though, and while I try to follow him with my mouth, show him that I'm okay with not talking about my stupid brain making me emotional and such a downer, he only kisses me again softly. Briefly. So quick I almost miss it.

"No offense, but you can't exactly trust your feelings right now. Your thoughts."

And he's right about that. Because all I can think about now that he's kissed me is how I want to keep kissing him. How I want to stay in his arms for as long as possible, and maybe, just maybe, one day he'll change his mind about a relationship and think of me.

At least there's still a small, rational part of my brain that's telling me to stop dreaming about impossible things. Zeus is an impossible future if I were to actually have a chance at one.

I'm sure Lemon would offer me my old job back at his new strip club, but while he might be forgiving, I know for a fact none of the other dancers would be happy to see me there.

I could go back to school. Get a college degree ... with all the money I don't have to pay for it.

When it's all said and done, I want to tell Zeus and the others not to go to bat for me. Their risk isn't worth the outcome if they pull it off.

Saving one lost soul and risking losing countless other lives … it's not worth it.

"I'm not worth fighting for," I whisper.

"That's what you think," Zeus says.

He doesn't kiss me again, but he does hold me. He lets me bury my head on his wide chest, and he's so tender and caring with me that seed of hope for more blooms in my gut.

Because I'm nothing if not a lonely, pathetic loser.

Just like Stephen used to tell me.

CHAPTER TWENTY-ONE_
ZEUS

I HATE, HATE, HATE HOW CALLIE SEES HIMSELF, BUT I have no idea how to deal with this. I can barely deal with my own shit, let alone his too.

The emotional toll a toxic relationship has on someone is deeper than I ever let myself think about. When I don't have to face the realities of being serious with someone, I don't have to take their baggage on board.

But here I am, holding all of Callie's baggage, and I don't seem to care about my needs. My wants.

He needs to realize that his life is worth living. He might not know what to do with himself when he's finally free, but that will come to him. Until then, Stephen still controls him, even from the grave.

He falls asleep in my arms, and he's so warm against me. His breath on my neck is steady. I'm not usually a cuddler, but with him … It's like I'm hoping our physical proximity will breathe new life into him.

If I had a wish, any wish in the world, I'd ask for his problems to go away with the snap of a finger. Actually, I'd ask for my sister back, but that's not even in the realm of possibilities. Callie's freedom is, but I'm all he's got.

Fuck, he's screwed.

Kissing him earlier was the only thing I could think to do to make him see that he's worth saving. All I have to give him is physical touch because for years, that's all I've done. It's all I've known.

I drift off at some point but am woken by Callie twitching, followed by him thrashing about and trying to fight me off him like I'm some kind of an attacker.

"Callie," I say, trying to wake him up.

He keeps going.

I let go of him so he doesn't feel trapped, but that only makes him shove me harder and say, "No."

"Callie," I say, louder this time.

Still doesn't work.

"Sam!"

That does the trick. His eyes fly open, and when he sees me, he lets out a loud breath.

"Fuck," he hisses.

Callie pries himself away from me and sits up, running a hand through his messy blond hair.

I sit up, too, and put my hand on the middle of his back. He flinches, and I pull it away as fast as I put it there. "Sorry."

A sob racks his body. "It's okay. I just ... I'm so messed up."

"Can I touch you?" I ask. "Comfort you?"

Those glassy blue eyes appear as he looks over his shoulder and nods.

This time, when I put my hand on his back and give it a rub, his shoulders lose some of the tension in them.

"I'll be okay. It was a bad dream."

"About Pierre?"

He shakes his head. "You and I were back in that hotel room where you and I had to put on a show, and the dream started out great because we did a hell of a lot more than a blowjob, but after you were done with me, you brought Stephen and David in and said that I now had to put out for both of them too."

I obviously haven't won any trust points with him. "I would never—"

He nudges me. "I know. Brains are dumb. I wish I could be like those people who have the ability to control their own dreams. Unfortunately, I can't."

"No, you can't. But you can control what happens between us in the lucid world."

"Well, that's a lie."

"How is it a lie?"

"Because if I had that kind of power, you'd be kissing me already."

I tell myself not to do it. Not to lean forward and make all his problems go away with more kissing. More sex. But I want to be there for him, and I don't know how else to do it.

Maybe he's not the only broken one of us because I do kiss him, and I let him kiss me back. I reach for him and grip his hips so that when I lean back with my head on the pillow once again, he moves with me and ends up straddling my waist.

My hands slowly travel down to his ass so I can pull him against me and let him feel how hard I am for him.

The voice in the back of my head telling me this is the third time I've hooked up with the same person is dull and muted. As if horny me is drowning commitment-phobe me in a pool.

Callie grinds his hips against mine, the friction as our cocks slide against each other being overwhelming as fuck. And that's still with clothes on because we fell asleep that way.

The tingles in my gut, the ache in my balls … It won't be long before I ruin more of my clothes while I'm here.

I have a go bag stashed at the ranch—we all do—but I don't want to be caught going to find my spare change of clothes. It would be bad enough if anyone saw me coming in here. I could use the excuse that all the other beds are taken and I don't want to sleep in a tent outside, but that would be a lie.

Knowing what we're going to do tomorrow, knowing that

Callie will be freaking out the whole time, I wanted to be in here with him tonight.

Not in the way we are now, but just … be there for him.

I didn't think I wouldn't be able to keep my hands to myself. I'm a strong man and have resisted many pretty faces before.

But Callie makes me weak.

He pulls off my mouth and sits up, stripping off his shirt and baring his miles-long torso with tightly toned muscles.

I run my hand up his body, holding myself back from gripping his throat and throwing him off my lap so I can pin him down and climb on top of him.

Callie leans over me and says, "Do it," but I freeze.

"Do what?"

"Manhandle me the way you're itching to."

I wonder for a moment if he can read minds, but he keeps talking.

"You look like all my clients from when I was stripping. Tempted to touch, tempted to take things further, but knowing you can't. I give you full permission."

"I don't want to scare you. Or hurt you."

His hand lands on mine where it sits on his pec, my fingers splayed out toward his neck. "After all that you've done for me and after showing me that sex can be about me, I trust you. I trust you know what you're doing and that you don't want to hurt me."

"I really, really don't." And it's surprising to me how much I mean it. Not only physically. He's had one too many jerks manipulate his emotions, and I don't want to be another one.

Even if it breaks every rule in my book. Even if I get shit for it tomorrow.

I won't let Callie down.

"Zeus," he whines. "Please."

That last thread of hesitance snaps, and I push him off me and onto his back.

My body blankets his, but I stare down at him and wait for

any sign of uncomfortableness. There is none. Only lust in his hooded eyes and desperation in his parted lips.

"Do whatever you want to me," he says, and fuck, he should not offer me such things.

"I don't have the supplies for what I want to do to you," I growl. "But I am going to get us both off again."

"Let me." Callie raises his hand and licks it before trying to reach between us.

I catch his wrist. "Nuh-uh. Same rule applies as before. You come before I do."

"Honestly, the idea of you getting off to me makes me so horny it won't take me long to come."

"Good. Because I don't want to have to hold back for long."

"Don't. Don't hold back at all."

I sit up and trap his legs under mine.

"No, I said don't hold back. Not move back." He reaches for me, all whiney and cute.

"I'm taking my clothes off, impatient one." I quickly get naked, but Callie still has his pants on.

"Here, I'll—"

Before he even has a chance to move to help, I'm pulling them down his legs and off. "I've got it."

"You're very efficient." He smiles.

"No." I lower myself back on top of him, my flush skin against his, hard cocks lining up. "I'm fucking desperate."

Callie tenses below me, and at first, I think it's because I've scared him or I said something wrong. Maybe something some asshole would say in the heat of the moment. But as he reaches between us, he grips his own cock and chants, "Don't come, don't come, don't come."

My lips quirk. "Aww, honey. You a bit too excited?"

"Shut up," he mutters. "You said you were desperate for me, and my dick was just trying to give you what you wanted."

I lean in, lips to his ear. "And I would've loved every second of it. This works both ways. If you don't want me to hold back, I don't want you to either. You can come whenever you damn well feel like it."

"Fucking hell." His hand moves again, but I can't feel what he's doing. Yet, when I look down, I can see him slowly milking his orgasm that's pooling between us. "How is it I can give people lap dances, grind up on them, and never get so turned on that I come, but you tell me you're desperate for me and beg me not to hold back, and suddenly, I can't control myself and I'm like a damn teenager?"

"I don't know, but I also don't care because I love that I turn you on so much. I want your load any which way you want to give it to me."

"Now it's your turn." Callie's cum-covered hand wraps around my cock, but his hold is gentle.

I move my hips, trying to get him to tighten his grip, but he doesn't.

"Put your hand on my throat," he rasps.

I narrow my gaze and search his face for that deal breaker. That feeling that he's only doing this because he thinks I want it or need it.

"I like it rough."

"Do you, though? Or do you act like you do because you think it's what the other person needs? I like getting rough, but I don't need it. I do need you to feel safe." I would love to hold on to his throat while I fucked his fist, but why does it feel wrong in this situation?

"You are my safety," he says, and I should be freaked-out by that, but I'm not. "Unless you're not comfortable with—"

"I am," I say quickly. "But you're—"

His blue eyes are shiny as he says, "I trust you, Zeus. Grip it as hard as you want me to hold your cock."

So, I unleash because I can't hold back after that.

My fingers dig into his skin, my large palm covering his entire throat area.

I move my hips, sliding in and out of his hand, where he

matches my grip. I want it tighter, a bit more firm. I adjust my hand, and he follows. He moans, and it vibrates against my hand.

I grunt because I'm so close.

"Fuck, Callie," I murmur, chasing the end. "You feel so good. I can't hold back. I can't—"

I push through his fist one more time, and every muscle in me tenses. My cock throbs as my cum mixes with his, and while my grip on his throat loosens, he doesn't let go of me. He strokes me through my orgasm until we're both breathing heavily, and everything becomes Jell-O.

I roll off him but keep one leg thrown over his waist.

Then, with my hand resting on his neck, I slide it upward and cup his cheek. "You okay? Was that—"

He turns his head toward me. "That was awesome." As he smiles, a dark cloud passes over us, and I know it's all because of me.

Because as I stare into his eyes and fall deep into his blue orbs, I realize that I might be in way over my head.

The excuse that I'm just looking out for him doesn't fly anymore because if it did, I wouldn't have done that with him. The first time could be rationalized. The second? It was paying back a favor. Evening the score.

And now?

Callie's quickly becoming a habit that I had no intention of picking up. But like any other bad habit, now that I've started, I can't stop.

CHAPTER TWENTY-TWO_
CALLIE

THE BED IS EMPTY WHEN I WAKE, AND PANIC SLOWLY trickles in. Not about being alone but that whatever is happening between Zeus and me is over now.

I didn't question last night as it was happening, but now I can't help thinking if it was a last-time thing. Because today, he's going to go and take out Pierre, free me, and then I'll start my new life. Whatever life that might be.

He's out there with his teammates, planning what's going to happen today, and we're now just ... done.

Okay. I can be cool with that. I knew it was coming. I do wish he could've plowed me at least one time, but maybe it's better this way. There's already the love-starved part of my brain sending signals to all my other body parts that this man could be the one.

They *all* could be the one.

I huff a humorless laugh because Zeus and I could not be more opposite. He sees no one as the possible one. For me, it's anyone who shows the slightest sliver of decency. In which case, in my defense, I should be head over heels in love with Zeus by now because he's been nicer to me than any other person.

He respects me, but that still doesn't mean he sees me as more than a fling. Or that he ever will.

Why am I so desperate for someone to love me? Even worse, why do I always want the ones who will never love me the way I want them to?

It's a good thing this is done because I can get my head out of the clouds and face reality. Today's the first day of the rest of my life ... or whatever that saying is.

I get out of bed and put on the same sweats Zeus bought me in Vegas, but there's a fresh shirt on the bed. Plain army green, a size too big, but it's better than the smelly I heart LV shirt.

Okay. I'm ready to go out there and make today my bitch.

Then I remember how many Mike Bravo badasses are in this house also getting ready to make today their bitch. All because of me.

The action, the commotion, everything stops when I enter the main living quarters. Some of the guys are eating breakfast at the table. Others are—I'm guessing—taking inventory of the mountain of weapons dumped on the couch. But the second I appear, everyone freezes and looks at me.

My heart stutters, and a lump forms in my throat.

I wish I could find my voice to thank them for what they're going to do today, but my mouth can't seem to work. So it opens and closes rapidly.

"This was a mistake." I turn to run back to my room, but the second I do, I run into a large wall of muscle and a familiar scent —Zeus's scent, which is somehow woodsy but also like sex.

"Geez. I leave you to take a piss, and you decide to face the lion's den alone?" He's smiling, so I think he's teasing, but little does he know that's exactly what it feels like with his team.

There were too many eyes on me to focus on any one individual face, so I can't tell if they were judging me, but it seemed that way.

"I ... I ..."

"They're not going to hurt you." He turns me back around

and marches me back out there. "Everyone, some of you have met Callie, and some of you haven't, but you've definitely heard about him. He would like to apologize for his actions last year—"

"Wait, what?" I cut in.

"Well, don't you?"

My mouth is doing the fish thing again until it settles on speaking so softly I'm not even sure Zeus can hear me a foot away. "You know I want to."

"Which is my point." He turns back to everyone else again. "But he's scared of all of you, and I would be, too, if I were him."

"Because we're so awesome?" that Iris guy asks.

"No, because you're all butt ugly." Zeus grins.

There's a round of groans like Zeus just said the cringiest dad joke ever.

"But seriously. Callie's been through some shit. Give him a break."

"Exactly." Lemon stands from one of the other couches that I glanced over at when I entered but couldn't see him. Probably because I was too busy focusing on everyone else staring at me. Lemon approaches and links his arm through mine. "If I, of all people, can get over Callie's mistakes, all of you should be able to too."

"We can get over it but not forget," some other guy says.

I nod. "That's fair."

"It speaks!" Iris jokes.

"I … I …" *Fucking hell, get it together.* "I can't look at you while I do this." I turn my back to everyone and close my eyes. "You have no idea how hard it has been living with the guilt of what I've done. I wish I could blame my ex for the way he manipulated me into every decision I ever made, but when it all comes down to it, it was my choices that led me there."

Zeus's warm hand lands in mine. "Still doesn't make it your fault."

His voice is soothing, and I manage to turn my head to look at him.

"If I could take it all back, I would," I say. "And I know no one here has the right to trust me, and I'll wear that. But I want you all to know that I appreciate everything you've done and are doing for me." I lose track of if I'm still talking to the group or only Zeus.

Trav's booming voice joins the fray. "It's time to move on. All of us. And Callie?"

I turn back to face the room and lock eyes on Trav, standing by the kitchen with his arms folded.

"Thank you for saying that. It means a lot."

"Thank you for getting me out in the field today," Iris says.

"Wasn't your dog eating glass last night?" Zeus asks.

"Yeah, Saint's taken her to the vet. I swear that guy takes vacations on Saint's and my dime. But anyway, he updated me. She'll be fine. Just needs to be monitored. Therefore, I am happy I get to go blow up casinos in Vegas. It's gonna be fun."

"No blowing up casinos," Atlas orders.

Iris deflates. "Fine." But then he holds up his fingers to indicate a small amount. "Only a little blowing up."

"Are we sure Saint can't come on this mission and we leave Iris with the dog?" Atlas asks.

"Nope. Ghost is on comms, and I'm a much-needed member in the field."

"How do you rationalize that?" Zeus asks.

"Because I can do anything. Need a pretend drunk to swipe a bad guy's phone? I'm your man. Need a distraction? I'll run down the Strip naked. Need me to get into small crevices to plant some C4—"

"No C4," Atlas reiterates.

"Either way. I'm a chameleon. The best one we got."

Zeus smiles and then leans in and says, "I hate to say it, but he's actually right. I'm thankful he'll be there today."

"You know, I'm smaller than you," Lemon says to Iris. "So if anyone was going to squeeze through tight spaces, it would be—"

"You're not going," Atlas says.

154 / MIKE BRAVO OPS: ZEUS

Damn. I've never heard the soft-spoken man that … dominant. I hate that it turns me on.

"I think there's something wrong with my ears," Lemon says and looks at me. "Can you check to see if they're red or blocked or anything? Because I swear I just heard my husband say I can't do something."

"Ooh" echoes around the room. Atlas is in trouble.

"I didn't say you can't," Atlas says. "I said you're not."

More mocking sounds fill the space.

Atlas holds up his hand to get everyone to shush. "Because he's needed here. With Callie."

Lemon assesses my face, as if trying to figure out if Atlas is telling the truth. Which he totally is. I might have apologized, and everyone might have been told to be nice to me, but that doesn't mean I'd be comfortable alone with any of them.

"Fine," Lemon relents. "But one day, you'll let me go after the bad guys with you."

Atlas scoffs. "Please. You hated the adrenaline last year when David was trying to kill you."

"That's not the point," Lemon says. I swear he's two seconds away from stomping his foot.

I think I've missed the point, too, then, but I don't say that.

"Love you," Atlas says and puts his hands in the shape of a heart on his chest. "Are we ready to roll out?" Atlas has obviously learned the best way to deal with a Lemon tantrum is to change the subject because with a simple I love you, Lemon goes from pre-diva to lovesick fool. If he were a cartoon, he'd have bulging heart eyes right now.

"Soon, boss," Zeus says. "I need a minute with Callie."

He grips my wrist and pulls me back down the hallway to the room we stayed in last night. "Are you going to be okay here?" He gently shuts the door behind us.

"I think the question should be, am I going to be okay anywhere because it doesn't matter where I am. Until Pierre is taken out, I'm not going to have the freedom of knowing the answer to that question."

"Okay, that was deeper than I was expecting."

I cock my head. "That's what he said?"

Zeus laughs. "If you're making jokes, you're going to be fine. Humor is the key to happiness. Or so I've heard."

"Don't believe it?"

"Humor helps, but I often find those who make the most jokes do it to cover how uncomfortable they are."

He's got me there. This is *weird*. He's checking on me before he goes? This is ... not what I thought would happen when he dragged me in here. Then again, I didn't know what to expect. A goodbye?

I avert my gaze. "I guess I should wish you good luck?"

"We don't need it."

"I know confidence is good and all, but don't be *overconfident*. That's when shit goes wrong, and I don't want the guilt of your death on my head too."

Zeus's lips purse. "I'll tell you what, if this plan goes to shit and some of us don't come back, I want you to remember this: the police have been after Pierre for a really long time, but he knows how to cover his electronic footprint. They'll never be able to charge him."

"How is that supposed to make me feel better if your guys get in the crossfire?"

"Because we might be using you as an excuse to go after him, but you can bet your ass that each and every person going today is going for the adrenaline hit. And maybe because getting assholes like Pierre off the street is for the greater good. But mainly the adrenaline thing. We live for it."

"Just ... don't let any of your team die, okay?"

"I'll do my best."

"No, I need you to promise." I grip his shirt and pull him close to me. "Please. I won't be able to take it if another person gets hurt because of me."

Zeus takes my shoulders in his big, calming hands, and with the most serious expression I've ever seen on him, he says, "This might be hard to believe, but not everything revolves around you."

I blink at him.

His lips turn up in the corners. "Seriously, though. I can't promise you that. Are the chances high that one of us will get hurt? Yes. Killed? Eh, less likely. I think we've all been shot at one point or another—"

"This isn't making me feel better." I try to fall backward, but he tightens his grip. "I think I'm going to be sick."

"Sit …" He moves me to the bed and lets me sit, but before he can kneel to my level, I wrap my arms around his waist and bury my head on his lower abdomen. "Look at me." He crooks a finger under my chin and lifts my gaze to his. "I want *you* to promise *me* something."

I can't find words, but I nod.

"If something happens, and that's a big if, promise me you won't blame yourself."

The lump in my throat is back. "I … I can't do that."

"Then I guess I am going to have to make sure everyone comes back alive."

"You just said—"

"I know. But I will do anything to lighten your burden. Do you understand?"

No, but again, I nod.

"Your burden is now mine. Got it?"

I swallow hard. "Why?"

"Because …" He pauses. "Because you need someone in your corner." He bends over and presses his lips to mine, kissing me like it's going to be the last time.

My newest fear is that it'll be the last time because he won't come back. Gone are the worries of him not wanting me in the future. I could handle that. I just want him to *have* a future.

Out of nowhere, the door flings open.

Zeus and I break apart, and he jumps back like his ass is on fire, and there, at the door, is Iris.

Staring.

There's a beat of silence. And then another.

Zeus points at Iris. "Say a word, and—"

Iris practically vibrates with excitement. "Oh, it's so adorable you think I can keep this a secret." He runs off, and Zeus looks up at the ceiling.

"This mission is going to be a fucking nightmare."

CHAPTER TWENTY-THREE_
ZEUS

Iris is in the back seat of Trav's Range Rover, on the other side than me, with Haz up front and Trav driving. Iris hasn't said anything yet, but I can feel his stare. His taunting smile.

"It's such a shame we'll have to destroy this suit," Haz says, running his hand over the smooth silk and wool blend. "This mission is one huge crime against fashion."

"Question," Iris says. "Does the new kid ever shut up? People might have important things to say."

I glare at him. "You have nothing of importance to say. Haz can talk all he wants because for once, we all don't have your voice in our ears."

We're all miked up with comms in our ears, ready for when we get to Vegas, and everyone snickers at my barb.

I shouldn't be playing with fire—the more I push Iris, the more likely he'll tell everyone I was making out with Callie—but I get the impression he's going to tell them anyway, so I may as well try to delay it. Or speed it up. The sooner he tells them all, the less on edge I'll be.

"Saint loves my voice," Iris says.

"Bet he likes it better when you're gagged," Ghost says in our ears.

"Don't we all," I say. "And I'm not even meaning it in the sexual way."

"As if you wouldn't have sex with Saint if you were allowed to," Decaf joins in. "You know, if Iris wouldn't rip your balls off and shove them down your throat."

Iris looks at me. "Normally, I'd agree with you. My man is so sexy, everyone would want to fuck him if they had the chance—"

"Can we stop talking about people wanting to fuck me?" Saint cuts in. He must've made it back to HQ with the dog.

"Shh, baby, your man is bragging."

"Please stop."

"No, no," I say, interrupting their private but very public conversation. "I want to hear more about how your relationship is on the rocks. Saint, why does Iris bragging about you make you uncomfortable?"

"Since when does Zeus care about other people's relation-ships?" Atlas, who's in the car behind us, asks. "First, he congrat-ulates me on getting married; now, he's playing relationship counselor. Is the apocalypse coming? Surely this is one of the signs."

"Nah," Iris says. "He's trying to deflect from—"

"The mission," I blurt. "Because it's a long way to Vegas, and maybe we didn't need to put our comms in so early. Right, Trav? Can we, you know, maybe not have them in the whole way?"

Trav doesn't reply. Just keeps driving.

"Trav?" I ask again.

No reaction.

Haz taps Trav's arm and then points his thumb toward the back.

Trav takes out what I thought was his comms this whole time, but it's not. It's his AirPods. "What? Sorry, I was listening to music. I came prepared after realizing I was going to be driving you three to Vegas. I'm thinking of implementing a new rule. Only one smartass per assignment allowed."

"That doesn't leave a lot of available teammates," I point out.

Everyone laughs.

"I'm going back to my music," Trav says.

"Wait." I stop him before he can put his AirPods back in. "Can we go comms silent for a bit?"

"Why aren't you all on mute to begin with?" Trav asks.

"Tell him it's because we love hearing his voice," Decaf says. "That, and some of us were ordered to stay behind and don't want to miss out."

"Decaf called you an asshole, boss," I say.

"Fuck you! I did not! I didn't."

"Ope, Trav said we're allowed to go on mute. Bye now." I hit the button on the tiny device in my ear, but all that does is mute me.

The others keep ribbing each other, so even though I'm panicked about what might be said if I take out my device, I should be able to hear it because it'll be Iris who's spreading shit. Like that Callie and I have become a couple or some other insane story that isn't true. Because we're not a couple. We won't be a couple. And once this is over, Callie can go and do whatever and whoever he wants.

Out of the corner of my eye, I see Iris hit mute on his comms too. "Well played." He tips his head to me.

I turn to him, and I get the impression he's letting the news hover over my head, and it's something he can use as a weapon anytime he feels like it. And while I don't want it to get out, I also don't want Iris to have that kind of power. Iris having any authority over me—or anyone—shouldn't happen. Especially when I have to concentrate on this Pierre job.

I reach forward to get Trav's attention.

"What now?"

"I'm still fooling around with Callie. Thought you should know."

And with the way Haz spins in his seat and points to his ear, he and the others haven't been put on mute. So now everyone knows.

"Damn it," Iris says. "Way to ruin my fun."

"That's precisely why I did it."

"Can you be impartial on this job?" Trav asks.

"Yup. Because it's not emotional. Only physical. And once he gets his freedom, I'll do what I've always done. Kiss my hookups goodbye and never see them again."

"I'm starting to see why you're perpetually single," Haz says.

"Because I choose to be. And there's nothing wrong with that."

Haz turns in his seat, staring at me with his baby face. "Isn't that a little cold?"

"No. It's realistic."

"Pessimistic, more like it," Haz mutters.

"Just don't let it get in the way of this mission," Trav says, and his word is final.

I finally get the quiet I'm looking for and without Iris holding any power over me.

Now, to get in there, get the job done, and be finished with this whole drama.

⸻

Haz and I are dropped at the Luxor, as far away from Pierre's casino as we can practically get.

"Ready, Douche?" Haz smiles up at me.

"That's Dushay, boy."

"I wonder if he calls Callie 'boy'?" Iris says in our comms.

"I wonder if you'll ever let this go?" I say through gritted teeth.

"Never," everyone replies for him.

Haz snorts.

"So glad I get to be your entertainment for the night. Let's head up to the monorail. Screw walking."

The monorail doesn't save much walking, but it's something. Plus, the more we're seen all over the Strip, the more chance of being spotted by one of Pierre's guys or security cameras that Pierre has access to.

It's our job to lure out as many of his guys as possible and even him if we can. Trav, Atlas, and Alphabet all have escape cars for us, stationed at different meeting locations for when we need to get out.

The challenge is going to be making sure Pierre comes after us himself and doesn't send his goons to deal with his problems.

We're being trailed by Iris, Scout, and Kevlar, who'll keep close to us but act like drunken imbeciles who look like they're coincidentally heading into the same casinos and in the same direction as us.

We get on the next available monorail, Iris and company getting on the next car over so they're close but not too close.

"How long do you think it'll take before someone approaches us?" Haz asks.

"Could be five minutes. Could be a couple of hours. We just need to make it look like we're trying to keep a low profile while also … not."

We could go straight to Pierre and offer him a fake deal that will lure him out to the desert, but he's more likely to sense a trap that way.

If it looks like we're desperate enough to do anything to make him let us go, we have more of a chance of getting him.

We have a whole backstory ready for him. We were hired to steal Callie but are using our reward money to gamble because we know how Pierre likes to take advantage of those with addiction issues. So, we'll act like the middlemen. Promise to take him to the man who hired us and to Callie.

Or trap is to pretend we're hiding while also feeding our

gambling habit and then wait until someone connected to Pierre finds us.

We don't plan to go to his casino. That would be too easy. We hit the casinos we know Pierre has associations with—whether it be personal or business partnerships—and make sure to cause a scene.

We hit the casinos on the South Strip, slowly making our way north but still far enough away that it looks like we're trying to avoid Pierre's vicinity. I pull Haz over to the craps table at the Catalina and make a whole song and dance over him blowing on the dice before I throw them. It's a fine line between showing off while trying to hide, but I think we manage it.

"And there he goes, spending more of my money," Trav mumbles.

"Calm down, we freaking won," I say under my breath.

On the next round, we lose, but I'm not saying that for all the money in the world.

"Allow me." Haz takes the dice from me and rolls them around between his fingers, going up over his knuckles and back into his hand again, like it's a basketball and he's a Harlem Globetrotter.

When he throws them, they barely roll, and when they land, the whole table erupts with elation because we all win.

"Maybe I should've had you playing from the start, sweetheart."

The attendant pushes the dice toward us again, and I pick them up.

"All yours. Let's win big."

And I have no idea if Haz is the luckiest person in the world or if he has some hidden talent when it comes to rolling dice, but he wins. Every damn time.

Which means we catch the eyes of everyone around us easily, and our plan unfolds exactly the way we want it to.

When a group of three intimidating men appears, heading right for us, I say loudly for everyone near us and the guys over comms to hear, "Babe, let's cash out while we're still hot. Our luck is bound to run out sooner or later."

That's Iris's cue to drunkenly stumble into the guys coming for us, heading them off, while Haz puts on a show about not wanting to leave but relents when I pocket our chips.

Then it's a mix of a fast walk but being patient enough to let them stay on our tail.

We make it outside and over the footbridge to the other side of the road before they catch up to us.

The three of them surround us.

"Can we help you?" I say. "If you're trying to mug us, here ..." I take out a couple of chips. "That's all we have. I promise."

Haz acts scared, shivering up against me.

He's really good at playing the role of helpless boy.

"Lies," one of the men says. "The owner of the Ruby wants to have a word with you."

"The Ruby? With me? Why?"

"No need to play games. We know exactly who you are and what you've done, Dushay."

"Here, take the money." I empty my pockets to Trav swearing in my ear.

"There goes Rogue's and my vacation this year."

I try not to laugh because that's so not true. This kind of money is a drop in the bucket for him. This job might be pro bono because Callie is like one of our own—or one of our own adjacent thanks to Lemon—but he gets paid a shit ton of money for the jobs we do. He's fair to us but also smart with his money.

"We're not after the money," one of the other men yells.

People pass by us on the busy bridge, but this is Vegas. Someone getting a shakedown from guys in suits with a casino logo on their pocket? No one's going to get involved in that.

"You took something," the original guy says. "Something that belonged to the Ruby."

"Not how I remember it. And from what I was told by the

guys who hired us to take it, that thing didn't belong to Pierre to begin with. We're squared away."

I grab Haz's hand and try to walk away, knowing they'll stop us. The three men practically form a blockade of bodies so we can't leave, and then they step closer, pushing us up against the railing.

Cars whiz by beneath us, and while we'd be able to escape them if we really wanted to fight our way out of this, we want them to take us. Sort of. We need them to take us where we want to go.

"Take us to Pierre, then," I say.

The one in charge reaches for his phone and hits Dial on a number. "We've got them." There's a beat. "We'll take them there." He ends the call. "Let's go. I'm warning you now, you try any funny business or try to escape, the pretty one gets a bullet in his head." He opens his suit jacket to show me he's packing.

I turn to Haz. "You heard him. If you try to escape, I get a bullet to my head."

Haz laughs. "Think he was talking about me, but okay."

"Don't scale down the side of any buildings," the guy says.

"Aww, our reputation precedes itself," I quip.

"Get walking."

One of them walks in front of us while the other two box us in between them.

"Iris, go get those chips on the ground," Trav orders. "Alpha, Scout, you stay on Haz and Zeus. It's game time."

LEMON AND I ARE AT THE SMALLER OF THE DINING tables while our "babysitter," Decaf, is asleep on the couch in front of a TV.

My knee bounces wildly, I'm fidgety, and every time Lemon types away on his phone, I ask if he's got news yet.

His answer is always the same. "No, it's the club. I'm checking in and making sure everything is running smoothly. I'll tell you if I hear from Atlas, but it's been my experience that we won't hear anything until they're on their way home."

My heart thuds and drops into my stomach. "How do you deal with it? Aren't you worried?"

He holds up his phone. "Why else do you think I'm checking in on my business that has perfectly capable managers running it?"

"That makes me feel somewhat better, at least."

"Knowing that I'm also freaking out?"

"Yes. Because at least I'm not being melodramatic."

"You're both melodramatic," comes Decaf's rumbling. "And you're keeping me awake."

"You've been snoring for the last twenty minutes," Lemon says.

Decaf sits up and rubs his eyes. "Need. Coffee."

"Uh-oh." Lemon stands. "I'll get it for you."

Decaf grunts.

"Wait, what?" I get up and follow Lemon into the kitchen. "I thought his name was Decaf. He drinks coffee?"

"His name is Decaf because he drinks so much coffee. Like, probably more than is recommended by health professionals."

"Is this like one of those weird nicknames like how redheads are called Blue?"

"Probably. If you haven't noticed, none of the guys have normal names. Not that we can talk, *California*." Lemon starts making Decaf's coffee.

I shudder. "That name feels so foreign to me, but at the same time, so does Sam. I'm used to Callie, though, even if *Callie* has done some horrible things."

"You should wear your name proud. You've made mistakes, but if you grow from them, that's what makes Callie a decent person. When you're ready to forgive yourself, you can use your name as a reminder of how far you've come, and maybe you won't repeat old patterns."

Old patterns.

It takes a second for me to realize what he's getting at. "By going for the wrong type of man?"

"You and Zeus … I can't ask if you're serious because it's Zeus, but I mean, how far has it gone? I thought it was just sex, but how many times has it been? I didn't even know Zeus knew that was a thing."

"Knew what was a thing?"

"Aftercare. He seems like the type to get in, get off, and get out." Lemon shrugs.

"That hasn't been my experience with him at all."

Does that make me … different?

Fuck, don't think like that. You can't afford to have your heart broken.

"Maybe I'm wrong," Lemon says.

"He did say his reputation was a bit out of control. Maybe

because I'm the only hookup he's kept around long enough to be told any different than the perceived notion that he uses people for sex."

"That's very insightful." Lemon finishes up with Decaf's coffee.

"Coffeeeeeee," Decaf whines.

Lemon rolls his eyes. "He's very dramatic when his blood drops below eighty percent caffeine." Then, the Lemoniest expression crosses my old friend's face. I know that face. He's scheming. "I know a way we can pass the time and stop thinking about our guys out there."

"Our guys?"

"The team. Mike Bravo. They're family here, and I'm like their annoying little brother-in-law who fusses over them."

He really is like a mother hen, but I can't say a little thrill didn't shoot through me at the thought of Atlas and Zeus being "our guys." Like Atlas belongs to him in the way I'm starting to want Zeus to belong to me. Stupidly, though. Because I still know that can't happen.

At what point do I cut out of here to save my own heart? I can't leave now because he's out there—they're all out there—doing this for me. What kind of thank-you would it be if I left before they've finished the job?

"Ready?" Lemon grins.

"Yes. Please show me how to turn all my nervous energy into fun."

"Follow my lead." He takes Decaf's coffee and serves it to him, but instead of going back to the dining table, Lemon takes the couch opposite, and I do as he says and follow his lead.

Decaf takes a sip, his dragon sleeve tattoo catching my eye as his muscles bulge. He lets out a loud moan that almost sounds sexual and throws his head back, rich chocolate-brown hair falling from his face. He goes for another swig.

"Is that the sound you made when you slept with Haz?"

Lemon asks, and Decaf sprays coffee everywhere. He gets it in his dark beard, on the coffee table, the carpet …

"What?" he splutters.

"That's what happened, isn't it?" Lemon blinks innocently at him.

"Where did you get that idea?"

"I hear everything that goes on around here because I'm like a ninja. I see and hear everything."

"Or maybe you're so short no one sees you and talks as if you're not there," Decaf grumbles.

"Shit. You know my secret. And hey, Angel is the same height as me, thank you very much. You all see her."

"Because she's scary. You're like a cupcake. All sweet. Or I thought you were until you asked me about …"

"Haz. Stalker ex-hookup. Following you to your place of employment. Joining the same team. Goading you and breathing in the same space as you."

"We didn't hook up. I would never hook up with him. He has some misinformation about me, and he thinks he can worm his way into my life, put himself in dangerous situations, and … and …" His face goes so red I'm worried he might pass out.

Lemon gestures to Decaf's cup. "Drink some more coffee to calm yourself down."

Coffee to … calm him?

Decaf might be the most interesting member of Mike Bravo yet. Other than Zeus, of course, but that's a different kind of interesting. Decaf is an anomaly.

After Decaf drains his coffee, he looks defeated.

"What misinformation does he have on you?" Lemon asks.

"It's a long story."

"We have nothing but time," I point out. "We need a distraction. Please?" Now it's my turn to flash my innocent face at him.

Lemon and I know how to play dirty.

Decaf sighs. "He thinks I killed his father."

In unison, Lemon and I gasp.

"I didn't," Decaf says quickly. "Not ... technically."

I glance at Lemon, and he looks at me.

"How do you not technically kill someone?" I ask.

"I need more coffee." Decaf stands and heads for the kitchen, but we're so not leaving the conversation like that. Lemon and I are quick to get up and follow him.

He jumps when he realizes we're right behind him. "Jesus. You really are like ninjas."

"It's our light dancer feet." Lemon lifts up onto his toes like a ballet dancer.

He has proper training from when he was a kid. My dance moves all consist of ways to get my clothes off in a sexual way. Put me on a stage where I don't have to strip, and I wouldn't have a clue what to do.

"Keep talking," Lemon says.

I have to admit, as far as distractions go, this is a pretty good one.

"Trav spoke to us both separately, so he knows what went down, but basically, Haz is here for some ill-informed revenge plot against me. That's what I think anyway. He somehow convinced Trav that he's here for legitimate reasons, but all I can say is if he offers to make me coffee, I'm saying no."

"But what did go down? How did you technically not kill his dad?"

"I need a double shot of espresso." He makes his shot along with a larger drink with creamer. He downs the espresso and then takes his mug and heads back out to the sitting area.

"Tell us," Lemon whines.

"His father. He ..." Decaf glances away from us. "He was the best friend I ever had. We grew up together, enlisted together, even deployed together, and I was best man at his wedding. I was there when Little Haz was born."

"Little Haz?"

"Their last name is Hazard. His dad went by the same nickname in the army."

"How did he die?" There's that lump in my throat again, and my voice comes out all raspy.

"We were stationed outside a village in a classified country and had strict instructions not to interfere with anything going on. Our only job was to count how many trucks were going in and out."

"Let me guess, you interfered," Lemon says.

Decaf sniffs. "I didn't. He did. He couldn't take the screaming of the little girl. She wouldn't have been more than seven."

"Do I even want to ask what they were doing to her?" I think I know, but I need to be sure.

"Oh, it wasn't her they were hurting. It was her mother. They dragged her out of her home and into the streets to show the rest of the villagers what they did to people who stole from their crops. The woman was pleading, telling them that she had no husband and was trying to feed her child. It wasn't working."

"That makes my stomach churn," Lemon says.

"Ours too. The commotion was so loud. The screaming, the crying … it has the power to break you. And Hazard broke. Little Haz was less than a year old at the time, so I have no doubt he was picturing what it would be like if it was his wife out there. His child. But our orders were simple, and we had to follow them."

"So you all sat there and watched and listened as they …" The lump is now the size of a baseball, and I can't swallow, let alone finish that sentence.

"Our CO ordered us to stay where we were, even as Hazard pleaded to go do something about it. To interfere. To save the mother and the little girl."

"You should have helped," Lemon says.

"But you had to follow orders." It's the exact same way I felt when I was put in the position last year to either follow Stephen's orders or run. I should have run. I shouldn't have done the wrong thing just because he told me to.

And in the army, it would be so much worse. Their whole lives revolve around following orders.

Decaf shakes his head. "I should've gone with him. I should've defied my CO, but I didn't. It was difficult enough being gay in our unit. I couldn't be known as the one who didn't follow orders too. They would've transferred me or given me a court-martial. Hazard would have got a slap on the wrist. If he'd made it back." He hangs his head. "He was killed right there in the street along with the mother. They took the little girl."

"Fuck," I whisper.

"It's the biggest regret of my life."

"Do you really think Haz is here to seek revenge?" Lemon asks. "Wouldn't he have killed you already?"

"Maybe he wants to watch me suffer first. Because I swear, the second he walked into that war room, I knew who he was. He looks so much like his dad at that age. It was like seeing a ghost."

"When was the last time you saw him?"

"When he was about five. For a few years after Hazard's death, I made sure to go see the kid, to make sure he had a decent male role model in his life. His mother would ask what really happened the day her husband died, but I refused to talk about it. I still refuse to talk about it. I don't even know why I'm telling you two." He lowers his voice. "Pretty faces always getting me into trouble."

I smile at that.

"I'm guessing she found out?" Lemon says.

"Yep. Rightfully so, she kicked me out of her life. Wouldn't let me see Little Haz. Now, he's finishing what she started by driving the guilt home. Every time I have to look at his face, I see my best friend."

"Damn. That must be hard," I say.

"My heart breaks all over again. Every damn time. And knowing he's out there, putting himself in danger like his dad did …" He grits his teeth. "I fucking hate it."

"You know," Lemon says, that glint in his evil, scheming eye back again. "If you took us to Vegas, you could watch over him and protect him."

Decaf's features morph from playful to his lips pressed together in disappointment. "Nice try, but keeping you away from danger is one order I have no issue following."

Lemon's shoulders deflate. "Damn. Was worth a try."

"What would you even do if he said yes? Go to Vegas and wiggle your ass in your yellow thong?"

Lemon throws up his hands. "I don't know. All I know is waiting around sucks."

"I'm sure everything is going to plan," Decaf says.

CHAPTER TWENTY-FIVE_
ZEUS

NONE OF THIS IS GOING TO PLAN. INSTEAD OF LANDING in front of Pierre, all we've managed to do is get thrown into a fucking cellar, deep under the Ruby Resort and Casino, where we're now bound by our wrists and waiting for whichever thug Pierre is going to send in next to beat the shit out of us.

We have two guard dogs watching over us, refusing to acknowledge anytime we ask to see Pierre.

This whole plan revolved around getting Pierre to follow us out to the desert, and yet we can't even lure him down to his own basement.

"This is extreme, isn't it?" I say. "Because we stole one of Pierre's whores?"

The two guards look at each other.

"We should've just paid for him," Haz adds. "Instead of abducting him the way we did."

"Can you tell Pierre we're willing to negotiate?"

Haz smirks. "What if we put Callie in the middle between Pierre and Dushay and let Callie pick whose whore he'd rather be."

"Like a puppy," I add.

"Do you two ever shut up?" one of our captors asks.

Echoes of "No" ring out in our comms.

"Not until we get what we want," I casually say.

"Maybe we should gag them," the other says.

Haz stares them down. "Maybe we'll like that."

I snort.

One lunges for me, but the other pulls him back. "Save them for Tommas. You know he likes a blank canvas to work."

"We're having our portraits painted?" Haz asks. "That's a nice gesture."

"The new kid really does have a death wish," Iris says in our ear. "That should really be a red flag if even I think that."

I want to tell them to stop distracting me from figuring this out—a way to escape, get Pierre himself to follow, and get back to the original plan. I'm not worried about being tortured or hurt or even getting out of this room because I have a full team figuring out how to get us out of here, but I want to end this. I want to take Pierre down and free Callie.

It needs to happen tonight.

A voice in the back of my head asks, *Why?* and I don't have the emotional capacity to answer it. Not truthfully.

I can lie to myself and vehemently say that it's because of the parallel between Callie's life and my sister's, but that's thin at best. Yes, I have that connection with him, but if that was as deep as it goes, I wouldn't be ready to blow a hole in the middle of the Vegas Strip so I could save him.

I wouldn't put my life, my teammates' lives, everything I love at risk by threatening to end the entire underground world.

And here I am, willing to do it. Not only willing but eager for it.

I'm not only lying to myself, but I'm lying to Callie as well. While most of us are here for the adrenaline, I'm here solely for him. But it needs to be done right, and we need, at a minimum, Pierre and his goons. If we could get his second and third in line, that would be helpful, but I doubt that's possible to do.

The biggest risk is cutting off the head of this snake, only for it to grow another one back. Wiping out organized crime syndicates isn't as easy as it looks in the movies. Killing the queen in this instance won't make the whole organization crumble.

The door to the cellar flies open, and in steps the biggest man I've possibly ever seen. Our boss, Trav, is six-five or six-six and three hundred pounds of muscle, but I think this guy could even overshadow Trav.

Maybe I take back not being scared of being hurt because this guy could Hulk smash us into a grave.

He dumps a duffle bag on the ground, and the rattling of metal tools echoes off the walls.

Haz tenses and shifts in his seat behind me, and when I turn my head, I think it's the first time I've ever seen him scared.

"Which one do I start with?" the giant rumbles in a French accent.

With how terrified Haz looks, it doesn't matter what I say. He'll be targeted because he looks easier to break.

"He's too pretty to get messed up," I say. "Besides, you'll be doing him a favor if you damage my face. Less competition for him in the hooking-up department."

Our assigned torturer cracks a smile, and I can't tell if he finds me funny or is excited to shut me up. Probably the latter, but I'm convincing myself it's the former.

"Question," I keep babbling. "Why are we being threatened with torture? Is it to teach us a lesson or to get information from us? Because you could ask us what Pierre wants to know. We're open books. If he wants Callie back, we'll tell you where he is. If he wants to teach us a lesson, lesson learned. Don't mess with Pierre. See? We're quick learners."

Even though I'm still being a smartass, it's working in making him think I'm desperate for him to not do his job. Which means he'll target me, and I know I can handle it.

Haz, I'm not so sure about. He seems strong, but he's new, and there's no way to tell the demons he's hiding underneath. What he's been through. He's still young too. Green.

And thankfully, my smartassy mouth wins again as Gigantor steps toward me and punches me across the face so hard I think he breaks my jaw. The crack sound bounces off the cold walls down here.

Motherfucker, that hurts. He's also dislodged a tooth. I spit it out of my mouth, along with a shit ton of blood, but that sends pain into the whole left side of my face.

"Let's see how well you can talk with a broken jaw."

One of my brothers in arms laughs in my ear and says, "Wow, he sure underestimates you, doesn't he?"

Trav, being more professional, says, "We've got you. We're breaching the tunnels of where you're being held. Your trackers are blocked by the walls, I'm guessing, but we have your last location before it glitched, so hang in there. We'll get you out."

When? I want to ask, but I'm not ready to let this mission go yet. I don't want to abort.

So, even though it's painful, I force my mouth to move. "Now that's over." I wince in pain. "Can we see ... Pierre?" I have to talk through gritted teeth, but it doesn't affect my pronunciation too much.

There's that smile again. Even injured, I'm hilarious to this guy.

"We're just getting started," he says.

Yep. That's what I thought.

He goes to his bag, and if I know psychos like I think I do, he's either going to pull out pliers to get rid of the rest of my teeth or to pull my nails off.

His hand reappears with the pliers, and oh, look at that, I was right. I hate being right sometimes.

Except when he turns back to us, he approaches Haz instead of me.

"You should do mine." I wiggle my fingers. "He's a total bottom and can have pretty nails. My babies need to be trimmed at all times, and getting rid of them completely would actually be doing me a favor."

Iris says into the comms, "I'm starting to think Zeus has a pain kink."

Like fuck I do. I just see the terror in Haz's eyes, which makes me think of the fear in Callie's nearly every time I look at him, and that protective instinct kicks in.

See? It really is an overprotective side of me and not a getting-feelings side of me. Because when it comes to Haz, I can't see him as anything but a young kid fresh off a military contract where he didn't see much action. I feel like his babysitter and have no desire to act out any of those kinds of fantasies with him.

With Callie? Sign me up.

There I go making it about Callie again when it's not.

It's *not*.

This time, my tactic doesn't work, and as the guy releases one of Haz's hands and brings it around to his front, no matter how much Haz tries to fight him, this guy is just too strong.

He presses Haz's index finger between the tips of the pliers and starts to pull.

I have to look away. I wish my hands weren't restricted behind my back because the coarse scream Haz lets out will give me nightmares for the next year. I'd give anything to be able to cover my ears. It's more psychologically scarring than the broken jaw.

I do what I did during torture training and go to my happy place. Orgies, orgasms, origami, and hot dogs.

Okay, not really origami, but I wanted my happy place to spell out OOOH for the acronym. Like the way I like to make people moan it while having orgasms and orgies. Or eating hot dogs.

Haz's constant yell for mercy finally stops, and I spare a look. One nail gone. Nine more to go, I guess.

But then, as if music to our ears, shots from the hallway ring out, and our knights in shining camo find us.

The door bursts open, and Atlas and Iris take out the two guards standing by the door. Trav moves in between them, and with pristine precision, he puts a bullet in Gigantor's head.

"About time you guys showed up," I say.

Iris approaches me, changed from his drunk disguise and dressed in tactical gear. He puts a finger to my lips. "Shh, you have a broken jaw. No more talking for you."

"Fuck you," I grit out.

Trav rubs his chin. "I'm actually surprised no one's broken your jaw sooner. Hell, I don't know why I hadn't thought of doing that before."

Atlas kneels in front of Haz. "You okay?"

Haz nods, but it's shaky.

"Let's get out of here," Trav says.

"No, we can't leave yet," I say, even though my jaw aches. We need to get this done. I can't go back to Callie with bad news.

"What do you propose we do?" Trav asks. "Scour this whole building, leaving a trail of dead bodies in our wake, and still, we might miss out on getting Pierre? This wasn't the plan, and this isn't the kind of mission where we can wing it."

I know he's right, but *fuck*.

"Do you even know where Pierre's office is? Or where he works out of?"

I deflate. "No. We were put in a suite for that high roller's game, and Pierre didn't even make an appearance."

"Then now's not the time. Let's get out of here with the least amount of damage."

"You say that like three dead bodies isn't a lot of damage," Atlas points out.

"Better than attacking an entire casino full of people and have all the other crime bosses fear Vegas is under fire and come looking for us," Trav says. "Let's roll out."

Reluctantly, we follow the guys back out the way they came in, which was breaking through a side door with a code scanner that replicates the data on a security or employee card.

Iris stays at our back, keeping an eye behind us to make sure no one else is on their way to take us out, and as we pass a security camera hanging from the ceiling, I grin up at it, bloody mouth and all, and send up a salute.

Maybe he'll come after us himself if I piss him off enough. They found us in that seedy motel, so they obviously have eyes on CCTV to track where we went, so if we go slow enough, maybe our plan will work after all.

"Hey, boss?" I say as we reach the alley behind the casino. "Would you object at all to putting traceable plates on our car on the way back?"

Trav looks at me over his shoulder and smiles. "Hopefully, he's the vengeful type who likes to take care of problems himself."

Dead henchmen and walking out of here like I don't have a care in the world?

Game on, Pierre.

CHAPTER TWENTY-SIX_

CALLIE

GHOST COMES OUT FROM THE MINI COMMAND CENTER he disappeared into when everyone left for Vegas. "They're on their way back."

"Are they all okay?" I ask.

Ghost and Decaf share a look. Decaf locks his phone screen, and they both avert their gazes.

My heart feels like it might beat out of my skin. "What? What happened?" I'm on the verge of panic.

"It's okay," Ghost says. "Nothing but a few bumps and scratches."

"So they're alive? Everyone?"

"Everyone," Ghost says, but there's something about how on edge Decaf suddenly is that makes me think they're not telling me something. And it makes the dread and guilt over this mission even worse.

Lemon went to bed a few hours ago, but I have no idea how he can sleep at a time like this. His husband is out there, risking his life, and he's sleeping it off like it's no big deal.

How does he do this on a regular basis and with someone he loves? I can barely stand it when it's Zeus, and I'm only hopelessly, pointlessly, in like with him. If the type of love I want does exist out there, I wouldn't be able to let it go so easily and sleep through them possibly not coming home.

But maybe this is my issue when it comes to relationships. I have what I think is forever, what I think is eternal—the person who'll take care of me until the day we die—and I hold on so tight I miss the giant red flags that tell me he's not the one.

Like the big, enormous red flag Zeus keeps waving in my face, telling me he's emotionally unavailable.

I'm yet to meet anyone who *is* emotionally available. We live in a fucked-up world where everyone needs professional help.

"You should try to get to sleep," Decaf says. "I'm going to stay up a bit longer to make sure they get back all right."

"Wait." I swivel my head. "There's a chance they won't make it back?"

Ghost and Decaf share another concerning look.

"You two are really bad at hiding your worry. What aren't you telling me?"

Ghost sighs and joins us in the living room, sitting across from me and next to Decaf.

"I may as well tell you because you're going to see for yourself, but Zeus is a little banged up. Haz too. But they are both fine. I want you to remember that."

"Fine how? How is 'banged up' fine?" My voice cracks.

"Because they're alive, and they're on their way home. They'll heal."

I swear Decaf is trying to kill Ghost with one glare, and knowing Decaf's history with Haz, I think I'm going to take my cues from him. "What's wrong with them?"

Now, Ghost side-eyes Decaf, like he's unwilling to say.

"What did they do to Haz?" Decaf asks.

"He's only missing one fingernail. I don't know the kid well, but I do know he'll be flipping everyone off to show off his war wound."

I'm confused. "That's it? He lost a nail? What happened to Zeus? Lose an eyelash?"

Decaf's glare turns to me. "You don't understand, do you? He lost a nail because some crime boss told his goons to pull it out. It's one of the worst but easiest torture techniques."

Thinking it was impossible for my heart to sink any lower, I'm gutted to know it can. "T-torture? Th-they tortured them?" As if in the middle of an exorcism, my head turns slowly until I meet Ghost's gaze. "What did they do to Zeus?"

Ghost stands. "This is why I didn't want to tell either of you. I know you're both worried, and I'm only passing on the message. Next time, Zeus can call you himself."

"Zeus told you to tell me?"

"He said to let you know he's on his way home." He walks off and mutters, "I should've stayed in the command center." Ghost disappears, but I only have more questions.

"Do you know what they did to Zeus?" I ask Decaf.

"They only told me about Zeus—he has a broken jaw. Trav didn't update me on Haz."

I don't want to know what they did to break his jaw. "Makes sense if he knows the story between you, though. You'd want to protect him. Just like …" What good would I be at protecting anyone when I can't even protect myself?

"You would want to with Zeus." Decaf smiles. "Can't. But would try with everything you have."

I nod.

"Zeus is fine. Broken jaw, some missing teeth. He wanted to keep going with the mission, even after he was told to pull back."

That's when it dawns on me. "Keep … going. They didn't get Pierre?"

"No, but they're not giving up. They're going to come back here, regroup, and then come up with a different plan."

"And we have to do this all again? They should cancel the whole thing. I'll go back into hiding where I should've stayed. I'll go back to when everything wasn't this messed up."

Zeus finding me set off a chain of events that never should've happened. Yet, the only thing I regret about it is not hearing him out before running. In my defense, I thought he was there to kill me, but still. I regret running to Pierre, thinking he would be the lesser of two evils.

Zeus isn't evil, and neither is Mike Bravo.

I'm so fucking broken that I couldn't see that sooner. If I had, Zeus and Haz wouldn't be injured, Pierre wouldn't have trapped me, and none of this would've happened.

"Stop," Decaf says.

I look up at him, his warm skin defined with small wrinkles and sun damage that somehow makes him look distinguished instead of old. "Stop what?"

"Blaming yourself."

"How did you know—"

He cocks his head. "It's an expression I see every day in the mirror. None of this was your fault. Got it?"

"People keep saying that to me. What Stephen did wasn't my fault. What David's business partner did wasn't my fault. But the truth is, when this shit follows you around and you're the common denominator, sometimes you just have to raise your hand and say, 'I'm the problem.' How am I supposed to make things right?"

"Maybe it's not your job to make it right. Maybe your job is to make sure that you take care of you. Don't rely on others. Live your own life."

"I don't even know how to do that."

"What's your passion? What do you like doing?"

I don't think I've ever been asked that before.

"You used to be a dancer," Decaf says. "Did you like that?"

"You say that like stripping could be compared to being a ballet dancer or on Broadway or something. Once upon a time, I had dreams of doing ballet, but my parents wouldn't let me, so I have no formal training."

"Stripping is still dancing. You have to have talent to be able to do it well."

"Lemon's the dancer. He really could have been on any professional stage. I, however, walked out there wearing board shorts, a Hawaiian shirt, and sunglasses that I'd throw into the audience. My whole routine was full of awkward finger guns and hoping my rip-away clothes didn't get stuck again."

Decaf tries to hide his smile.

"You're allowed to laugh. I have to, otherwise I'd cry."

"Okay, so stripping is out. I need more coffee so my brain does its job."

"You don't have to help me come up with a life plan or anything. That's not your job. It should be mine."

Decaf stands. "Oh, I know that's not my job. My only goal is to distract both of us until Zeus and Haz come back."

My stomach does the little flip it always does when someone does a single decent thing for me, only this time, it's not followed up with the urge to throw myself at them simply because they're giving me attention.

Progress?

Decaf and I are no closer to figuring out what I should do with my freedom should I ever get it, and as the hours tick by, both of us stare at the front door.

Finally, somewhere around sunrise, the team bursts through the quiet house, feet stomping, endless loud teasing, and only what I can assume is adrenaline pumping through their veins. How can they still have so much energy?

Decaf and I stand, but all the up-nods in our direction aren't going to make the nauseous feeling in my gut go away. That won't leave until I see Zeus really is okay.

Of course, Zeus and Haz come in last. It's not just that they're silent compared to everyone else; it's that there's something simmering between them. A vibe they're giving off.

It's uneasy, and I don't like it.

Haz keeps his head down as he speed walks past everyone and down the hall.

In the moment I watch Decaf follow Haz with his gaze, I miss Zeus approaching me. I miss being able to check him out completely to make sure all of his body parts are where they're supposed to be.

So when I nudge Decaf to go after Haz, because we both know he wants to—feels obligated to—I startle when Zeus takes hold of my hand.

But that's nothing compared to the flinch I make when I look into his eyes ... or eye if I want to be accurate. The whole left side of his face is swollen.

I step toward him and cup his good cheek because the other looks like it would be painful. "What did he do to you?"

Through gritted teeth and struggling to talk, he says, "Nothing I can't handle."

"Mm, sounds like you've got this under control. You can barely speak."

He smiles. "Trav says he's mad he didn't think of breaking my jaw sooner."

I frown.

"He was joking. Obviously."

"No, I wasn't." Trav appears out of nowhere, and now I know what Lemon means when he says they're all so stealthy. Apparently, Atlas announces when he walks into a room now so Lemon doesn't jump a mile high when his husband simply sits next to him.

Zeus drops my hand and steps away, making my hand fall from his face.

"Did you get any sleep?" Trav asks me.

I shake my head.

"We're all going to crash for the next few hours before heading back out for plan B. I suggest both of you do the same."

My eyes widen. "You're going back out there?"

Even though I'm clearly looking at and talking to Zeus, Trav answers for him.

"Oh, he's not going back out there. The rest of us are."

"You're letting Haz back out there when he's injured too," Zeus argues.

"Yes, but unlike you, you know how to handle what you went through. He's been quiet on the way home. Too quiet."

"Sure, when I can't talk, you're happy, but when he's silent, it's a problem."

Trav taps Zeus's shoulder. "Can you blame me? Even with a broken jaw, you don't shut the fuck up. Go sleep. I'll wake you when we're going to head to the safe house so you can keep updated with Pierre."

"And in the meantime," I say, taking Zeus's hand, "I'm going to make sure you're in the least amount of pain possible. Anything you need, I'm here."

Trav puts his fingers in his ears like a child. "I'm not hearing that."

"I mean soup!" I call out to him as he walks away.

"Lalalalala," he replies, fingers still in his ears, though they're obviously not blocking any noise whatsoever.

I lean in and whisper to Zeus, "And blowjobs, of course. You might not be able to use your mouth, but I can use mine."

Proving to me that a broken jaw can't stop him, he lifts me over his right shoulder and carries me back to our room.

I don't want to think it, and I hate that I immediately do, but I could really get used to this.

Having him with me.

Having him have his way with me.

Making me feel like his possession.

I shake my thoughts free because I can't afford to think that way. I can't.

It'll only end in more heartache and pain.

CHAPTER TWENTY-SEVEN_
ZEUS

I WISH I COULD KISS HIM ALL OVER, WORSHIP HIS goddamn body the way I want to, but I fucking can't. My jaw aches, and my eye twitches. I can feel my heartbeat in my brain. That can't be normal.

But even through all that pain, I can't take my hands off Callie.

As soon as I get him back to our room, I dump him on the bed and pounce on him.

"Are you sure you're okay to do this?" he asks.

"Mmhmm. Make me feel better. Take all my pain away."

Trav was right about one thing. Talking with a broken jaw is horrible, but it's still not going to stop me from doing it. Especially when I'm asking for things that will distract me from the pain.

I roll off Callie and lie on my back, pulling him with me so he's now on top. "Besides, you promised me something about blowjobs."

"I could blow you," he says. "Or ..." He reaches over to the nightstand and opens a drawer. "Lemon stocked up for us." He holds a condom and lube in his hands.

"That's one way to distract me."

He leans over me and kisses my good cheek. "I'm just glad you're okay."

"Relatively speaking." It's so difficult to talk without moving my teeth.

"Do you want to talk about what happened?"

"No." I grip his tight ass in my big hands. "I want to watch you ride me and fill you up so fucking good."

"I want that too."

I smack his butt. "Get up so we can get naked. I want to see all of that body as it moves on top of me while you take what you need from me."

Callie slowly climbs off me and takes off his shirt.

I should start on getting rid of my own clothes, but I'm too mesmerized by the miles of bare skin he's revealing. He drops his sweats to the ground, having been freeballing it, and his cock is already hard, pointing straight up.

"You need me to undress you, or will you do it while you watch me prep myself?"

I groan. "That one. Definitely the watch you thing. It'll be so hot."

Callie climbs back on the bed, facing away from me, and I shuffle over to give him the room.

My gaze doesn't leave his tight little hole as he leans forward, resting one hand on the mattress. I keep staring, even when I kick my legs to remove my pants and then do a mini sit-up to get my shirt off.

I watch intently while he lubes up his fingers and plays with his taint. Pressing his finger against his tight ring of muscle before easing off and doing it again. He loosens himself up and lets one finger inside.

My cock aches as much as my jaw, but it's not in a painful way. It's in that needy way that begs for mercy.

I have to touch myself. I can't not. The issue will be having the control to stop stroking myself before I reach the point of no return, come too early, and then ruin this moment.

This perfect moment, where instead of sympathy, he offered pleasure. Instead of anger from failing the mission, he's offering himself to me.

I wrap my callused fingers around my shaft and squeeze tightly.

There's nothing hotter than seeing someone turning themselves on for you. It doesn't matter what gender, what parts they have, or how they do it. Knowing they're doing it so you can share that pleasure is everything to me.

It's the kind of connection I've never gotten outside of the bedroom. That whole give-and-take thing.

Maybe I've been fucking the wrong people, or maybe I just don't have that in me, I'm not sure, but I do know that there's something about Callie that piques my interest that has nothing to do with sex.

It's like that protective instinct I have over him, the drive to fix his life and hurt those who are trying to hurt him ... It's as if all of that only makes moments like this more intense.

He slowly fucks his fingers, slicking up his hole for me, and I have absolutely no control when it comes to him.

While I continue to stroke myself, I use my free hand to run up his thigh and land on his ass cheek.

"I'd love to see this a nice shade of pink."

Callie lets out a stuttery breath. "Oh God. Do it."

Even though we've established he's okay with being rough in bed, I hesitate a second.

"Do it, please." He turns his head to look over his shoulder at me. "I want it. I want to feel the sting. I want—"

I lift my hand and bring it down again, but the sound of palm hitting skin isn't as satisfying as it usually is because I didn't spank him hard.

"Harder," he demands.

I do it again, still hesitant to use all my strength. This time, there's a better sound, but Callie whines in frustration.

"Make it sting red," he rasps.

This time, I don't hold back. How can I when he says things like that? The second my hand connects with his delectable ass, he clenches around his fingers and moans.

"Fuck, I'm ready. I'm so ready." He pulls his fingers free, and I can't help myself.

I reach for his hole and press the pad of my digit at his entrance while he retrieves the unopened condom on the bed. When he leans back again, he takes my finger all the way inside him, and just the sight of him doing that with my bright red mark I left on him makes my patience snap.

"Hurry up and roll the condom down my cock. I need to be fully inside this sweet ass."

He turns to do exactly that, but when he's done and he climbs on top of me, he's still facing my feet.

"Nuh-uh. Turn around. I want to see your face as you come. As you make me come."

Callie pauses, but it's only for the briefest second before he does as I ask.

The sheepish smile on his face is the brightest thing I've ever seen in my life, but as he stares down at me, it turns into something more teasing.

Confident.

And it's sexy as fuck when he straddles my waist, reaches behind him, and guides my cock inside him. Inside the tightest ass I've ever been inside of. The pressure around the tip of my dick as he takes his time lowering himself builds and builds. His ass squeezes me tight, and I have the very real fear that it will be all over before I give him the chance to come.

I can't do that to him.

He will always come before me.

That's my rule for him. Because he still needs to know that he's worth every sensation, every feeling that he gives me.

I want him to take everything from me. Everything he could ever want or desire.

"Fucking ride me, Callie."

When he starts moving up and down my shaft, rotating his hips, and slowly gaining more traction, more speed, I watch his face.

His hooded blue eyes, which look almost black in the dark. The way his lips are parted. He looks like a feral animal in heat, possessed by the need inside him.

It's euphoric.

Callie focusing on what I can give him instead of what he can give me shouldn't turn me on the way it does. I have hang-ups about being used, about only being seen as a pretty face, but with Callie, it's an honor to be the one who brings him pleasure. To see him filled. And to see him be the one to take it instead of asking for it or going without because he's too busy focused on me.

I didn't know it could be like this. I didn't know that sex could include emotions. To me, it's all sensations and an end result. It's getting lost in the satisfaction an orgasm gives, not getting lost in each other.

And right now, I'm so lost in Callie.

I want more, and even though that thought is terrifying, I didn't realize that meeting someone I could genuinely have feelings for would be like this.

All the mocking I did at Atlas's wedding, all the extreme protests against relationships, it's only because I didn't understand it.

I still don't understand it, but I feel it.

And if it's like this with someone I'm interested in, I want to know what it would feel like to be with someone I love.

The inner fuckboy in me scoffs at the idea, but I've never felt closer to anyone than I do with Callie on top of me, writhing, taking my cock as deep as he can get and making sinful noises through every moment of it.

"I'm getting close," he says. He has almost no voice left.

I slap his ass once more and reach between us so I can jerk him off at the same time.

"Oh, fuck." He drags out the word. "Again."

With one more hard crack of my hand meeting his flesh, my hand fills with his release. His body changes from moving rhythmically to stiff and jerky.

He continues to use my dick, moving up and down, no doubt rubbing that magical place I like to call my cum trigger, and he rides wave after wave until he has nothing left.

It's so amazing to see his walls come down, his hesitations disappear, and this confidence in his expression. It's so entrancing, in fact, that I totally miss that I didn't come. I'm still hard as a pipe inside him, pulsing, aching, but if he was done and asked to stop, I'd do it.

It's as if thinking about it makes him realize too.

He stiffens on top of me. "Oh shit, you haven't come yet."

"I don't need to. Not after seeing that. That was ... that was ..." What the fuck was it?

"I wish I could kiss you," he says.

"Then do it. Pain be damned." I lift up to try to meet his mouth halfway, but he pushes me back down.

"I don't want to hurt you, but I can kiss you somewhere else." He slowly rises so my cock falls out of him, and then in the next minute, he shuffles all the way down so he's practically straddling my ankles, rips off the condom, and then swallows me all the way down.

As if all my synapses were taking a break, one second of his mouth on my cock has them firing on all cylinders again.

And because I know I don't have to hold back anymore, because Callie has gotten what he wanted, I let myself go.

I thrust up into his mouth, and it only takes a couple of pumps before I'm filling his mouth with my cum. A white-hot orgasm rushes through me, making me grit my teeth so hard that when they slip to the side, something in my jaw snaps, and it's so excruciating I have to yell out. But the second the sound leaves my mouth, the pain stops.

So does Callie. He sits up, startled by my outburst. "Did I do something wrong?"

"No." My brows must shoot up into my hairline because I'm able to move my mouth properly again. I open my mouth wide and then make an O shape with my lips and repeat it. "I think my jaw was only dislocated." I try side to side now. It's tender but so much better than it was. "It's fixed."

"No broken jaw?" he asks, looking hopeful.

"Not broken, no."

"Then can I kiss you properly now?"

"Fuck, yes."

With Callie wrapped up in my arms, his head in the nook of my shoulder, and his gentle breath on my chest, it's without a doubt the most intimate position I've ever been in. I'm finally under-standing the difference between sex and intimacy.

The me at Atlas's wedding would be cursing up a storm over this, but current me ... It's like my blinders have been taken off, and I see it now.

Eww, feelings really are contagious. Soon, the entire team is going to come down with a case of the feels. At least if they're all busy in their own love lives, they won't be interested in mine.

Not that these blips of connection I'm having with Callie could be considered love, but it is the closest I've ever come to contemplating it. Or a relationship. If that's what you can even call this.

Ugh. I'm too in my head.

This feels good, so I'm going to do it. The end.

"So, what happened on the mission?" Callie pulls back slightly so he can see my face.

"We were hoping when we were caught, we'd be led to Pierre. We were supposed to lure him out with the promise of handing you over at a location in the desert, but he was too smart for that. We never got in the same room as him."

He runs a finger over my jaw, so gentle it sends a shiver down my spine. "How'd the jaw happen?"

"Instead of facing us himself, he sent his henchmen after us. Took a punch to the face by a guy who has no right to be called a human. I'm pretty sure I came face-to-face with flesh-colored Hulk."

"I heard what happened to Haz. Is he okay?"

That's a hard question to answer. "Physically, he'll be fine, but I think it was his first ever run-in with that kind of situation, so he's processing at the moment. He'll either deal with it and move on or realize that maybe Mike Bravo isn't for him."

"Then what would he do? Go back to the military or …"

"Who knows? Hell, I wouldn't even know what *I'd* do if I didn't have Mike Bravo."

Callie chuckles softly and reburies his head on my shoulder. "It must be the night for people to have an existential crisis."

"What do you mean?"

He continues to talk into my chest, unable to give me eye contact again. "Decaf was keeping me distracted while you were out there by asking me what I'd do with my freedom. I couldn't come up with anything."

"You could work at Lemon's club," I suggest.

The shudder that racks his body is answer enough.

"Okay, so not that. What about …" Shit, I don't know. "Accountant."

Hey, at least his body is shaking with laughter now. "Decaf and I went through all the options I'm qualified for, and I think I landed on possibly going back to Nevada and working on Extraterrestrial Highway. It was remote, easy job … not a lot of money, but livable."

"Weren't you living out of your car?" I hate the thought of him living like that.

"Only because I was worried about when I would have to run

again. I could afford at least a trailer if it was going to be a permanent thing."

Okay, no, I hate the thought of that even more.

"You deserve so much better."

"Hey, it's a roof over my head. I don't think there's anything to be ashamed of doing that."

"That's not what I meant. I mean …" I bite my lip. "You deserve to have the life you want, not the life you're willing to settle for. You could go to college. You could—"

"That implies I finished high school to begin with."

"Then get your GED and then go to college. Be whoever and do whatever you want."

He sighs in my arms and snuggles closer. "One can dream."

After this is all done, I'm going to do everything I can to make sure his dreams come true. Whatever they might be.

CHAPTER TWENTY-EIGHT_

CALLIE

Z EUS AND I ARE WOKEN BY A KNOCK AT THE DOOR.

"We're heading out," a deep voice says.

"Shit." Zeus jumps out of bed so quickly I'm almost dragged with him. "I can come!" He scrambled for clothes.

"Don't need to know, man."

"On the mission, fuckface." He gets pants on and swings open the door.

The guy I know as Scout stands on the other side.

"My jaw wasn't broken. Only dislocated. Look."

I can't see from here, even when I lean up on my elbow, but I'm assuming Zeus is doing that fish mouth thing again that he did when he realized his jaw had clicked back in place.

"It fixed itself last night."

This Scout guy looks skeptical. "Also don't need to know how it was fixed, but let me have a feel."

Scout cups Zeus's face, and Zeus grunts, but Scout pulls away with a small nod. "I can clear you to go back out there, but you're still tender and in pain, so good luck getting Trav to sign off on you going."

"So we don't tell him it's still sore."

"Don't give me those damn puppy eyes, dude. They didn't

work when we served together, and they aren't going to work now. Talk to Trav."

Zeus quickly turns to me. "I have to go."

That's all I get.

That gross feeling of being abandoned so quickly and easily washes over me, and I know they're my issues and Zeus hasn't promised me anything, but I wish I could make it hurt less.

Scout tips his head. "Callie."

I nod back, and then he's gone too.

I slump back on the bed and stare at the ceiling.

I hope this mission is over with today because I don't know how much Zeus I can handle before my heart is wrecked when I have to leave.

It's not like I can hang around the Mike Bravo quarters after they're done like the annoying houseguest that won't leave.

Twenty minutes of wallowing time is all I allow myself before I force myself out of bed to shower and change into more of the clothes others in Mike Bravo were able to lend me.

The place is silent when I first walk out there, but then I find Zeus setting up a computer at the small formal dining table I've never seen anyone eat at. They usually all eat together at the long-ass table that will fit them all.

"I thought you left?" I ask.

From over in the corner of the living room, where Decaf is nursing his cup of coffee, he says, "Daddy didn't let him go on the mission."

Zeus looks up from what he's doing. "I thought the aim was to keep you and Haz separated. Why did you stay when he's still in his room?"

Decaf stands. "One, because Lemon and Callie still need a babysitter and Trav doesn't trust you to do it because you'd most likely let them tag along with you to interrupt the mission. And two, I volunteered."

Zeus narrows his gaze. "But why did you volunteer? You hate that Haz joined the team."

Decaf's face goes a tinge of red like he's trying not to explode.

I know why he hates that Haz joined Mike Bravo, but considering how vulnerable he was about it, I'm not about to blurt it out. I need to diffuse the situation.

"Is that empty?" I say sweetly and point to Decaf's cup. "Want me to make you another?" I turn to Zeus. "And you? Let's all have coffee."

Coffee fixes everything, right?

"I'll help," Decaf says, following me into the kitchen.

We hear Zeus call after us, "Callie, make sure he doesn't poison mine."

"I promise," I yell back.

"I dunno. Poisoning him wouldn't be the worst thing," Decaf mutters.

"Let's agree to disagree with that one." I move about the kitchen, searching drawers and cabinets for cups, which Decaf doesn't even help me with. He, of all people, should know where the mugs are kept.

Then I realize why he's not helping. He's too busy studying me. "Thank you, by the way," he says when I finally find the cups.

I pull three down. "Thank you for what?"

"Not telling Zeus what I told you yesterday about Haz."

"It's not my place to say."

Decaf opens his mouth to say something but then closes it again.

I turn to him. "What's going on?"

"I appreciate you not saying anything because you're right, it's not your place. Which is why I hope you forgive me when it's not my place to say this, but I want to protect you."

My mouth goes dry, and I lick my lips. "What is it?"

"I don't want to see you get hurt, so I'm only going to say this once. Don't get attached to Zeus. It won't end well for you."

My chest sinks, but I think it's more from relief than disappointment. I thought he was going to say something like the mission is failing and I'm on my own from here on out, or if they can't get Pierre, then I may as well accept that my life is over. This? This I can handle.

"Thanks, but I already know that. It's not a secret that he doesn't do relationships, and I'm okay with it."

Or I will be. Once it's over and I have the space to get over it.

"Then I'm sorry I said anything."

I smile at him. "Don't ever be sorry for looking out for someone's well-being. It's actually nice you care."

Again, he goes to open his mouth and then shuts it just as fast. "It's hard to turn it off. Caring. About people, I mean. Not you specifically. I'm not trying to hit on you."

"Thanks for the clarification because I hate to tell you, but I'm not interested in you like that."

"Ditto, but I can't help looking out for you, you know?"

I want to ask if it's because I remind him of someone else, maybe. Someone around my age who's currently injured in one of the bedrooms, but I don't. He told me the story. I'm not going to bug him about it.

"Does everyone in Mike Bravo like to play big protectors? Zeus is the same. Atlas."

"We were all cut from the same cloth."

"That's some mighty fine cloth."

Decaf laughs. "That's so cheesy. I don't like cheese with my coffee. Which, by the way, isn't making itself."

"You distracted me with all the talking! Your fault. Besides, you said you were going to help."

"Okay, get out of my way, and let me show you how to make the perfect coffee."

I watch him as he adds more coffee grounds to the filter than recommended and then stand there frozen in horror as he fills his cup to the top with the black sludge.

Look, I love coffee. I'm a fan of caffeine. But how does he drink that?

"That can't be good for your arteries. How much caffeine is that?"

"The perfect amount. Just enough to show up on a tox screen."

"Have you ever tried to quit?"

"Do you have a death wish?" There's a moment of silence where we stare at each other before both of us burst into laughter. "I probably should quit, but I won't."

"At least try to cut back. If you're going to look out for me, I'm going to look out for you."

He smiles over at me. "Then maybe I will."

Zeus's voice makes us flinch. "Am I interrupting something?"

CHAPTER TWENTY-NINE_
ZEUS

THIS IS A NEW EXPERIENCE TOO—SEEING SOMEONE I'M interested in openly flirt with someone else. I don't like it.

No, I fucking hate it.

Callie's warm smile takes away some of the growliness, but I've never wanted to hurt Decaf more, and I have no idea why.

It's taking all my effort to anchor myself to this wall and not advance on him.

"Decaf was telling me how to make the best coffee."

So he can ask you to fetch him some like a good little house husband?

"Don't listen to him. His coffee is lethal," I say, trying to keep my voice as level as possible.

"Yeah, I figured that one out on my own. You want me to make you a pot of regular, normal-person coffee?"

"Let me." I push off the wall and stalk over to them, eyeing Decaf as I go.

"Huh," Decaf says and takes a sip of his coffee. Then he turns to Callie. *My Callie*, the voice inside my head growls.

I shake that thought free. I'm clearly going insane. Hearing voices and all. That's what this is. It's a mental breakdown. Psychosis. Anything but the J-word. I'm not jealous.

I'm not.

"Maybe I was wrong about him after all." That's all Decaf says before leaving Callie and me alone.

"Wrong about what?" I ask.

Callie shrugs. "I have no idea."

I want to call bullshit, but I don't. Because if there's one good thing about having to stay back from the mission, it's that I get to spend more time with Callie.

I squeeze his hip as I pass him to make us both coffees, just needing that physical touch. To remind him that I'm the one who gets to touch him. At least while he's here.

Don't ask me why he and Decaf getting along made me want to reinforce that, but seeing them together ... it gave me the ick. Like watching someone touch your things.

Possessiveness is a trait I didn't even know I had.

Interesting ...

"So what's with the computer setup?" he asks as I pour the coffees.

"Ghost kicked me out of the command center early. Said he won't deal with my attitude all day and to connect to the system in any other room. All I did was insist I sit in his chair and he work at an angle. Is that so much to ask?"

Okay, so maybe it was irrational, considering how much Ghost does while we're out there. If we need traffic directions for the clearest path, he's on it. If we need to research someone or something, he gets background information in seconds.

I still choose to believe I'm not too close to this mission, as he implied. I just want it over with. I want Pierre dead so the world could be that little bit better.

It will still be a mess, but just less of one.

"I know you don't want to hear it, but I'm kind of glad you weren't allowed to go on the mission." Callie steps closer to me. "And that you're not holed up in Ghost's cave. We didn't see him at all yesterday until the mission was over."

I try not to let my smile show at the idea that he wants me here.

He blinks up at me. "When you ran out of the room earlier, I kind of felt like we were unfinished."

"Unfinished? You came last night. Geez, greedy much? But I'll tell you what. We can head straight back to that room, and I'll finish you off."

Callie's eyes narrow. "What if all I meant was you hadn't kissed me good morning?"

That shouldn't be as cute as it is. "I'll fix it right now."

I grip the backs of his thighs and lift him, putting him on the kitchen counter with his legs wrapped around my waist.

Damn, he feels good against me.

I run my hand over his hair and grip it tight, pulling his head back enough so that he has to look up at my face.

Then, without a word of warning, my mouth meets his, and I dive in. My tongue strokes his, and I swallow the moan that escapes his throat.

His hips begin to move as he ruts against me, but then, as if he comes to his senses and realizes we're in a very public kitchen, he pushes me off him, accidentally scraping his teeth along my bottom lip as we part.

I grin as I run my thumb along where it stings. "Didn't know you were into biting. The kiss was that good, was it?"

"What is wrong with you?" he asks, and his tone is so serious I'm confused as to what's going on.

I glance around the room. "Uh, did I miss something?"

"Yeah." Callie jumps off the counter and puts his hands on his hips. I don't have the heart to tell him he looks exactly like a bulkier Lemon when he does that.

"Did you not want me to kiss you?"

"Of course I wanted you to kiss me. I just didn't think you would."

I cock my head. "Why would you think that?"

"Because when I said we were unfinished and I didn't want sex, only to kiss you, you should have run away from me. It should've been too much commitment for the man-slut."

"What kind of reputation do you think I have? Being scared of kissing? Are you high? Did Decaf give you drugs? I'll kill him. I'll—"

He points at me. "That. Right there. That doesn't belong in what we're doing. You really want to know what Decaf meant when he said maybe he was wrong about you?"

"I did, but not so much anymore." Why am I getting yelled at for giving Callie what he wanted?

"He came with me to make coffee because he's worried I'm developing feelings for someone who can't love me back. But for all this talk of not doing relationships or repeats or any of that ... nothing seems to scare you off. What if I told you I was falling in love with you?"

"Whoa, wait, back the truck up." I stumble away from him.

He throws up his hands. "Thank you. Was that so hard?"

I'm still so fucking confused. "You want me to run away from you? Is that what you're saying?"

"No, but I have the expectation that you will. I can't get my hopes up or think that I'm special because everyone here knows I'm not."

"Don't talk like that." Oh, look, Mr. Growly Pants is back. "You've been through a lot, and you deserve a break. You are special, okay? And you're particularly special to me."

"As what?" Callie asks, exasperated. "As a pet project? As someone to fuck? What am I to you?"

Shit, that's a heavy question, and he's right, it's one I would normally run away from. But for whatever reason, I don't want to with him.

I run my hand over the back of my neck. "Umm, you're ... you? And I ... I, umm, like you? And want to spend time with you. And fuck you? Is ... umm, that okay?"

Callie frowns, making him look as confused as I feel. "Are you saying you want to ... date me? Is that what all the stuttering is about?"

"Is that dating? I don't know. I've never dated someone

before. All I know is that when you say things like you want to kiss me, it doesn't make me want to run away."

"Okay, kissing good. The L-word, bad."

"D ... d-did you mean the L-word?"

"Calm down. I did not. I was getting confused, is all. I was happily living in the *this will only be while I'm here* realm of possibilities, so when Decaf said maybe not, I might have freaked out."

I step closer, boxing him in against the counter. "Why did you freak out?"

"Like I said. I didn't want to get my hopes up."

I smile. "Because you want to date me too."

He nods. "Even if I worry it'll be a mistake."

"Mistake?"

"I don't have the greatest taste in guys, and it's no secret you've never done this before. What if I'm repeating old patterns?"

I give him some physical steps between us when I say, "You don't think I'd hurt—"

He follows me, closing the gap and holding my hand. "No. You wouldn't physically hurt me—"

"Unless you ask," I add.

"Right." His cheeks turn the very same shade of the palm print on his ass last night, and I love it. "But the thing is, I'm the worst person a commitment-phobe should get involved with because when I'm in a happy relationship or dating someone new, it's easy for me to be blind to red flags because my little abandoned inner self needs it to be my happy ending. Always. I'm ... I'm scared that I might not be falling in love with you yet, but that's only because I thought it couldn't be a possibility. I guess I've been holding back to protect myself. If we do this ... there's a good chance I will fall. I fall too easy. Too fast."

And that's a lot of pressure. That means if I'm in this, I need to be all in.

"I ... I ..." I have no idea what to say to that.

"See, I'm already scaring you off." He is, but probably not for the reasons he's thinking.

"I'm not scared off because of the possibility of that happening. I'm scared because hurting you at all will kill me. I don't want to break your heart."

This time, when Callie laughs, it's humorless. "It figures when I finally meet someone willing to put me first, there would be one major catch."

"My cock is too big? That's the catch, isn't it?" Making light of the mood doesn't help like it usually does, and when a heavy silence falls between us, I regret not learning how to be a normal, well-adjusted human.

"That, obviously. But also that he'd be way too nice to take advantage of me." He wears a small smile as he disappears back into the living room.

I have no idea where we stand now, and I don't know what to do. If I keep going, there's the likely chance that I'll hurt him, and that's the last thing I want to do.

As much as I want to be selfish in this situation, it's unfair of me to promise things I can't actually promise.

So what do I do? Stack the odds and take the risk, or ignore that I have an actual genuine connection with someone for the first time in my life and keep everything as it always was: carefree and unserious.

It's too hard a decision.

I can't make it. At least not without a lot of thought.

CHAPTER THIRTY_

CALLIE

WHY IS ZEUS SO FUCKING PERFECT? AND WHY AM I SO messed up over it?

When he finally emerges from the kitchen, where I've probably scared him by getting too serious too quickly, I expect him to ignore me or be dramatic and break things off now to make it easier.

Not that there is really anything to break off. I knew the deal.

But he doesn't do any of that. He comes right over to me, takes my hand, and drags me over to where he was setting up his computer earlier.

"We can watch the mission from here."

We sit side by side, and while he's not ignoring me, he's definitely avoiding eye contact with me.

At the moment, all we can see on the body cams is the interior of all the different cars.

"How many ended up going out for this?" I ask.

Zeus hesitates, so Decaf, who's back on his couch, answers from across the room.

"Everyone we had available."

"What is the new plan? Ambush? Blow up Vegas?"

"I suggested that," Zeus says. "But Trav said I wasn't allowed to blow up any casinos. Something about collateral damage and pissing off all the other organized crime syndicates on the Strip. This plan is much simpler. Last night, while we were in Vegas, we put traceable plates on our car and made sure CCTV picked us up and could follow us out of town. The plates connect back to a safe house Trav owns, so we had Angel and her right-hand man, Proxy, out there last night, keeping an eye on the place in case we were followed, but we knew it would take a while for them to track the address down. Angel's last update was there wasn't any action, so it's really a waiting game now."

"How do you know Pierre will even chase you down?"

"Oh, he'll send someone after us. Hopefully, I pissed him off enough last night to make him do it himself."

"And if he doesn't?"

"Then we move to plan C."

"What is plan C?"

Zeus purses his lips. "We'll come up with it if we need to. There's always an alternate plan."

This doesn't fill me with confidence. "So we're supposed to sit here and watch them all wait?"

Decaf cuts in again. "It's good to be connected at all times in case something goes awry, but you don't have to watch it all the time."

"Don't *have* to," Zeus says, "but if you want to, you should be able to."

Decaf sips his coffee. "Hey, I'm not going to yuck anyone's yum. Go nuts."

So, as the seconds and minutes tick by, and all we're watching and hearing is them driving to this safe house, the more nervous I become. It's not that I still feel guilty over them doing this for me when they have no stake in the game—though that is still an issue—but it's as if I'm there with them. The outcome of today might not be the one we want, but I'm so close to freedom I can taste it.

After talking about what I want to do with my future, I'm

beginning to believe I could actually have one. Whether it's going back to living in the middle of nowhere with a simple job or being brave enough to chase my GED, I'm realizing I really want it.

I want to look at my life and have something to work toward. It's been a long time since I've had that because my ambition has been drowned out by those heavy questions of why I'm even here to begin with.

Every life has purpose, and I want to find mine.

It's just the waiting around that's killing me.

"I don't think I can watch this," I say. "Is there something I can do to distract me?"

"He's sitting right next to you," Decaf snarks.

Zeus throws up his middle finger without taking his eyes off the screen. "Maybe you could go see what Lemon's doing."

Okay, he's not ignoring me, but he is pulling away. And I get it.

It's better this way. Even if it hurts more than it should. But that means this is the right move.

"I'll go find Lemon." I stand, yet part of me yearns for him to grab my hand to stop me. Maybe to pull me down and kiss me.

Of course, he doesn't, and then I'm walking away.

It sucks, just like I knew it would.

Lemon keeps me distracted for most of the day by telling me all about the club he now owns and what shenanigans the guys I used to work with are up to. When I ask him how the club is doing after the rebuild, he admits that business without the side hustle of dealing drugs isn't as lucrative as one would think, so I try to come up with ways he could bring in more business.

"What about theme nights? Peaches was always a gay strip club, but what if you host a ladies' night once a week? Get a drag queen to host it? Women go nuts for things like that, don't they?"

He smiles. "That's actually a really good idea. Diamante and Romeo said they got way better tips working for that *Magic Mike* rip-off club than at Peaches. That could also be more like a show too. Like, with actual dance routines I could choreograph and—"

"Why limit that to the ladies' night, though? You could have it as a regular thing. Not every night, but you could capitalize on it and bring in new patrons, bring back old ones who were over the same routines every night who want more than a strip show with a bump-and-grind lap dance."

"I need to write all this down. Wait here." He runs off and comes back with a notepad and pen.

But in the middle of writing down ideas, we hear, "Fuck. No!"

Both of us don't waste time running out to the living area.

Zeus is practically pulling his hair out from the roots as he paces in front of his computer.

The urge to throw up builds in my gut. "W-what happened?" I must also look pale because Lemon grabs me and directs me to the couch.

"Sit down. You look like you're going to pass out."

"I'll get you some water." Decaf jumps up.

Lemon glares in the general direction of Zeus. "What's happening? Who's injured, what's wrong?"

Zeus appears next to Lemon, and he immediately drops to his knees in front of me. "I'm sorry to scare you. Everyone's okay. No one is hurt. I promise."

"I've heard that before," I rumble. "Then you came home with a broken jaw, and Haz is still hiding in his room, nursing his hand because he was literally tortured."

"Okay, I'll rephrase. Everyone on Mike Bravo is unharmed, but I didn't think you'd care to know that all of the men Pierre sent are dead."

"Then what's with the huge overreaction?" Lemon asks.

And I know the answer. "Pierre didn't show up himself, did he?"

"No," Zeus says.

If I didn't know Pierre personally, if I hadn't seen him, smelled his expensive cologne, and shuddered at the thought of having to have sex with the man, I might begin to believe he's not actually real.

"How many henchmen does he have?" I ask.

"A lot less now." Zeus smiles.

I can't help it. A laugh bursts from me, and then I cover my mouth. "Fuck, I shouldn't be laughing at that."

"Aww, we'll make you one of us yet." He slaps my shoulder.

Sure, one of them. When fantasizing about my future, I don't picture living in the Mike Bravo world. Especially not if I had to see Zeus on a regular basis.

I'm so certain what we have is something special. Temporary but special. It's as if I already know he's the man who's going to bring me out of my funk and give me purpose again.

And that is exactly why I can't hang off him like a leech. Because then I'll be attached and lose my sense of self for the millionth time with the millionth different guy.

"So does that mean we're doing plan C?" I ask.

Zeus nods. "Plan C."

"And what is that, exactly?"

The word "Zeus" booms from the speakers of the computer. "You there?"

"We're about to find out." Zeus takes my hand and helps me off the couch while Decaf, who's hovering behind him, hands me the water I no longer need but I'll take anyway.

Trav's face appears on screen, his hair wet with sweat.

"What's the damage?" Zeus asks.

"Six dead minions. They had no idea what they were walking into. I get the feeling Pierre did, though. That's why he didn't show up himself."

Zeus runs a hand over his hair again. He's lucky he has a full head of hair and can spare some with the rough way he grips it. "How do we lure him out, then?"

"I think you know how," Trav says.

"No," Zeus growls. "No fucking way."

"What am I missing?" I glance between them.

"He wants to use you as bait."

I'm confused. "Isn't that what you have been doing?"

"He wants you there. Physically."

"We can keep him safe," Trav says.

"Doesn't matter what we can do because it's not happening."

I've gotta say, I do love me a growly Zeus, but this isn't his decision. Do I want to put myself on the line like that? Fuck no. But just like I can't rely on Zeus being the one to breathe life back into me, I have to be the one to step up and get my own future back on track. This whole thing is about me, after all.

So, I take a deep breath, scared shitless as I am, and say, "I'll do it."

CHAPTER THIRTY-ONE_
ZEUS

"LIKE FUCKING HELL YOU WILL."

The whole point of this was to get him out of danger, not put him right in front of the firing line.

"No," Callie says softly. "It's time I contribute instead of hide away. If I really am going to be free after this, I need to be able to do things for myself. Otherwise, what's the point in fighting for my future if I don't have any autonomy over it? I'll do it."

I want to be proud of him, but at the same time, I want to slap him upside the head. Metaphorically. I wouldn't actually hit him. That's what all those other assholes did to him. "Sure," I deadpan. "*Now* you're ready to stand up for yourself."

"What's that supposed to mean?" Callie asks at the same time Trav, Decaf, and Lemon wince.

I shake my head. "It's a good thing you're ready to fight for what you want. But couldn't it have been after this was all over and the thing you fight for is a college degree? That's a lot less violent."

"No time like the present and all that," Callie says.

I turn my attention back to Trav. "I don't leave his side. We meet somewhere where Angel can get off a shot before Pierre comes anywhere near him. And I swear to God—"

"You don't believe in God," Trav says.

"Fine, I swear on the Kama Sutra, if one hair on his pretty little head gets hurt, I'll go on a rampage that will take down all of the crooks in Las Vegas."

There's a sharp intake of breath beside me, and when I look at Callie, I don't know what it is I'm seeing in his eyes, but I want to bottle it.

"I didn't go through all of this for your story to end here," I say.

Nobody is speaking. Everyone is staring at me.

"What?" I ask.

That breaks them out of whatever trance they're in.

"Nothing," Trav says. "Let's get to work. You need to call Pierre. FaceTime him. Whatever. Make sure that you warn him that if he keeps sending other people, soon he won't have any employees left to protect him."

"We could take him down that way," I say. "Keep taking out his team of henchmen until there's none left. Sounds better than having to put Callie in danger."

"You know how this business works," Trav says. "When lower-rung thugs are taken out, there's a long list of desperate people behind them to take over."

Sadly, that's true.

"When negotiating places to do the trade, your life for Callie's surrender, you have to make sure he agrees to come. You want to hand Callie over face-to-face so you can have his word firsthand that he won't come after you. Also, make sure it's somewhere with access points, an escape plan, and nowhere he can pull one over on us. Ask Saint and Ghost to pull up maps and find a few places that will work and hope that Pierre will agree."

"And if he doesn't?"

"The deal is off, and we'll keep killing his men."

I love the way my boss thinks.

I wouldn't have thought agreeing to meet on the rooftop of the parking structure across from the Ruby would benefit us in any way, but of all the places we suggested, it actually turns out to be the perfect spot.

I was even able to act like it wasn't my idea when Pierre and I finally came to settling on somewhere.

But this whole thing still makes me uneasy. Having Callie in the back of this car with me is the worst idea Trav's ever had. And of course, it was a bad decision for Callie to put himself on the line to dangle him as bait, but I guess I should've expected it. He's notorious for bad decisions.

Okay, that's unfair on him, I know that, but fuck. He's had this self-preservation instinct for the last year, and now he decides to throw it out the window? Now he decides to grow as a human being and take charge of his own life?

Screw being mentally stable and shit. Though I'd argue offering yourself up to be shot at doesn't exactly scream pillar of mental health.

Yet, the Mike Bravo guys do it on nearly a daily basis.

Why is he getting in my head so much? Why does my chest hurt at the thought of losing him?

When Trav pulls the car into the parking structure, and we start making our way up, circling the ramp over and over again, I begin getting dizzy.

Then a hand lands on my leg, and I turn toward Callie.

He's staring at me with this weird expression, something like a mix of apologizing and fear, and I know I need to be strong for him. Even if it's killing me to hide how much I don't want him here.

I want him back where he's safe. Where no one can hurt him.

"Don't worry," I force out. "We got this."

And we do.

Even though Angel is our top marksman, that doesn't mean the rest of us can't hit a target. Saint is an amazing shot, and though he's usually in command, Ghost is in there for this particular mission. Because on all the surrounding rooftops, we have our guys with long-range sniper rifles and a thirst to be the one to put a bullet in Pierre's head.

Knowing my team, there are probably bets placed.

Then we have Haz on the other side of Callie, Atlas up front with Trav, and those two will act as our sole bodyguards.

Yep. Just two of them. That was the deal. A deal I'm sure Pierre has broken also, but we're prepared for that too.

Proxy has eyes on the buildings that surround us. So far, he's found no one, but I wouldn't be surprised if Pierre didn't have anyone with a good enough aim to set up there.

Which means his extra hands will either be on the roof with him or hiding in cars on these lower levels. If I were him, I'd do the latter.

Little does he know, our shooters will take them out before they could even get to us.

Our Range Rover hits the last speed bump and turns into the open rooftop and empty parking lot. Empty of all but one Escalade facing us. Or, perhaps more importantly, the exit.

Pierre said he could close off this level, seeing as this is his parking lot that guests of his casino and hotel use. That way, he'll know we didn't bring anyone else with us. But there's no way I trust it. He shouldn't either, considering how many guns he has trained on his car right this second.

Trav pulls the car to a stop with a good hundred feet between us. The Escalade's headlights don't turn off until Trav makes the first move by killing ours first.

Las Vegas is lit up all around us, so even though the rooftop only has four lights connected to one single light pole in the middle of the parking lot, our sight isn't affected.

I'll be able to see that slimeball's face the minute he steps out of his car. Which ... he doesn't do. Not yet.

No one moves on either side.

"Are we going to sit here and play a game of chicken all night?" I ask.

"You want to get out and make the first move?" Trav retorts.

Pierre is the one to break, sending out two of his bodyguards first. They stand in front of their Escalade in suits, no doubt with concealed weapons under their jackets.

"We've got eyes on them." Angel's voice has never sounded sweeter over our comms.

"Aimed and ready to go," Saint adds.

Trav signals for Atlas to get out, and unlike Pierre's guys, who are dressed all nice-like, Atlas isn't even trying to hide his badassery. He's in tactical gear, Kevlar, and has his trusty assault rifle strapped to him. He doesn't point it at anyone as he gets out, just pets it like it's his baby to let them know what he's packing.

"Okay, now you three," Trav says.

And this is it. I squeeze Callie's thigh and open my door, holding my hand out for him to take it. When he's out, I put him at my back, and Haz boxes him in between us as we move to the front of the car.

I purposefully take a long glance around the rooftops, trying to pretend like I don't know half a dozen men and one woman are up there, but at the same time, I'm trying to see if Pierre has anyone obviously positioned around the place too.

When Pierre finally makes an appearance, it's with two more bodyguards, and while that means we're outnumbered on this rooftop, there's no way Trav will get out of the car. He knows our key to escape is to get back inside the safety of the Range Rover and to get out of here as quickly as possible.

I've never seen Pierre in person, only in photos and things we could dig up online. He's shorter than I'm expecting but every bit of the rich, arrogant crime boss I knew he'd be.

As he walks between his henchmen, buttoning up his suit jacket, I can't tell if he's moving in slow motion to try to be intimidating or if his performance is so mind-numbingly boring that time stands still.

"I can't get a lock on him," Angel says. "His bodyguards are too big."

"They don't look that big from here," Proxy says.

"Well, compared to the little man," Angel adds.

"Blocked shot here too," Saint says, which is followed up by everyone saying the same thing.

I'm starting to see why Pierre might have picked this place. He knows how to cover his ass. We might have access to the buildings around us, but that doesn't matter when he's too protected with literal bodies in our way.

"Let's get this over with," Pierre says in his French accent. "Give me the boy, and I'll spare your life. As discussed."

"How can we have your assurance?" I ask. "What's going to stop you from killing us as soon as we let him reach you?"

"Good faith?" Pierre smirks.

"I'm not going to just take your word for it." I fold my arms, making myself look bigger while trying to cover Callie from any potential crossfire.

"You need to get him out in the open," Angel says.

He's not going to leave his posse. I know that. So all I need is to get him to shift his position. Because unless we can order our guys to take out the bodyguards first and then get to Pierre, there's going to be gunfire. We all know that's where this is headed anyway, but the main goal is to take Pierre down. He's the priority and can't be an afterthought.

"You're the one who wanted this trade, this meeting," Pierre says.

"I was. But ... I'm not really getting much out of this trade, am I? You've promised me and my partner our lives, but I have no guarantee of that, do I?"

"What do you want instead? Money?"

"You willing to pay for him? Doesn't he owe you money?"

"He can owe me more."

Trav's voice now joins us in our ears. "Keep pissing him off. He's getting antsy. He might move into the line of fire if you ... be you."

Gee, thanks, boss.

"Why are you so obsessed with this one?" I wrap my arm around Callie. "He's a great lay, and I've fucked him so many times over that I could play with him forever, but he's a hole, just like any other. Why do you want him so badly? That's what I want to know. Did you make him swallow smuggled contraband? Like, you're gonna cut him open and pull out drugs or gold or ..." I gasp. "Is he full of gold? That would be cool. Though, what if it melts from the body heat, and then his organs get covered in it, and—"

"Would you shut up?" Pierre yells.

I pretend to think. "Hmm, nah. The more I think about it, the more I want to keep him. There's something special about him if you're willing to go to this much trouble to have him back. Have to say, though, I'll be disappointed if his dick doesn't turn to gold. Oh, I've got it. You want to keep this one because of how big his dick is, right? That's why you hate him? Overcompensating for something? Aww, size doesn't matter. It's how you use it. You shouldn't let people emasculate you like that. Body shaming is not cool. Want to whip yours out now, and I'll compliment it? Will that make you feel better?"

"Jesus," Iris says. "He's so going to get himself shot."

Yeah, probably, but better me than Callie. To be safe, I push Callie further behind me. As if following my lead, Haz steps closer to us too. My body will slow a bullet down but not necessarily stop it, and I won't let Callie get hurt.

"What is wrong with you?" Pierre asks.

"Ah, the question every single one of us has been asking for years," Trav says.

While everyone is goofing off and being assholes, I'm focusing on our next move.

"Wrong? Nothing wrong with being the life of the party. I could give you a few pointers. Your party sure was fun, but why didn't you make an appearance? Can't make any friends? Wow, short, misplaced emasculation insecurities, and no friends. What's it like to be you? Does it hurt—"

And finally, my taunting works. Pierre charges through his protection, pulling a gun from behind his back. "That does it, you fucking—"

"Take the shot," Trav orders, and that's the moment all hell breaks loose.

Angel hits her target, the middle of Pierre's torso, but before she can finish the job with one to the head, one of his bodyguards jumps in front of him and takes the bullet in his shoulder.

The other goons start shooting at us, but their pistols have got nothing on what Atlas is packing.

The sound of rapid fire rings in our ears as Atlas advances, his automatic weapon shooting round after round.

"Get Callie back in the car!" I shout to Haz while I arm myself with the gun at my back to join the mess of bullets flying all over the place. Atlas is holding them for now.

"Trav, you got backup coming, man?" I ask.

"They're too busy shooting from all sides," Trav says in my ear, then tells me to get back in the car. I ignore him.

The guys opposite have retreated behind their car, dragging Pierre with them, but we don't pull back. This isn't going to be a shootout that ends with us all going back to our respective corners and then trying again later. I won't let it.

I'm not decked out head to toe in Kevlar like Atlas is, so I can't really afford to get shot, but I need to make sure Pierre is dead. Callie's freedom is my priority, and you'd think with how selfish everyone thinks I am that they'd allow me to be chivalrous for once.

"Get back in this fucking car," Trav yells.

"Sorry, what? Can't hear you." I aim my gun toward the Escalade, waiting for someone to pop their head around the corner, but they don't.

The second Atlas runs out of ammo, though, I know they'll be back on the offense.

"Zeus!" Callie calls, his voice laced with fear.

"Can't talk right now, babe!" I reply. One of Pierre's men

finally peeks out from around the trunk and takes a shot, but he's clearly not aiming well because it goes nowhere near me.

I return fire and make him drop back behind the car.

"Fucking hell," Trav mutters in my ear, and the next second, he's out of the car too, joining the fight.

"Zeus, please," Callie cries.

I make the mistake of turning to face him. He's refusing to get back in the car, even with Haz pulling on him and trying to force him.

The worry, the sheer angst in Callie's scrunched brow, it breaks my heart but only makes me more determined.

Something behind him catches my eye, and at first, I'm thankful for reinforcements, but then I really look.

The guys encroaching on us with guns are not our guys.

"Get Callie in the car," I growl and then open fire on the people approaching us. They were trying to be stealthy, but as soon as I give them away, they shoot back.

Haz finally manages to throw Callie in the back seat and covers him with his body.

Good. Stay there.

I'm open and exposed, and my guess is that my hunch was correct, and these assholes were hiding out in the cars parked inside the lot, but bullets have stopped flying from the Escalade's direction, so Atlas and Trav change their focus too.

"Is Pierre down?" I yell. "Angel, Saint, you got eyes on him?"

"A little busy saving your ass," Angel replies.

Then, as if in slow motion, a guy getting way too close to me for comfort falls to the ground, but not before his head explodes with blood and brain matter.

"Nice shot," I say.

"Duh," Angel replies.

"I have eyes on Pierre," Saint says. "He's down, and he's bleeding, but he's still moving."

"Can you take a shot?"

"Not from this angle."

"I'm ending this. Boys, cover me." I turn and run toward the Escalade, expertly changing over magazines in my gun as I do.

Gunshots continue to ring out, but it's all background noise at this point. That is, until fire rips through my right arm, and I know I've been hit. Then, my ankle burns next. Not as bad. Probably a ricochet off something, but enough to make me limp.

All it does is slow me down. I'm not coming this far without finishing the job. Not this time.

So even if I'm gushing blood down my arm, covering my fingers and gun in thick, red stickiness, I continue on. It hurts to even lift my hand, so I swap arms and hope I can aim just as well with my left than I can with my right.

On a shooting range, in controlled environments, I'm decent no matter which finger is squeezing the trigger, but this ain't no controlled environment, and the burning sting of being shot makes my vision blurry.

Still, I keep going. Limping. Aching. Determined.

I'm going to get this fucker. When I round the back of the Escalade, I don't even have time to aim, only shoot. Because while my team have taken out some of Pierre's guys, they didn't get them all.

If I'm going to get out of here alive, I need every shot to count because it's not as if I can put my hand up and say, "Hold up, you mind not shooting at me while I reload? Timesies outies. Thanks."

All I can think about while I shoot to kill is the promise I made Callie that none of my team or I will go down. None of us will let this get us.

It's not our time.

It's not my time.

I'm going to get out of here, and it won't be in a body bag. I'll reserve that for Pierre.

And speaking of fuck nuggets who are the scum of the earth, while his bodyguards drop around him, I stand tall over the piece of shit, and I don't even hesitate as I put a bullet right in between his eyes.

At the same time the life drains from his eyes, the adrenaline leaves my body.

It's as if my body says, "Mission accomplished? Good. Let's crash."

And then I go down.

CHAPTER THIRTY-TWO_
CALLIE

I STRUGGLE TO GET HAZ OFF ME AS HIS BIG BODY covers mine in the back seat. I hit, I kick and thrash, but nothing gets him moving. "Let me see," I whine.

"No. It's my job to make sure you don't get hurt. If a single bullet grazes your skin, Zeus will kill me."

"How are you so strong? You're half the size of Zeus."

"Fuck off, I'm not that small."

"Okay, fine, I'll stop struggling."

He eyes me as if he can tell I'm bluffing, but then he finally untenses every muscle he has, and I take my chance.

But even as I scramble to throw him off me and sit up, I don't get far before he pins me back down again. I do, however, get the chance to see Zeus fall to the ground in the split second I have a view.

"No!" I scream, and Haz sits up.

I don't even fight him off me anymore because I know what I saw, and I don't want to accept it. If I sit back up, what I saw will be real, and no. No, no, no, no, no. It can't be. He can't.

Even when Haz's weight leaves me completely and he exits the car, I don't look. I don't move to even try to see.

He slams the door, and I flinch.

All I can do is curl into a ball and wish to be anywhere but here. Be anyone but me.

I don't know how long I stay like this, sobbing with my arms wrapped around my knees, but when the door flies open again, I'm too numb to care if it's one of Pierre's people and they're here to end me.

Just do it, I think.

"Get your ass up," Haz yells.

The door near my head opens too, and when I glance up, Trav's there.

"Up you get." He grabs under my arm and pulls me toward him.

What are they going to do? Hand me over now one of their own is hurt? Abandon me here? Kill me themselves?

Where I'm expecting him to pull me out of the car completely, all he does is order me to sit up properly.

I'm confused for all of two seconds until Atlas and Haz help lower Zeus into the back so he's lying across the seats with his head in my lap.

He's covered in blood, his normally flawless skin a pasty white.

But he's alive.

Barely.

"Zeus," I whisper.

"Sam." The barely there croak of my real name both breaks my heart and fills me with something warm.

Hope.

But that hope is dashed when the other guys climb in the car, and we speed out of the parking lot.

"Scout, you better be close by," Trav says, expertly driving the narrow, winding parking ramp.

"It's just my shoulder." Zeus can barely get the words out.

I stare down at his body, at his clothes covered in red, and where Haz is half in the footwell of the opposite seat, half under Zeus's legs while he puts pressure on Zeus's stomach.

"Fuck," Atlas hisses. "Scout, it's bad. He's been shot multiple times. He can only feel his shoulder."

My gut drops even more, but I try to hold strong because Zeus is looking up at me, his clear eyes shining.

He places his bloody hand on my chest, gripping my shirt in a tight fist. "If there was ever a way to go ... this would be it."

"Don't talk like that," I plead.

"Saving you. Saving a life that hasn't yet had the chance to live."

"Stop," I try to say forcefully, but it comes out more like begging.

"I did it."

"Did what?" Tears fall freely down my face.

"I set you free." His grip on me loosens. His eyes slowly drift closed.

I shake him. "No. Don't go to sleep. Keep talking to me." I cup his face. "Zeus."

He opens his eyes quickly before they flutter closed again.

"Oren," I cry.

"We're losing him," Haz warns.

"Fucking, fuck, fuck shit, fuck," Trav lets out.

"I'm still here, fuckers," he says, but his eyes are still closed, and his voice is weak. Weaker than I've ever heard it.

Trav careens the car out of the parking lot, bouncing and jostling us in the back with every bump he takes without braking.

"We have to go to the hospital," I scream.

"No hospitals," Trav orders.

"He might not make it to the safe house," Atlas says low, but I hear it.

The car screeches to a halt, and Trav turns in his seat and yells to "Get out."

At first, I think he's talking to me, but he's not. I'm too self-involved to realize he's talking to Haz.

With hasty movements, he's gone and is replaced with someone I vaguely recognize from the ranch but forget his name.

"Damn, bro," he says. "I thought we had a deal. If we serve together, we survive together." He has a bag with him and pulls out a bunch of medical equipment.

"You gotta keep him hanging in there, Scout," Trav says. "If we can get him to Fort Irwin, I've got a guy there who can help."

Scout works on Zeus, taking over applying pressure with bandages and gauze and whatever else he has in his bag while also injecting him with a bunch of stuff that I have no idea what it is or what it does. It's like the dude grew eight hands in two minutes.

"Push down on here," he says to me, and I put my hand on top of Zeus's stomach. "Harder. You won't hurt him." Scout's sad eyes meet mine. "He can't feel anything."

My breath stutters.

Scout turns to Trav. "Sorry to say he won't make it to the Fort Irwin. Can you get Doc to come to the hospital here? Slip money up front to the ER for discretion?"

"Fuck." Trav turns the car around, still not taking it easy. He's going to need to replace his tires after this with how much they're screeching along the pavement. "Change of plans. We're headed to the nearest hospital."

Traffic is a bitch, and we get held up.

"What the fuck is going on?" Trav's frustration grows.

Seeing the big guy, the one in charge, get rattled, it does nothing to ease the dread building. The doubt. My heart is in my throat, and the little faith I had that I could truly have a shot at happiness is fading as quickly as the life draining from Zeus's face.

I want to say he looks terrible, but even with him on death's door, he's still unfairly attractive. His strong jaw and chiseled features. Trust him to look amazing, even in death.

"Fucking hockey," Atlas says. "Game just let out. Those fans are nuts."

"I dunno. I'd go nuts for the Mitchell Brothers," Scout says absentmindedly.

"Who?" Atlas asks.

"The Mitchell Brothers. They're married. And hot."

Atlas turns in his seat. "There are brothers who play hockey who are married? To each other?"

"They're not really brothers," Scout says. "They're—"

"Screw this." Trav throws the car in reverse, goes up on the curb, and then weaves in and around pedestrians on the sidewalk like they're mere traffic cones.

All of us quiet and hold our breath, waiting for him to hit someone. Yet, he doesn't.

After the initial shock of a car being on the sidewalk, everyone's smart enough to get out of the fucking way.

Somehow, don't ask me how, we make it to the hospital. But no one even reaches for their door handles.

"Are we moving him or what?" I ask.

"Multiple gunshot wounds, bodies on that rooftop, have to call the cops …" Trav's thinking out loud.

"What? What's going on?" The panic in my voice is something I'm not used to coming from me. And that's saying something because I panic about everything.

Zeus has gone cold. Hasn't said anything for a while. Scout keeps checking his pulse and doesn't seem too worried. Well, he seems worried but not frantic.

"Why aren't we moving?" I yell. Every moment counts.

"Because I have to make a phone call and ask for a favor."

"From who?"

Atlas turns to me with a grin. "His boyfriend."

Trav disconnects his Bluetooth and hits Call to his boyfriend. "Hi, honey!"

I swear Zeus chuckles, or maybe that's wishful thinking.

"Nothing's wrong. I just love you. I love you sooo much." Trav doesn't sound like any of the versions of him I've met so far. "Okay, fine. I need a massive favor. Who in the Las Vegas police department do you know who isn't … and I mean this with all the love in my heart, as big a stickler for the rules as you are?"

And that's how they get Zeus into the hospital without having to worry about being surrounded by a SWAT team for what went down on the parking garage roof.

━━━

Zeus's teammates are overbearing, loud, intimidating, and as a whole are giving off a very stressed vibe. It's no surprise when the hospital staff moves us to some private conference room in the basement. Or maybe they do that because Trav pulls some strings to get Zeus VIP treatment. I'm not complaining.

This room is smaller, and because it's filled with muscular men, all of whom are in a different state of anxiousness, denial, and numbness, I'm able to slink into a corner and melt into the wall.

Hide.

Pray.

I don't even believe in God, but I'm asking him to save Zeus anyway.

I'm on the floor, my knees to my chest and my head tucked between my legs. I'm an invisible ball of guilt.

Zeus wouldn't be in surgery if I'd done what I should have a year ago and let myself burn in that club fire. Or taken a long walk in the desert until it would've been impossible for me to return.

I should've ended it before I hurt even more people.

There's a hand on my knee, and when I look up, Saint lands by my side. He lowers himself to the floor and rests against the wall, mirroring me. But he doesn't say anything.

We haven't had a lot to do with each other, but as soon as our eyes meet, I know he understands.

"I ... uh-I ..." I can't talk.

He shakes his head. "You don't need to say anything. Zeus getting hurt wasn't your fault, and even though you're not going to believe that purely because I say so, I'm not going to let you sit here by yourself and continue your cycle of self-loathing and regret."

I blink at him. "You sound like you're talking from experience."

"I lost my entire team of people. People I trusted more than my blood family. And when it turned out that one of them lived, I had to eat the guilt of leaving him behind. Abandoning him. There's a lot I could blame myself for, and if it weren't for Iris, I probably would've driven myself crazy by now believing the lies my head tries to tell me. So, I'm just going to sit here and be that person for you because Lemon is back in LA, and Zeus is ... you know."

"What if he doesn't make it?" I rasp.

"We don't need to think about that."

"Eventually—"

"Nope. We don't talk what-ifs until something actually happens."

I grip the sides of my head, pulling on my hair just for the distraction. "Can you ... just talk to me?"

"What about?"

"Anything. I need to think about anything but him."

Saint's lips quirk. "I have something for that." He lifts his head. "Iris, get over here. I need your services."

"In front of everyone?" Iris makes his way over and reaches for his fly. "Didn't take you for the voyeur type, but I'm game."

Saint turns to me. "He's bluffing. To have sex in front of the rest of us, I'd have to get naked, and he won't let anyone else see that."

Iris slumps. "I hate when you call me on my bullshit like that." He sits in front of me, crossing his legs. "What do you really need me for?"

"You're already doing it," I say.

"Looking sexy?" Iris asks.

"Being a fool," Saint clarifies.

"I hate to say it, but Saint's correct. I need a distraction."

"Ah. I'm king of distractions. Want to hear a joke?"

"Warning," Saint says. "They're dad jokes and not very funny, but you won't be able to help it. You'll laugh anyway."

"What do you call someone who's gender fluid and lactose intolerant?"

I glance over at Saint. "Do I really want to know?"

"They're non-buy-dairy." Iris laughs at his own joke, and I think I understand why Saint says I'll laugh too. Because Iris finding himself entertaining is funny in itself.

"Ooh, ooh. This one isn't a dad joke. What do you call a slutty T. rex? A dino-whore."

"That's still a dad joke. Just not suitable for kids," Saint says.

Iris smiles proudly. "But it made Callie laugh."

It did, but not enough to bring me out of my head.

When the door to the conference room swings open and a doctor in scrubs is standing there, the small laughter dies. My gut sinks. My heart stops.

"Mr. West, can we step outside?" the doctor says to Trav.

I stand, intending to run out after them so I can hear the news too, but as soon as I'm upright, my head spins, my vision blurs, and if it weren't for Saint and Iris reacting so quickly, I would fall right back down.

But they're there, holding me up on either side.

Seconds turn into minutes, each tick of the clock on the wall echoing in my ears.

Trav needs to hurry up and come back in. Or if it's bad news, he can stay out there as long as he wants.

Ugh, waiting is killing me.

The unknown.

I'm worried if I hear the words I don't want to hear that I'll crumble. I can't face losing Zeus. I can't lose him at all. He's quickly become the most important person to me. The only one who has always been on my side.

I can't go on without him. I won't know how to. He has to survive.

CHAPTER THIRTY-TWO / 233

When Trav comes back in, his eyes meet mine, but I can't get a read on his expression.

"It's touch and go," Trav says. "He's been put into an induced coma so his body can heal from the trauma. We have to keep waiting before we get any answers."

More waiting?

More of this hell?

The urge to run is so fucking strong. Start again. Forget about everything that ever happened here.

It's how I've survived. How I live. I need to run.

"Uh-oh," Iris says. "We've got a runner."

I turn to him, eyes wide. "W-what?" Can he read my freaking mind?

"You look like you're about to bail, and we're not going to let you do that."

"Not after what Zeus just did for you," Trav adds.

"I deserve it," I say. "I deserve to be alone."

"Does Zeus?" Trav asks, his tone cold.

I glance around the room, at all of Zeus's teammates, his family. "He has all of you."

"Was I seriously this dumb when it came to admitting my feelings for Rogue?" Trav asks.

"Yes," everyone says at the same time.

"W-what do you mean?"

"Look," Trav says. "I'm not saying you and Zeus are in love or what-the-fuck-ever. I don't care what you two do with your lives. But I will say that I've never seen Zeus like this with anyone before. Whether it's friendship, sex, love, whatever, it doesn't matter. You're important to him, and he disobeyed orders *for you*. If you abandon him now when he needs you most, that would be the worst thing you've ever done."

"Agreed," Atlas says. "And you tried to kill me once."

Run, stay, run, stay, run … *stay*.

They're right. I can't abandon him. I can't leave.

I have to stay. If not for me, then for him.

CHAPTER THIRTY-THREE_
ZEUS

I'M GOING TO THROW UP. I'M ON SO MANY PAIN MEDS that I think I'm supposed to be high, but all I am is nauseous. I haven't actually vomited, though. It's almost as if I can't.

Part of me wants to force myself to do it because maybe then I'll feel better, but no matter what I try, I can't move. I can't even lift a finger.

It may be hell, and hey, maybe I died and I'm actually in real-life hell if there is such a thing, but even with the pain, I can't be brought down.

I did it.

I freed Callie.

Now, he gets to live a normal life. He'll get a job, find a man ... settle down.

Ergh, the nausea is back, but this time, I don't know if it's physical or emotional. The thought of Callie living the life he deserves—the one he's always wanted—makes me happy, but the idea of him settling down with someone who isn't me doesn't.

Which is a new concept for me.

Murmured voices echo around me, but I can't understand what they're saying. It's a constant buzz of activity; why won't they let me sleep?

I know I'm loveable, but come on. I've been shot. Multiple times. Let me rest.

"We should let him rest," a voice I don't recognize says.

Thank you! I want to yell but can't.

"I'm not leaving his side," Callie bites back.

I smile. At least on the inside.

Everything is too heavy. My eyelids, my face, my arms …

"He's not waking up anytime soon," Trav says, his voice surprisingly sweet for him. "We can come back."

It's selfish of me to love the idea of Callie being by my side, but I want him to stay anyway.

"No. You guys were right when you said I can't abandon him. Not after what he did for me. He put his life at risk for me. I owe him now. I owe him my life."

Is that what he really thinks? He's totally missed the point of taking out Pierre. I don't want Callie to owe me. I want to set him free. And that's including from me.

Even if I'm not done with him physically, I have to be. Because emotionally, I can't be the one for him. I'm not the one for anybody.

It's not a fear of commitment or not even a fear of not being able to keep my dick in my pants. It's a fear of hurting someone I'm supposed to love or vice versa. Who wants to put themselves through that?

Callie has already been hurt by the assholes in his past. That might have been physical, but from witnessing my sister's spiral, it's the emotional toll that does the worst damage.

I can't be the reason Callie wants to stop living. I can't be the entire reason he wants to stay alive either.

"It's not healthy for you to be by his bedside day in and day out," someone says.

"I have to." Callie sounds so damn broken. He sounds like he did back when I met him. After all the manipulation, the abuse he's suffered … for him to think he has to do anything for me breaks my heart.

You owe me nothing, I want to say. *Go live your life.*
Forget me.

———

"His eyes are moving! Quick, someone get the doctor," Callie exclaims. He's so cute.

Slowly, the bright room comes into focus as my eyes blink awake.

It's the first time in days I haven't felt something pulling me under and keeping me down. I'm partially in a seated position, the back of the bed at a thirty-degree angle.

When I can finally see the figures hovering above me, I flinch. "Who wants to see your ugly mugs when they first wake up?" I'm unable to turn my head, but I can glance out the corner of my eye toward Callie. "Except for yours. I could wake up to yours every day."

Fuck, why did my mouth say that?

"Damn." Iris whistles. "Either he's on the really good drugs, or I was right about Zeus being next to fall."

"Drugs," I croak. "Plus, he's so pretty."

Again, what? Maybe it really is the drugs because I can't stop spewing shit I should not be saying to Callie.

Callie's hand holding a cup of water appears in front of my face. "Sip." He lifts the straw to my mouth, and the cool liquid feels like heaven, easing my dry throat.

Scout pushes his way through between Iris and Trav. "Dude. You've been in a coma for three years."

My eyes widen. "What?"

The guys laugh, but Callie scolds them.

"It's not nice to joke with trauma victims."

"Eh. I probably would've done the same," I admit.

"Pretty sure you did back when we were Marines," Scout says. "Remember that time they thought I had a TBI and you kept making me think I was going crazy by moving all my stuff around in the barracks?"

"I'm hilarious."

"Okay, I take it back. You deserved that," Callie says.

"I probably deserve a lot worse, if I'm honest. What's the damage? Give it to me straight."

Trav's hardened features are surprisingly soft as he says, "We've got some really bad news … You're going to live."

"How is that bad news?" I ask, knowing I'm walking right into his trap but wanting to do it anyway. Because if they're joking, it means I'm going to be okay.

"Oh, sorry. I meant bad news for us."

Everyone laughs again.

"You know what? Fuck all of you." I manage to move my hand so I can take Callie's. "Except for you."

"Hmm, I'd prefer if you didn't fuck any of them and only fucked me." It comes out as joking, carrying on the light mood, but it makes every muscle in my body tense.

Callie frowns at me, perhaps sensing my mood shift in the tightening of my grip on his hand, so I let him go and face everyone.

"Okay, but what's the real outcome? Is there a doctor I can talk to?"

Scout goes to open his mouth, but I cut him off.

"A real doctor."

"Hey, if it weren't for me, you wouldn't be alive."

"Multiple times, but I need something more than a trauma medic." I might not feel heavy anymore, but it's still impossible to move. I can only shift slightly, but even that hurts.

Trav's hand lands on my shoulder. "You've got a long recovery ahead of you, but you'll be back to one hundred percent … eventually."

"What are we talking? Three months?"

They're all silent.

"Six?"

Slightly freaking out, the machines I'm connected to start beeping with my erratic heartbeat. For a moment, I'm scared I'm paralyzed or something, but I'm able to move my legs and wiggle my toes. Barely, but it's possible.

The room is swarmed by medical professionals.

"What's going on in here? We told you to get us as soon as he woke." A doctor or nurse pushes Trav and Iris out of the way and shines a torch in my eyes.

I squint and silently complain about proper bedside manner.

She smiles at me. "Welcome back. We were beginning to think you were enjoying your sleep too much."

"What do you mean?"

"We took you off all the drugs keeping you in your coma a few days ago."

"Coma? Haven't I been in and out of consciousness?"

"You had extensive internal injuries, and your body needed time to recover."

"And it's been days?" It has felt like days, but I also thought I was in and out for most of it.

"It's been over a week since you were shot," Callie says.

I'm finally able to turn my head toward him. "What? Is this another joke like Scout's stupid three-years thing?"

Callie doesn't need to say the words for me to know that answer.

I close my eyes. Kept in a coma for a week? I'm scared to hear my prognosis. "When can I get out of here?" I ask.

The doctor's pretty green eyes flash sympathy toward me. "You'll be able to go back to LA in a few days but not home. We're organizing a transfer to your private facility, where you'll need to go through some rehab on your shoulder and leg, and you'll need to see a gastroenterologist because they had to do a resection of your bowel where a bullet was lodged."

"What the fuck?"

"You got shot in the stomach," Scout says. "You really think you can walk away from that without messing up your intestines?"

"I did? I thought it was only my shoulder. My ankle."

The doctor turns to my teammates. "Confusion is common after trauma like this."

Shot in the stomach.

Coma.

I would say I regret all my life choices, but I don't. Because I gave Callie the thing he needs and the thing I needed to let go of my sister.

I wasn't able to save her, but I saved Callie.

"He's probably overwhelmed. We'll let you get some more rest," the doctor says. "Everyone out."

I'm thankful for that, but when Callie turns to go, I reach for him again. "Can you stay?"

He breaks into a wide smile, and I immediately hate myself for it because he won't be smiling after I say what I need to get out.

As the room empties, my nerves kick up.

"I thought you were going to die," he says.

"Eh, takes more than a few bullet holes to slow me down."

"I ..." Callie takes the seat next to my bed and reaches for my hand, taking it in both of his. "I don't think I could live with myself if anything ever happened to you."

"I feel the same way. But Callie ... what did I tell you? If something happened to me, you couldn't let it go to waste. Nothing has changed with that."

"But you're fine. You're going to be okay." The relief in his glassy eyes is touching, but the unmoving loyalty as he keeps talking does me in. "I'm going to wait on you hand and foot until you're better. Until—"

"No." I shake my head. "You're not."

"W-why not?"

I slip my hand out from under his. "Because I don't want you to.

I want you to do what you promised me on that rooftop. I want you to go out there and live. You're free now. You owe me nothing. Actually, no. You owe it to me to go and make something of yourself."

And this is the part I wasn't looking forward to. Where Callie's smile would drop, his eyes would dim, and where he'd bite his bottom lip and look utterly *rejected*.

"Hey." I squeeze his hand again. "I want you to know that you're possibly the best friend I've ever had, and that's saying a lot because Scout and I served in the Marines together, and we've seen some shit. But he's more my brother than my friend. You ... you know more about me than a lot of the people closest to me in my life. I don't think I would've run through that hellfire of bullets for anyone else."

"Then why are you—"

"Because I did that for you so you could live your life. Not get tied down serving me out of some false sense of obligation for saving you. I don't want to hold you back like every other man has. I want to set you free and watch you soar."

"Zeus ..." He sniffs.

"It's your time to shine, and I want to see you succeed."

"I don't want to run," he says. "I don't want to leave."

He's never going to chase his real dreams if I lead him on. Keep him here until I get bored, and then let him go. I need to sever this now.

"Then don't," I say. "But if you're going to stay, you have to know that whatever we had outside of friendship is done. I admire you, but by setting you free, I was also able to forgive myself for not being able to help my sister."

Callie lowers his head. "T-that's all this was to you? It was about *your sister*?"

I should tell him the truth. That it was way more than residual guilt. But if I do that, he might stay, and he's too big for this life. Too big for stripping or going back to that cafe in the middle of nowhere. He's too precious to be doing something menial.

"You know what we had wasn't real," I lie. "Like I said, you're maybe my best friend, but I told you from the beginning, and you knew from my reputation that this had an expiry date. I can't offer you any more than what I've already given."

"I'm ..." He scrunches his forehead.

"I know you're probably confused, but—"

"I'm not confused. Just ... disappointed, I guess. I knew it was coming, but I wasn't prepared for it to be so soon. Or without an amazing goodbye fuck."

I stare down at my broken body. "I don't think I'll be having any amazing sex anytime soon."

He mock gasps. "How will you survive?"

"It'll be really, really, really hard. Literally."

Callie wears a sad smile. "So you can survive bullets but not celibacy? Checks out."

And even though our fling or whatever it was is ending, I'm glad we could end it on good terms. He's taking it better than I expected. Which actually ... kind of hurts. But it's better this way. I know it is.

I force a smile at him. "Hey, they don't call me Zeus for nothing."

CHAPTER THIRTY-FOUR_

CALLIE

I LEAVE THE HOSPITAL WITH MY MIND SPINNING. I'M free.

I have no one chasing me.

No debts.

It's surreal, terrifying, but also depressing. Because even though the world is at my feet, I have nothing.

No money.

Nowhere to live.

No boyfriend. No one to rely on. On the plus side, there's no one to rely on me.

My life is a blank canvas that I can fill with what I choose, and the most fucked-up thing about that is I've never had a choice before. I've never had this privilege. This right.

Which makes everything so damn overwhelming.

Okay, Sam. Let's start with something small. Transportation.

I haven't seen my car since we ditched it at the park and ride, and it's most likely been towed, stolen, or trashed by now, but it's the only option I have at this point. If I can get that back somehow, I'll at least have somewhere to sleep and a way to go wherever I want to. As long as I can scrounge up some money for gas.

I literally don't have a cent to my name, so it looks like I'm walking. I go to take a step when I hear my name.

"Callie, wait up."

I turn to find Atlas walking after me.

"Where are you going?" he asks as soon as he reaches me.

"That's a loaded question."

He cocks his head. "Is it?"

"Zeus told me to go, so I'm going. Starting over. Clean slate."

Atlas looks back at the entrance to the hospital and then back at me. "Really?"

"He did what he promised, and he says now I have to go do what I promised. I need to stop running and start living."

"Like it's that easy?"

I throw up my hands. "Right? Okay, so I'm not being dramatic when I'm all I have no idea what I want to do? Where do I go? Where do I stay?"

"I know Lemon wouldn't mind if you stayed with us."

"I can't."

"Why not?"

"Because even though it's daunting, I can't keep relying on others. Zeus saved my life, and you guys told me to stay and repay him by looking after him or whatever, but that's obviously not what he wants. He wants me to stand on my own two feet."

Atlas mutters, "More like he wants to avoid his feelings."

Whatever that means. I don't want to know. If he's implying that Zeus has real feelings for me, I can't hear that. I can't have hope.

Walking away from him feels wrong, but I know it's something I have to do. For me and for him. We were never going to work, and the sooner I can accept that I felt more for him than he did for me, the easier it will be to fulfill his request. I'll be able to move on and make myself happy without relying on someone else to do it for me.

"This is something I need to do on my own. Taking a handout from you or Lemon would still be surviving any way I can."

"Starting over with no money isn't a walk in the park, though. He can't let you go and then expect you to instantly land on your feet."

"The most I'm willing to take from you is cab fare to my car."

Atlas folds his arms across his wide chest. "Counteroffer. I drive you to your car and give you enough gas money to at least get back to LA, where you can get your life in some sort of order before you run away again. Give you a chance to say a proper goodbye to Lemon."

I bite my lip. I do need to give Lemon the decency of a proper goodbye after everything he's done for me, but at the same time, I still feel like I owe him so much, and it hurts to see him because he's so damn nice, and I haven't let go of all that guilt toward him yet.

"And if you really want to start fresh, maybe you could stop by Juicy and make amends with the other guys."

Go to the rebuilt strip club where everyone almost died because of me? No, thank you. But again, Atlas makes a point.

Can I really start fresh if I haven't made amends for my past? If I'm going to do this right, the way Zeus wants me to, I have to say goodbye to my old life completely. Own up to my mistakes with everyone I've ever wronged.

But fuck if I have the guts to do it.

"You're right. I need to put everything behind me if I want a real start."

Atlas reaches for my shoulder, squeezing it as if to say I made the right choice, and surprisingly, I think it's the first time someone's touched me uninvited in recent months that I haven't flinched.

Because of that, I now have a true sense of freedom.

I don't know what I want to do with my life. What I could do. But I do know that it doesn't matter. Whatever I land on, it will be because I choose it.

That's real freedom.

Surprisingly, my car is still where I left it, albeit covered in parking fines. I'm already starting my new life in debt, but I'm not going to let it pull me down into doubt or insecurity.

A new start doesn't mean I won't experience setbacks.

Setbacks are a part of a normal life, and if I had a choice between running for my life or paying a few fines, give me the fines. I have no money to pay for them, but I'll figure it out.

Baby steps. One thing at a time.

First step: LA.

Next step: anything I want.

I distract myself on the drive back to LA with ideas on what I might want to do with my life. What job. I could go back to stripping until I get on my feet, but I know if I do that, I'll never get out again. It'll become my comfort zone.

Zeus suggested going for my GED, and if I want to maybe go to college or get a good job, that would be a good path to take.

It's when I get to the Nevada-California border that my mind drifts elsewhere. To everyone at Juicy. To the guys I haven't seen since disappearing a year ago. The ones I owe apologies to. The ones who may not forgive me.

Lemon did, but he has a heart of gold. The others I used to work with are fiercely loyal to Lemon because Lemon always looked out for us. He deserves loyalty, and I deserve to be shut out.

It's not something I want to experience, but it's something I will do. Because I need to.

It still doesn't make pulling up to the club any easier.

The best move would be to charge in there and get it over with, but I've never been a take-charge kind of guy.

Zeus's voice fills my head as if he were right here in the car with me. "Now's your chance to change that. Be that guy. Take charge. Own your life."

I take a deep breath, swallow my nerves, and get out of the car.

There's a split second where I pause and almost turn around and get back in, but it's Zeus that gets me going again. His faith in me. His sacrifice.

I'm starting fresh and owning up to my past.

I push through the doors, and I'm sure it's my imagination, but I swear the whole place stops.

Bartenders freeze midpour, patrons turn to stare at me, the stripper onstage—someone I don't recognize—stops sliding down the pole, upside down, legs spread wide.

It's only for a second before everything resumes, and I shake it off. No one is staring at me, the world continues on as it was before, and I'm not even going to contemplate the possible mental breakdown I'm experiencing.

Lemon appears through the staff entry to the back. Instead of the yellow thong he used to wear in this place, he's in a suit. All managerial-like. It's a good look on him. "Hey, you're here."

"I am. This new place is ..." I glance around. With the rebuild, it's got all new furnishings, fancier tables and chairs, and the bar is lit up in neon while the lights are kept low everywhere else except onstage. "An upgrade," I finish. Because it is in the basic sense, but it's still a strip club. Seen one, seen them all.

"I like to think so, but it still feels like home."

Lemon belongs here, and that's something I never felt while I was stripping. I was waiting for my life to start, hell-bent on believing someone would come rescue me from it instead of trying to rescue myself.

"Are the others here?" I ask.

"Yeah, they're getting ready out back. Come through."

I hesitate. "They're not going to douse me in gasoline and set me on fire as some form of payback, are they?"

Lemon chuckles. "No. But I told them all to play nice."

They're not going to be as forgiving as Lemon, but I'm ready to face them.

When we get to the dressing room area, I can tell this is where Lemon really made improvements to the place. Separate, huge cubbies, comfortable chairs, and maybe if I keep focusing on everything around me, I won't have to face the three guys standing in the room with their arms folded and scowls on their faces.

"Hear him out," Lemon orders.

They don't budge.

"We'll hear him out," Romeo says.

"Doesn't mean we have to forgive him," Diamante adds.

I wait for Frenchie to add his opinion, but he doesn't.

"I don't expect you to forgive me. I haven't yet forgiven myself." My voice barely comes out, so I clear my throat and try again. "I don't have any excuse for what I did other than I was only thinking of myself. I was selfish—"

"And brainwashed," Lemon cuts in.

I nod. "And brainwashed, but that makes me sound like I'm trying to get out of accountability, and I'm not. I hurt people I was close to because I believed that without Stephen, I was nothing. I've spent a long time thinking that, and it was only recently that I realized I have to stop. I'm a victim, but that doesn't mean I have to keep living like one. I hope one day you can all forgive me, but I completely understand if you don't. Just know, I love you guys, and you made the days and nights here bearable. The only reason I got through it."

Lemon frowns. "I didn't realize you felt that way. I was going to offer you your old job back."

"Thanks, but I know if I come back that I'll be stuck again, waiting for something or someone to come and fix my life when the only person who can do that is me."

"If there's anything I can do," Lemon says.

"Anything we can do," Romeo corrects.

Diamante backhands Romeo's chest. "We said we'd be tough."

"I can't. I hate what he did, but look at him."

248 / MIKE BRAVO OPS: ZEUS

Ugh. I'm still not a fan of pity, but I'll take it over their anger.

As if being given permission, Diamante deflates. "Do you need a place to stay? Some money?"

Frenchie reaches for the wad of cash in his thong. "I have tips."

I hold up my hands. "I don't need anything from any of you. I wanted your forgiveness, but even if I can't get that, you're all putting our issues aside for me and ..." I sniff. "I ... fuck, I told myself I wouldn't cry."

Lemon hugs me, and then the others all pile on for a group hug.

"Let it out," Lemon says.

And I do. Everything. From what I've done to where I am now, to not knowing where I'll go from here. I let it all fall from my eyes as I'm hugged by the sweetest, most important people I've ever had in my life.

I don't know if we'll move forward from this. I'm not sure they'll ever completely trust me. But I do know I'll never screw them or anyone else over ever again.

Maybe one day, I'll deserve their real hugs instead of the pity one they're giving me, but until that day, I'm going to do the very best I can to become a better man.

CHAPTER THIRTY-FIVE_

ZEUS

I GRUNT THROUGH MY LAT PULLDOWN REPS, POSSIBLY pushing harder than I need to at this point in recovery. "Nineteen." Another grunt. "Twenty."

It's been a slow process, but after six weeks, I'm cleared to start getting my life back into my regular routine.

I'm weaker than I was, my arm needing extensive rehab, my leg less so. Low weights, high reps, and I'd be lying if I said it wasn't driving me crazy. I want to be back to where I was. I want to be one hundred percent and to get back out there.

Because of how everything went down with Pierre, we didn't get a chance to go back to the Ruby and free any of the other people being held against their will. Those being trafficked.

I'm desperate to try to find them and make sure they were able to escape when Pierre didn't come back, but I'm not that naïve. One of Pierre's most trusted partners would take over the organization, maybe sell off people like Arabella to others. I want to chase them down.

But every time I bring it up with Trav, he mentions some bullshit about avoiding the real reason I told Callie to leave and trying to hold on to him by chasing down his demons.

I argue they're not his demons anymore and he's thriving, and he asks me how I know when we haven't had any contact.

Internet stalking. Duh.

I don't say that, though. I never say that. I say something like "he promised" and leave it at that.

"Uncle Oren!" The rehab center fills with the happiness of my nephew and the pretcen attitude of my niece, which might actually be louder than Nick's excitement, and all she did was roll her eyes.

Little Nicky—something he hates being called because he's ten years old and is already the same height as his sister, who's two years older—has always looked up to me with this kind of awe in his expression.

He thinks I'm a real-life hero, and I'd be lying if I said it wasn't a huge ego stroke.

I stand and grip his hand, pulling him against me for a hug with our intertwined hands between our chests. "What's up, little man?"

"Shouldn't I be asking you that? You're the one who decided it would be a good idea to volunteer to be a bullet target."

"Smartass," I mumble.

My mom appears behind the kids, looking tired.

"You told them what happened?" I ask. I'd called her when I was in the hospital but asked her to keep it a secret from the kids. I didn't want to remind them of when they got the call about their mom.

"Not ... exactly," Mom says.

"Trinny heard Grandma and Grandpa talking," Nick supplies.

"Ah. Well, I'm fine. Just need some rehab." I'm still healing, and because I'm shirtless, they can see the ugly red scarring all over my body. "I promise it looks worse than it is."

Trinity avoids eye contact with me with her arms folded as she kicks at the ground.

I look at Mom and mouth, "She okay?"

Mom glances at my niece and then back at me with a subtle

shake of her head. Okay, we'll be talking about that later, but right now, I need to show them I'm fine.

"So, did you come all this way to see how I am or to take me to lunch?"

"Can you tell me about getting shot?" Nick yells a little too loudly.

"Sure"—I catch Mom shaking her head more vigorously now —"can't. You don't need to know those details."

"I need to take Nick to buy new shoes. He's grown another size again in only a couple of months," Mom says.

"If you need money—"

"No, honey. We have plenty. But I was hoping maybe you could look after Trinny while we're gone?"

"Oh, so Trinny's going to take me to lunch? Deal." I throw my arm around my niece, but she ducks out of my hold.

"You're all sweaty. Gross."

I nod to Mom. "I got this. You go."

She mouths, "Thank you."

"Let's go for a walk, kiddo," I say.

"Don't you have to, you know, shower first?"

"Do I really smell that bad?"

"Yes," she answers immediately.

"Fine. You're not going to run off while I'm in there?"

"Only if you take forever."

"I'm trusting you here—"

"I was joking. Go. I'll wait at reception." She walks off, taking her phone out of her pocket as she does.

And even though I should trust her, I don't. Something is obviously going on with her, or Mom wouldn't have brought her here. It could be regular preteen hormonal stuff, or maybe over-hearing about my accident is dredging up stuff about her mother, but I hope I can help.

So after the quickest shower in history, I let out a loud breath of relief when I find her still waiting for me.

"There's a nice burger joint a short walk away."

252 / MIKE BRAVO OPS: ZEUS

She doesn't reply, just stands and starts walking. Okay then.

We don't even make it one block before I'm asking, "So, what have you done to piss off Grandma and or vice versa?"

She stops walking. "I'm not pissed off at Grandma. I'm pissed off at you."

I wince. "I didn't want you to worry about me, and I am fine."

"You're so dumb."

"Hey. No need to talk to me like that. Just explain what's wrong if I'm completely missing the point."

She grits her teeth as her eyes water, as if she's trying to hold her tears back. "Grandma always used to tell us that after you were done playing hero, we could come live with you. When you grew up. And here you are, still playing with guns, getting shot, and ..." She sucks in a sharp breath. "And I thought you were going to die. When I heard Grandma and Grandpa talking, I thought ... and then it reminded me of Mom. And ... and—"

"Shit, Trinny." I step toward her and wrap my arms around her. "I had no idea."

"No idea I'd think you were dead?"

"I had no idea you or Nicky were waiting for me to grow up to come live with me. Grandma and Grandpa ... they didn't think I would be a suitable guardian for you."

Trinity wipes her eyes with her sweater sleeve. "Mom died seven years ago now."

Fuck, has it really been that long already?

"Have you really not grown up at all in that time?"

Ouch, Trinny. Hit me where it hurts. Because the truth is, I haven't. I haven't even tried.

There are two types of people in this world: those who hear they can't do something and spend all their energy proving they can, and then those who are told they're too immature to step up and be responsible, so they lean into it. They accept defeat before even trying.

And as I get schooled by my twelve-year-old niece, I realize how being the second type has affected not only my family life but my love life.

Instead of proving to everyone that I can be an amazing guardian for my niblings, a serious person, and faithful partner, I just … let everyone believe I'm shallow, immature, and unworthy.

What I don't know is if it's because I don't believe in myself or that I wanted to take the easier route. It's possibly both.

I feel the ache in my shoulder, the twinge in my ankle with every step, and even though the doctors say I'll make a full recovery, I'm realizing how fragile I really am.

My body's tired. It's had enough adrenaline to last a lifetime, and while I love that high, I can't keep chasing it forever.

I love my niblings more.

"I'm going to step up," I say.

The pure look of relief on Trinity's face is the only thing I need to know I'm doing the right thing.

<hr/>

"You're not ready for this kind of commitment," Mom says, pacing around her kitchen. Dad's sitting at the dining table, staying out of the argument.

Asking for custody of my niblings is going as well as can be expected.

It's why I came over to their house while the kids are at school. I didn't want them to hear this.

"There's a reason you brought the kids to see me. There's a reason you look exhausted and at the end of your rope when it comes to Trinity. I spent all of ten minutes with her to realize she's struggling, which means you and Dad are struggling, which means it's my turn to step up. And if I'm honest, I should've done it the moment Olive passed away."

"You were only twenty-three then," Mom says quietly. "And it's not like you've grown up since then. I've been waiting since you were a teenager for you to wise up and quit playing with your toy guns and pretending to be Captain America."

"I don't really see serving my country as pretending to be Captain America, but you never did understand that part of me." I lower my voice. "Also, Captain America was in the army. I was a Marine."

"No, I never understood your need to put yourself in harm's way. For the last seven years, I've been worried about losing my only other child. And when I got that call …" Her eyes water, and she chokes on a sob.

"Hey, I'm okay."

"You were so close to not being okay," she cries.

I approach her, hobbling as I do, and I wrap my arms around her. "I'm so sorry. I never considered what you might be feeling when it came to what I do for a living."

She pulls away from me. "And that's why you're not ready for this. If you're going to be their parent, you need to think of others before yourself."

"Jesus Christ, Karol." Dad stands. "You've wanted him to tell you this for years. That he's ready. Now that he's here, taking this step, you're telling him no. This is why he never stepped up to begin with—because you wouldn't let him."

I'm … speechless. Mainly because in my entire life, I've never heard Dad speak to my mom like that. Growing up, my parents always had a playful relationship. Barely took anything seriously. They were the type of couple to throw insults at each other and then laugh and make out in front of Liv and me. Of course, the last seven years, I haven't really seen that side to them, but I figured they were grieving the loss of my sister and trying to remember how to be parents to small children again.

"I should've fought harder back then," I say. "But when I heard you didn't have faith in me that I could do it, instead of proving you wrong, I went the opposite way. I behaved childishly, acted wild, and didn't consider other people's feelings because I believed that was all I was good for."

And ouch, that hurts admitting that out loud.

"I never should have made you feel that way," Mom whispers.

"No, we never should have," Dad says, a lot calmer now, and steps up behind Mom, resting his hands on her shoulders. "We were holding on to those kids so tightly because they were part of Olive."

"Maybe I pushed you away because deep down, I didn't want you to take them from us." Mom sniffs. "I still don't think you're completely ready for this, but ... maybe that's our fault. Because we didn't let you prepare for it. After Olive died, you ran off to join your group of immature gun nuts, and we let you."

I step closer to my mom. "So don't let me this time. I'm under no delusion that this will be easy or that I won't miss my job. I'm going to need your help. A lot. I'll need your support."

Dad grips my shoulder. "And you'll have it."

Okay, I guess I'm actually doing this.

I thought I'd be more scared than I am, but it actually feels right. I'm going to miss Mike Bravo, and I have no idea what I'm going to do for a living to even support Trinity and Nick, but I'll make it work because I have to.

Callie never put himself first, and that's all I've ever done. If our time together showed me anything, it's that I can be awesome and unselfish at the same time.

I hope Callie's out there realizing the opposite. He can be selfish and amazing.

I've wanted to check in on him since he left, but other than internet spying on him, I haven't taken that step. Maybe now I'm all mature, I can swallow my ego and ignore the shit the guys would give me for it.

Because if I look at the real reason I haven't contacted Callie, it's because my feelings for him were becoming too real.

It's true I didn't want him to lose himself all over again. That I worried he would feel like he owed me forever. But the truth is, if I wanted something more with him, we could navigate those issues together.

I could make sure he remained independent and didn't rely on me or Lemon or Mike Bravo. We could've had a chance.

But just like when I used any excuse to run from responsibility seven years ago, I did it again with Callie.

The only thing preventing me from going after him is the knowledge that my life is about to drastically change. I want to go and beg him to give me a chance, but I can't do that when I don't know what my next six months are going to look like.

From wielding weapons and explosives to … school drop-off and PTA meetings?

I can't promise anyone anything, but maybe once I'm settled, I can at least go see him. Make sure he's okay.

Of course, it's also possible I'll be serving jail time for accidentally murdering my Mike Bravo teammates with the news that I'm leaving to become a single father of two preteens. Group panic heart attacks is a real phenomenon, isn't it?

CHAPTER THIRTY-SIX_
CALLIE

TECHNICALLY, I HAVE A PLACE TO LIVE, A JOB, AND I'M
in school. I'm doing it. I'm living and working toward a real
future.

Sure, the place I live is my car, the job is janitorial at a homeless shelter, and the school I'm in is an online school that I can
only access because of the computers the shelter lets us use.

But I'm already making a difference.

Because I've decided what I want to be now that I'm apparently a grown-up.

I'm studying social work, and I hope to build up enough
online credits to get into college to major in psychology, special-
izing in the psychological impacts of domestic violence. I want to
help others the way Zeus helped me. Only without the sex part.
Obviously. I would make a terrible therapist if that was my
intention.

While Zeus setting me free hurt because I really thought we
could be something good, I'm grateful to him that he did it.
Because I wouldn't have had the strength to, which means I'd
still be following him around like a puppy, taking care of him,
putting his needs first, when he was right. It's time I put my own
needs first.

258 / MIKE BRAVO OPS: ZEUS

It's not easy, not by a long shot, but I'm in a good place. The manager of the shelter, Coco, wants to help me in any way she can with working toward my goals, and while my income from cleaning the place is low, I know it will only be temporary.

I'm contemplating going back to Lemon and taking him up on a job offer, not to go back to stripping but possibly doing a similar job to here. Cleaning is the fucking worst, and humans are disgusting, but I'm not going to be able to be independent if I don't put in the work.

I never want to rely on anyone else ever again, so if that means scrubbing toilets in a shelter and cleaning cum off furniture in a strip club, I'll do it.

What I haven't been willing to do, and what I won't do, is take more of a handout from Lemon or his husband or anyone else offering a leg up. I'm not a total stubborn head. If Lemon wants to buy me lunch, I'll let him, but I'm happy with where my life is at the moment.

I'm starting at the bottom and working my way up, but my achievements will be so much more rewarding if I do them myself.

The only problem with this plan is I haven't had the guts to go see Zeus.

I know he's in recovery. He's in rehab and still battling the scars my chaotic life brought him. And it's not the guilt holding me back or the urge to want to help him because I feel like I owe him.

It's because I don't think I have the strength to stay standing if I see him. I'd fall to my knees and beg him to fuck me again. Even if it's only the once. I want his mouth on me, his breath on my skin, his cock moving inside me.

I miss his body.

I don't miss his support because it has never left me. It's inside me, and it gives me courage every day. It gives me the motivation to carry on. To work my ass off to build the kind of life I want.

In movies or TV shows, when someone decides to start over, that's usually when they cut to years later, where they're already living their life to the fullest. It never shows the unglamorous parts. The hard parts. It implies that the in-between time isn't living life to the fullest, and you can only be living your best life if you're successful. But I don't see it that way.

My life might not be enviable to many, but to the women and men who come into the shelter covered in bruises, the ones who have no one, nowhere to go, and they have to choose between staying living on the streets or going back to someone who's abusing them, I would have everything in their eyes.

And I do.

Living doesn't have to mean success.

Living is the feeling of being content. And I am content.

Lonely but content.

CHAPTER THIRTY-SEVEN_

ZEUS

"Everyone, arm up," Trav orders. "Saint, get on the phone. Call Domino, call my cousin, call the goddamn president of the United States. The world is under attack. The only chance of survival—"

"You can stop being dramatic now," I say, unimpressed. "I knew you would all freak out at my news, but you're being downright ridiculous."

Iris, who's staring at me, unblinking, finally says, "Zeus ... is calling us ... ridiculous. *Zeus*."

"We really do need a direct line to the president," Scout says, and I pout at him.

"My own brother from another mother. The disappointment in you stings, Scout. It *stings*."

Scout throws up his hands. "I'm sorry, but when Zeus, the god of fuckery, says he's going to become a dad, we always assumed this would happen accidentally. Not ..." He waves a hand over my body. "Like this."

"I'm not becoming a dad. Well, I am, but it's not like I'm their father. I'm their uncle, and they need me. And they've already lost the one person they were supposed to be able to rely on, so I can't work here. I can't be putting my life in danger and having them constantly worry that it's going to happen again. My parents have done an amazing job with raising them to this point, but they're getting older, the kids are getting more difficult, and …" I hesitate to say this part. "I actually want to do this. It's not from some obligation or being forced. I'm going to show everyone, including you assholes, that I'm not that surface-level guy you've known all these years. Believe it or not, I have fucking layers, thank you very much. Maybe you've never seen them because I haven't wanted to show you them, and really, that says more about you than me."

"Agreed," Haz pipes up. "If anyone hasn't seen your layers, they haven't been paying attention."

Across the room, Decaf growls.

"See, the world isn't ending. That's still the same." I point to Decaf. And I still have no idea what the story is there.

I can't tell if Haz is sticking up for me because of our mission or if he's purposefully trying to piss Decaf off. Either way, I'm not interested in the drama.

Holy fuck.

I'm not interested in the drama.

It's already happening. I'm already an enlightened, adultlike human. Maturity for the win!

"I'm going to go clean out all the crap I have lying around HQ if any of you dickwads want to help."

So close. I'm *almost* an adultlike human.

Maybe this parenting gig will be a breeze because I'm emotionally closer to Trinity and Nick's age than my own.

I'm not expecting any of the guys to help, but it does sting when no one at least follows me to try to talk me out of it?

Maybe they're still in too much shock. I can't really blame them.

Part of me still can't believe it myself.

I empty my locker slowly, making sure I go through each and every item and decide if I want to keep it or not. There's some random crap in here because over the years, it's become more of a storage space than somewhere to stash a change of clothes and a go bag.

My Marine Corps lapel pin is on the top shelf, and I hold it in my hand, quickly reliving my career in the military, being recruited by Trav, becoming … me.

A whole life reduced to a decorative pin.

If the next ten years of my life could fit into a pin, I have no idea what it would look like. A pin representing family? A single man and two kids?

Would there be enough room for another man in there? Or woman. Person.

Because even though there's only one man I'm thinking of, I can't upend Callie's life like that. His new life. It would be cruel to tie him down after he only recently got his freedom.

The easy choice here is to focus on the kids and only the kids, but there's something about my time with Callie that has changed me.

Old me would've said it was for the worse. New me? As scary as it is choosing to raise my niblings, it's like I've finally stopped pushing back. Stopped being what everyone expects—what everyone assumes.

Which is why I'm torn between doing the easy choice and doing what I want.

What I really want is to find Callie again. Ask him out. Date him. Be with him. It would be difficult with the kids and having to find a job. In a way, we're both starting over.

The timing is wrong, and I might be terrible at being a boyfriend and a parent, but I've never once backed down from a challenge.

The only issue with this one is, as much as I want it, it's not what's best for everyone involved.

Yet, staying away from Callie, only getting small updates from Lemon or Atlas or anyone else I try to casually ask but totally fail and give away I'm digging for information, I can't get him out of my head.

Considering everything that's happening with me with my recovery, my parents, my niblings, all I can think about is Callie. That has to mean something, right?

The fact I'm walking away from Mike Bravo without hesitation—I'm sad about it but not hesitating—shouldn't staying away from Callie be easier than this?

"Zeus." Trav scares the shit out of me, and when I glance up, he and Atlas are standing in front of me.

I didn't even hear them come down the stairs to where we keep all our stuff in the basement.

I check my pretend watch. "It took you way too long to come down here and beg me to stay. I'm so disappointed."

"If we had rushed after you, it would've fed too much into your ego," Trav says.

He's right. Even them just being here has given it a boost.

"Is that why you're really down here? To beg me to stay? Because as much as I want to, I can't. The kids need stability—"

"And you're totally what I picture when I think of stability." Trav smirks.

"You're not my boss anymore, so ..." I throw up my middle fingers.

"Like he hasn't done that to you in the past five years," Atlas says to Trav.

And yeah, true.

"I can't be risking my life and traveling constantly," I say. "It sucks, but I have to prioritize."

"Here is where you're going to regret flipping me the double bird." Trav's smiling, arms across his chest. "What if I told you that you could remain as part of the team, without the risk, with minor travel where you could probably take your kids along, and that I'd put you on a full-time base rate salary so you would know exactly how much money you've got coming and going?"

"I'd say sign me up, but wait ... Is it become like your housekeeper or something? I ain't changing your and Rogue's sheets."

264 / MIKE BRAVO OPS: ZEUS

Atlas cocks his head. "Really? You would be grossed out by cum-covered sheets? You ...?"

"No, I'd be too horny at work every day," I bite back.

Atlas looks relieved. "He really is still in there. I was about to jump on the body-snatching theory Iris was talking about."

"Body snatching?"

Trav nods. "Yeah, after you came down here, we were all trying to figure out if we were on a prank show, you were possessed by an anti-demon, or if we were right in the beginning and the world was ending. Among other things."

I scratch my head. "Should I be more worried that you're this shocked or that you think the opposite of demon is anti-demon and not an angel?"

"The second thing," Atlas says.

"I want you to recruit for me." At Trav's words, my eyes fly wide.

"What?"

"When Brix left, we found Saint. When Dom left, Haz came to us. If people keep fucking quitting, we're going to need new blood. And who knows if Haz is going to work out."

Throughout our one job, Haz and I have formed a bond, and the need to stick up for him is strong. "He's green, but he's determined."

"And because you can see that in him, I think you could find us some amazing people to come work for us. Most of it would be researching candidates online and then flying to bases around the world to talk them into joining us."

"I'd have to fly to see them?" I ask. "Couldn't recruit them over video call or voice chat?"

"Did you ever do a rotation in the recruiting department for the Marines?" Trav asks.

"Yeah? So?"

"The art of the sell is all about you. You're not really selling the military. You're selling a lifestyle. And you are this lifestyle, man. It's why we were so shocked that you were giving it up."

CHAPTER THIRTY-SEVEN / 265

"Plus, your gorgeous face doesn't hurt," Atlas adds.

"Aww, you think I'm gorgeous?" I blow him a kiss.

"Objectively speaking. I personally think your mouth isn't closed enough for me to find you attractive. There's a difference."

I wipe a fake tear away. "I'm hearing you find me so hot you want to shut my mouth by kissing it."

He throws up his hands. "I give up with you." Atlas walks away, but I call after him.

"You call that a goodbye?"

He spins on his heel and faces me. "We both know you're taking Trav's offer."

Damn it. He's right.

"I do need an income now," I say.

"Job's yours if you want it."

"I want it."

Trav reaches out to shake my hand. "Then it's a done deal."

We shake, but when I try to pull my hand back, he squeezes tighter. "Now. About your other issue."

"My niblings aren't an issue. I love them, and I'm looking forward to spending as much time with them as possible. I've missed out on a lot in their lives, and—"

He lets go of my hand but only so he can slap me upside the head. "Not them. Callie."

"Oh. Him. He's not an issue either. Last I heard, he was working toward his GED and doing some online college-credit course. He's living his best life and all that jazz."

"He's also living out of his car near a homeless shelter."

Okay, that part I didn't know. "I can't believe none of you have offered to help him. You have a million properties to the Mike Bravo name. You could—"

Trav puts up his hand. "I offered. Atlas and Lemon offered. He's stubborn as fuck and doesn't want any outside help. He's determined to do it on his own."

I respect that, but he's an idiot. A cute, adorable, stubborn fucking idiot.

"Maybe he'll listen to you," Trav says.

"Maybe," I murmur. Or maybe I'll see him, break down, ask him to give me a chance, and guilt him into being with me. It's a toss-up.

Trav goes to say something else but quickly closes his mouth again.

"Say it. What is it now? You want to use my knife to cut me to make sure my blood still runs red?" I turn to my locker, where I also had a knife stashed in there for unknown reasons, and hold it out to him.

"No. I was going to say that I'm proud of you, but then it felt like it would be awkward, and now it is awkward, and let's pretend I never said anything."

Trav tries to walk away, but I grab him and slam into him, wrapping my arms around him in a hug because having Travis West's respect means everything to me.

When we pull away from the hug, Trav stares at me with this look of ... something I can't decipher. Sympathy? No, wisdom? I don't know.

"Don't be afraid to put yourself out there. You've always been so wrapped up in having to have a certain image, be portrayed as a slutty fuckboy, because you thought that's all anyone could ever see you as. But Callie never once looked at you like that. You two ... you make sense." He punches my shoulder. "And I'm not saying marry the guy, but give it a chance. You've never done that in the whole time I've known you."

He's right. Of course he's right.

Maybe we're in two different stages of our lives. Maybe it won't work out. But all we have to do is give it a chance.

Otherwise, we're giving up before we can even begin.

I just hope he's easier to convince than myself.

CHAPTER THIRTY-EIGHT_

CALLIE

ROBBIE IS A CUTE KID AROUND SEVEN YEARS OLD WHO came into the shelter with his mom a couple of days ago. I could tell right away that her situation was similar to mine. Bruises. Nowhere to go. Constantly looking over her shoulder.

As much as I want to tell her things will get better, it's an empty promise she won't believe anyway. In her eyes, her future seems bleak, so instead of giving her false hope or placating her, I do all that I can to help her. Which, for the most part, is making sure Robbie is entertained and his mom gets a break.

We're sitting on the floor, bouncing a tennis ball back and forth, and even though he's been through some shit in the last few days, he doesn't seem fazed. He was a bit shy in the beginning, but the more time I spend with him, the more he relaxes.

I feel like I'm making a difference, even if it's only small.

"Sam," Coco says behind me.

I stop playing and turn to her. "What's up?"

"Someone is here asking for you, but you know why I can't let him in. I didn't tell him you were here, but he said he'll wait outside for you if you decide to see him."

I love how protective she is over me. Not only me but of everyone at the shelter. If Stephen were alive out there somewhere, I might be scared, but I'm sure it's Lemon or one of the guys from the club.

"Thanks, I'll head out. You good, Robbie?"

His innocence shines in the happy "Yup" he lets out.

"I'll come back and play more later."

His smile is bright, and I give him a fist bump as I leave him. Coco walks out with me, her lips pressed tightly together.

"What's up?" I ask.

"I just want to make sure you're safe. The person here for you …"

I stop walking, a bit of dread passing through me. What if it's whoever took over for Pierre? Or someone else Stephen threw me under the bus for to save himself?

"What about him?"

"He looks scary. Intimidating. I mean, he's gorgeous, but he gave some obviously fake name."

Now my heart kicks up for an entirely different reason. "Gorgeous military-looking dude?"

"I can tell by your smile that he won't be a problem."

"Not if it's who I think it is." Though, if I run out there and Atlas is waiting for me to take me to go see Lemon, I'm gonna be so disappointed. Because all I've been able to think about since being here, since starting over, is him. Zeus.

And as I burst through the doors of the shelter and see him waiting by his car, leaning backward against the trunk, I have to resist the urge to run into his arms and wrap myself around him. He's way too sexy.

I pause in my tracks. He grins over at me, and I melt.

"Get in." He gestures to the car and then moves to the driver's-side door.

"Where are we going?"

"I have something for you."

Please be his dick. Please be his dick.

I jump in the passenger seat, and we take off, heading toward

East Los Angeles, but I don't care where we're going. The only thing I'm focused on is him. That he's here.

He glances over at me and then back at the road. "You look good."

I think that's a lie, but I don't call him on it. "So do you."

"I hear you're being stubborn." The amusement on his lips makes me smile.

"So what if I am?"

"Maybe you should stop."

"Maybe you should stop being so damn good-looking."

He laughs. "Never going to happen. I made a deal with the devil, and I'm going to look this amazing always."

I shrug. "Hey, I'd believe it."

His tone turns serious now. "How are you doing? Really?"

And for the first time in my entire grown-up life, I can say, "I'm optimistic. I do wish I could be moving through everything faster, but it's a marathon, not a sprint."

"Good. You got any solid plans in place yet?"

"Why? Hasn't Lemon told you?"

"I …" Zeus side-eyes me again. "I know some things, but I've made it a point not to ask about you anymore."

Ouch. "Why?"

"I knew it would be too tempting to come see you."

I pull back in shock and hit my head on the backrest of the car. For him to say something so openly romantic … I shake my head at myself. No, he can't have meant it the way I'm taking it.

"Don't you start with the whole 'the world is ending' crap," he says. "You, of all people, should know I'm capable of missing people. I have emotions."

"That's … that wasn't the part I was shocked at. It's that you were missing *me*."

"What can I say? You're special to me."

My gut swoops, and my heart gives out. "You are to me too."

But nothing has changed, and I know that.

"I should be getting my GED soon. Coco, the woman you met

at the shelter, she's been helping me. She thinks I could take it now because apparently I'm smart—who knew?"

"I knew," Zeus says confidently.

"If you say so. When did I ever have to show off my brains in your presence?"

"When you ran me over. Everyone in Mike Bravo thinks you're a genius for that."

"I didn't run you over! You jumped on the hood of my car."

"Yeah, no one will ever look at it that way. But you were saying? GED?"

I start rambling about my plans, and the more I talk, the bigger his smile gets.

"Sounds like a solid plan," Zeus says.

"It is. And once I'm doing my social work degree, I can work at the shelter as a trainee. At the moment, I'm scrubbing toilets and doing anything that will make money, but it's an honest day's work, and I feel like I'm actually accomplishing something. Have something to work toward and look forward to."

Zeus's features are soft as he reaches over and squeezes my hand. "You have no idea how happy I am to hear that."

"What about you?"

He licks his lips. "I, uh, have some developments in my life too. My parents finally realized that maybe they aren't the best choice to raise my niblings. Trinity and Nick are moving in with me."

"Whoa. Really?"

He frowns. "That hurts."

"No, that's amazing! I'm just surprised because when you talked about them, it seemed like you wanted it but didn't think it was an option. I'm so happy for you. But wait, what about your jobs for Mike Bravo? Aren't you away a lot?"

"Trav gave me a new position. There will be small amounts of travel but no danger. I don't want to put those kids through losing someone else."

"Wow. Lots of changes." We're both going through major life

events, and I wish I could be there for him through his changes. Before I can tell him that, though, he pulls the car over.

"We're here."

I look up at an old two-story apartment building in Monterey Park. "What's here?"

"You'll find out once we're inside."

"If this is Trav or Atlas or Lemon trying to get you to use your good looks into me taking their charity—"

"Geez, paranoid much?"

"You have no idea how much they've been pushing this whole *let me take care of you* thing. I appreciate it, but I can't take advantage of them like that. Not again."

"The good thing about this place is it has nothing to do with them. Let's go."

I don't want to get out of the car because if this is another offer for a handout, I don't think I'll be able to say no to Zeus.

He could ask me for just about anything, and I'd give it to him even if that thing is taking his help.

When I don't get out of the car immediately, he comes round to my side and opens my door. "Come on. Out we get."

I move slowly. Cautiously.

Zeus takes my hand, dragging me up the outer set of stairs to the second floor.

He lets go when we stop outside apartment number six and takes a key out of his pocket.

I hold my breath when he leads me inside. It's small but well maintained and completely empty of furniture.

"I can't afford this place," I say. I still don't even know what he's offering, but I'm immediately on the defensive.

He walks over to the kitchen island, which is the only bench space in the whole room. He runs his hand along the fake marble top as he rounds it. "Did I ever tell you how I was recruited to Mike Bavo?"

"Nope. The only thing I know about getting recruited by Trav is that he looks for queer military guys or girls to join."

"I had a reputation," he says. "Slept my way through my platoon, broke rules, pissed off the wrong kind of people."

"Why am I not surprised?"

"When Trav found me, I was pretty much in my peak 'If you're not going to take me seriously, then I'll show you how stupid I can be' era. One of my superiors knew Trav, knew what he was doing, and he contacted him. Told him I'd be perfect because Mike Bravo was more free rein than the military. Trav approached me, gave me an offer of a lifetime, and before I knew it, I was discharged with no money to my name because I was a reckless spender back then, a job that wouldn't pay until I actually did a job for Trav, and no one really to turn to." He holds out his hands. "This was my first apartment when I got my new start."

"How did you—"

"Trav paid for it, and I paid him back when I started getting good money coming in. And then when I was ready to move out, I didn't want to let it go. I bought it and leased it to someone else who needed a leg up."

"And it just so happens to be empty now?" I ask.

"It's been empty for about a year. I haven't been bothered to find a new tenant. The place is paid off, I don't need the money right now, so it hasn't been a priority. Maybe I knew deep down I'd need it one day soon."

"Need it?"

His blue eyes pin me to my spot. "To give to you."

"No—"

He cuts me off before I can protest properly. "Same deal that Trav gave me. You can stay here until you're earning money. And who knows, maybe one day you'll be in a position to buy it off me."

"On a social worker's salary?"

He laughs. "Okay, maybe not. But you can at least pay me back rent. I don't even want all of it. Just whatever you can manage."

It's so fucking tempting, and I was right in being cautious about this because Zeus is impossible to say no to.

"You don't think this will complicate things?" I ask. "You said you needed space from me so I could live my new life without owing anyone anything. Isn't this the definition of owing you everything?"

"No."

"Why not?"

Zeus bites his lip, hesitating. "Because ... loving someone means there's no keeping score."

I blink. Blink again. Am possibly having a stroke.

"I know we never even went on a proper date, and it's way too early for the L-word to come out of my mouth, and I know we're not together, but I was stupid when I told you to go live your life. I changed my mind."

"You don't want me to go live my life?"

"I do. But I want you to do it with me. Alongside me. Or, you know, diagonally. Relationship adjacent."

"Are ... are you trying to say you want to date me?"

He snaps his fingers. "Yes. That's the one."

I glance around the apartment. "Is this a bribe to get me to say yes?"

"The apartment has nothing to do with it. It's yours to move into whether you want to be with me or not. Whether you're willing to give me a chance and then forgive me if I fuck it up. I can't promise that I'll be perfect. I've never done this before. I'm really terrified I'm going to do something to hurt you."

I step closer. "I know you'd never. I don't know how I know that, but I do. I trust you."

He steps closer now. "I want you."

We keep moving, inches disappearing with each step.

Is this really happening? Is this my Prince Charming moment? The one I've thought I've gotten so many times only to be disappointed?

Even the idea that I'm still looking for that after all I've been through should scare me, but it doesn't.

Because Zeus doesn't scare me.

We step in front of each other, less than a foot between us.

"What do you say?" Zeus asks. "Will you give me a chance?"

What else can I really say to that?

"Yes."

━━━

I don't know who moves first, but the next thing I know, I'm naked, on my back atop the kitchen island, and Zeus is sucking on my cock like I'm his last meal.

My hand is fisted in his hair, my hips writhing to push me deeper inside his warm, wet mouth.

"Wait, wait, wait." I can't catch my breath. I'm so dangerously close to the edge. "I want you to be inside me when I come."

I'm finally given a reprieve, but not for long. Zeus stands upright and pulls me with him so we're standing chest to chest.

"You're so hot when your skin is all flushed and you can't breathe," he rasps.

Precum leaks out of my tip, dribbling down my cock. "I need you to fuck me."

I need him.

No, correction, I *want* him.

I need to learn the difference between those two things. I'm getting on my own feet, and sure, I might be taking a little help, but the important part is if this apartment falls through, if something happens and I'm back to sleeping in my car, I will be okay. Because I can handle anything.

After everything I've been through, I can honestly say I've got this.

Instead of doing what I want him to, he kisses me deeply. I wouldn't complain normally because his mouth is so talented. It's forceful, dominating, and damn, kissing him is like having a mouthgasm of emotions. It's more intimate than fucking. It's claiming me in ways I've never been claimed. I love it but also hate it because even though we're giving this a chance, I'm terrified of it all going away or turning to shit.

I can't let myself give in to those feelings yet because I have no idea how this is going to work. Dating, together, boyfriends?

Kissing him fills my head with daydreams of happily ever afters.

I use all my strength to push him off me, and while it's a piss-poor effort because his muscles are so much bigger than mine, he goes easily because he knows I need him to. That's one major difference between Zeus and anyone else I've been with. If I ask for something, even only with body language, he does it. If he's uncomfortable, he confirms verbally.

We might not be able to communicate well with our emotions, but our bodies definitely talk.

Zeus's hands run down my back, our bodies pressed together, our mouths only mere inches apart. My cock is aching, but this moment, right here, breathing one another in ... my cock can wait. Because I want to keep a hold of this feeling a little longer. It's him and me, bare. Raw. Naked in every sense. Physically, emotionally ...

We're giving each other every piece of us.

Zeus stares into my eyes, a look of complete lust, adoration, and respect shining from his.

He's perfect.

Probably too perfect for me, but I'm not going to let that get to me. Because he's choosing to be here. He's choosing to be with me.

My hands run up his arms to his wide shoulders, one snaking to the back of his neck. Something inside him snaps, and his soft look turns hard.

"Callie, turn around."

My lips quirk. "If you insist." I try to, but his grip on me tightens. "Kinda need to be able to move to do it, though."

"One thing first." He cradles my head and kisses me softly, his tongue slowly parting my lips.

I let him take the lead and sink into the kiss. It's heated, needy, and passionate, yet still gentle and supportive. It turns me on and makes me feel cherished.

He breaks away. "Okay, now I'm good."

"What if I want more?"

Zeus smiles. "I'll give you a choice. More of my mouth or finally giving us what we both want." He reaches around my back, dipping his finger between my ass crack and pressing against my hole.

"Okay, fuck."

"That your answer?"

Instead of using words, I turn for him and stick my ass out, folding my arms on top of the kitchen island.

"I'll take that as a yes." Zeus leans over, using one of my ass cheeks to hold on to while he grabs his pants off the floor. He pulls out a lube packet and condom, and I watch him over my shoulder as he covers his cock.

"You knew this was going to happen," I say.

"I was hopeful." He covers my body with his, kissing my shoulder blade. "And I'm so damn happy you said yes."

"It's not like I had a choice." That comes out of my mouth before I can think it through, and he freezes. "Wait." I reach behind me. "I mean because I couldn't resist you, not that you were forcing me. I worded it badly."

He relaxes and lowers his weight on me, bringing his mouth to my ear. "As long as you know you always have a choice with me."

"Always. And right now, I choose to feel you inside me."

"Like this?" He reaches between us and teases my hole with his thick finger.

"Mm. And more."

Zeus works me open, pushing his way inside with one digit while exploring my back with his spare hand. He runs his fingertips over my muscles up to the back of my neck and then into my hair and grips tight.

I moan because the zing of pain from my scalp drives me wild. Zeus adds another finger, pushing two inside me now over and over.

When he brushes over my prostate, I shudder. He presses against it, teasing and playful.

"Fuck, Callie—"

"Sam. Call me Sam." I'm taking back my name after being detached from it for so long.

"Fuck, *Sam*. You're so hot like this. Trusting me. Baring yourself to me. Letting me inside that tight hole of yours."

I groan and push back against his fingers. "Then do it. I need your cock. I need it now."

Zeus pulls my head back and growls. "What else do you need?"

A gasp escapes my lips.

"Tell me," he encourages.

"Make it rough. Because I trust you."

I don't need pain to get off, but it does heighten the experience. Zeus knows that, but he won't do it lightly. He needs the reassurance that this is what I actually want. And I will reassure him every single time if he needs it. Him checking with me is sexy, and it only makes me want it more.

He releases my hair, removes his fingers, and then puts his hand around my throat and pulls me up against him.

I breathe hard. Fast. And as he guides his cock to my hole, I remind myself to keep breathing and let him in.

I love how he feels inside me, filling me up. He eases inside at first, taking his time, but his grip on my throat never wavers.

"You feel so fucking good." He pushes deeper.

It's impossible to reply. He's gripping my throat that little bit too tight to be able to speak, and I love it.

I swallow hard and move my hips to meet his short thrusts until he's all the way inside, his body flush against mine, and he pauses just long enough for me to brace for what's coming because we both know it won't be nice and easy from here on out.

I don't want it to be.

With one last reminder to tap out at any time, he unleashes on me and doesn't hold back.

The sting of the stretch, the punishing pace where I get half a second to adjust before he slams into me again. Over and over.

His grip on my throat, other hand on my hip and digging into my skin.

The pain both excites me and stops me from falling over the edge too quickly. It's a tease. A big one. And it doesn't take long for me to need it even faster. Harder.

I want him to use my hole like I'm using his cock. I'm going to come hands-free, even if it takes all night, because this is ... it's ...

Okay, maybe it's not going to take all night. "I'm gonna ... gonna—"

"Me too," he breathes. "You first. Let go, Sam."

My name on his lips, his raspy, needy tone ... it only takes two more thrusts before I come all over the side of the kitchen island. My cock twitches, releasing a stream of cum, and a few thrusts later, Zeus stills inside me and lets out a loud grunt as he fills me up.

His grip on my throat and hip tightens, and he stands upright, but he doesn't pull out of me yet. With his thick cock still inside me, I lower my chest to the counter, my arms lax, all of me completely spent.

The air is filled with loud breaths and the smell of cum, and it's another one of those perfect moments with him where for the first time in a long time, I feel safe. I'm not on edge. I don't fear he's going to turn on me now.

He eventually goes to pull out of me, but I reach back for him.

"One more minute," I murmur.

"We have a long relationship ahead of us where I can stay

inside you as much as you want." His big hands run down my back.

"Promise?" I ask.

"Unless I suck at this relationship thing. It's new for me. But I promise with my whole fucking heart that I'll try."

Trying is more than any other partner has ever done for me, so he's already the best boyfriend I've ever had.

EPILOGUE_
ZEUS

I'm so glad Trav didn't let me quit Mike Bravo. The whole team has been a godsend in the last couple of months, giving me a break from the kids, giving me an income, and even helping me through this whole having-a-relationship thing. Which is still a foreign concept.

I am loving it, though. I love Sam. Not like how I love my family or my brothers in arms around me. It's something I've never experienced before, something I didn't know I could.

There is one thing that's bugging me, though, but I don't want to bring it up. To Sam or to the guys.

"Hello? Earth to Zeus," Iris sings.

I snap out of my worry. "Huh?"

"It's your call." He points to the bets on the poker table in front of us.

"Oh. Right. I fold." I throw my cards down and then realize I was in with a chance to get a straight flush.

I'm too distracted to be gambling with my money right now.

The kids are with the grandparents, and the team is having some downtime, so we're all at HQ having a game night.

"What's with you tonight?" Atlas asks.

"What's with you? Where's your husband?"

"Contrary to what you all think, Lemon and I aren't glued to each other's sides."

"Lies," Iris says for me.

Atlas sighs. "Fine. He's at work."

"Knew it." Iris raises the bet. "We're just your backup husbands who you only spend time with when your real husband is busy."

Atlas doesn't answer because he's too sweet to, but it's true. Hell, if Sam were available to be with me tonight, I wouldn't be here.

Which I still don't get. He is available. He said he had to study and didn't want me distracting him. I might have been guilty of that in the past, but all it takes is one quick orgasm to make me leave him alone.

"Okay, Zeus didn't laugh or have a smartassy comment to that," Iris says. "Something is definitely up with him."

"How do you know if your boyfriend is hiding shit from you?" I blurt.

The entire room goes silent. I wasn't really that loud, was I?

"What do you think he's hiding?" Atlas asks.

"Money issues? Getting in more trouble again and not wanting to bother us with it? Seeing someone else?"

"He would never cheat on you," Atlas says.

"If he did, he knows we'd all rip his balls off," Haz adds from across the room.

"Agreed. You don't fuck around on someone who doesn't do relationships," Trav says. "That would cause relationship trauma for years."

"What makes you think he's hiding something?" Atlas asks.

"Gut feeling, I guess. He moved into my old apartment six months ago, but I don't think I've stepped foot in there since. For the first month, I had, but after that … it's like he's got a secret or something. Like he's hiding something there. Whenever I pick him up now, he's always out front waiting for me. He insists we stay at mine because my place is bigger, and that's

282 / MIKE BRAVO OPS: ZEUS

true, but ... I don't know. It's my gut. It's telling me something's not right."

"Then something's not right," Trav says. "It might not be cheating, but something's going on."

"Unless," Atlas cuts in, "Zeus could be projecting. He hasn't had a relationship before. Maybe he's the insecure, untrusting type of boyfriend and there's nothing to be worried about."

I narrow my gaze. "Do you know something?"

"No. I just think partners deserve the benefit of the doubt."

"You're right. I should trust him. He's given me no reason not to. Except ..."

"Except what?" Trav asks.

"Isn't it really weird that even when I asked to use his bathroom after I dropped him home last week, he refused? Like, why couldn't I go inside and take a leak? What was he hiding?"

"Mess?" Atlas asks. "Some people are real weird about their places being messy."

"Or maybe he felt like you were trying to invade his space," Decaf says. "I know what that's like." He glares at Haz, but I can't tell if it's genuine or playful. I will never understand those two.

"You know, there's a way we could all find out what's going on right now," Trav says.

"How?"

"We show up unannounced," Trav says as if it's not stalkery and weird. "Who's with me?"

Suddenly, I'm trying to hold back thirteen rowdy badasses hell-bent on defending my honor.

"No, no, no, I have to trust him. Atlas was right. And I do. I do trust him." I don't think he's cheating on me. But I do think he's hiding something. "If it's not someone else, though, I'm worried ..." I bite my lip. "What if he got himself into trouble again, but he doesn't want to say anything because he's sick of us bailing him out?"

"Okay, that I can get on board with checking out." Atlas stands. "I haven't been drinking, so anyone can ride with me."

"Wait, are we really going?" I ask him.

"You want answers or not?"

Everyone is staring at me expectantly, waiting for me to make the right choice. But what is the right choice here?

I'm so out of my element—something I've thought frequently over the last six months. Not only with Sam but with Trinity and Nick too. I'm hanging in there, and I'm loving it all, but I'm still learning.

What if I choose wrong?

"Zeus?" Trav asks.

I go with my gut. It hasn't steered me wrong yet.

We pull up outside the apartment block, and Sam's car is out the front. That means he is actually home, so that's one question down, only a million more to answer.

Maybe he does only want to study, and I'm too sexy and distracting. It's possible I'm insecure and all that other negative bullshit Atlas said I was. And if I'm honest, I'm hoping for that because at least then I'll know he's not keeping something from me.

"Going in?" Trav asks.

"I'm getting there," I say, even though I still don't make a move to open the car door.

"Uh-huh." Trav cocks an eyebrow.

"Ugh. Fine." I throw open the door and march toward the building and up the stairs, but I have to pause as I get to his doorstep.

Because if he is cheating on me, or is in trouble again and hasn't told me, or anything else that will break my heart ... I'm not sure I'm ready to hear it. Or see it.

I might not have done the relationship thing, but there's no way I could go back to how I was before. I won't admit it aloud, but Iris and Saint were right when they said at Atlas's wedding you can't help who you fall for.

I was against it. I didn't want *feelings*. But now that I have them, I'm terrified I'm going to lose him.

Instead of hating it or giving my old way of life validity because of the worry and fear I'm going through now, it gives me a sense of living. In a *I know I'm alive because I hurt* kind of thing.

If my world is about to implode, I'll be able to move on. Eventually.

But I hope that I'm wrong about this. I'm not ready to let Sam go. I don't want to. Ever.

I glance down at where my team has formed a group on the small grass patch lining the street.

Just get it over with.

I raise my hand and knock, and then two things happen simultaneously. A woman from inside yells, "Get out of here, or I'm calling the cops," at the same time Sam from somewhere else yells, "Zeus, no!"

My hands fly up like I'm under arrest, and I step back while Sam comes bounding up the outside stairs.

"What's going on?" I ask.

Sam goes to the door and knocks. "Delilah, it's okay. It's my boyfriend."

The door slowly opens, and a small, meek woman stands there, brown wavy hair messy from sleep.

A woman?

She's a gorgeous woman, but as far as I know, Sam is very, very gay. "I'm so confused."

"So am I," the woman says.

"Fuck," Sam curses.

"Are you cheating on me? Where even were you? What ..." I'm having one of those out-of-body experiences where I don't know where I am, which way is up, or if any of this is real.

"Cheating?" Sam laughs. "Why would I do that when you're the best thing that happened to me?"

"Aww," the woman says.

"Zeus, this is Delilah. I met her at the shelter, and I needed help and a place to stay. She has a young son, and her husband was not a nice person, and he found her at the shelter, and I ... I know you gave me this place for me, but she needed it more. I've been sleeping in my car. Just sleeping. I still shower and everything here, and sometimes I look after her son, Robbie, but I didn't want to tell you because I didn't want you to think I was taking advantage of your generosity, and—"

He keeps rambling all these excuses as to why he was worried I'd be mad at him, but the truth is, I've never found him more attractive. If I wasn't sure I loved him before this, I definitely know now.

"Why are you looking at me like that?" Sam asks.

"Like what?"

"Like ... you're not mad?"

I step forward and cup his cheek. "Because I'm not. I love that you're paying it forward. I love that you're looking out for others. Some would say that this is called—" I mock gasp. "Growth."

Sam smiles, and my heart swoons.

"Are you going to kick me out?" Delilah asks.

"No," Sam and I say at the same time.

"But I do need to talk to this moron." I thumb in Sam's direction.

Delilah smiles. "Go easy on him."

Oh, I won't. But she doesn't need to know I mean in a way Sam likes.

"It was nice to meet you," I say to her. "Stay as long as you need to get back on your feet."

She sighs in relief. "Thank you so much. You have no idea how much I need this."

I have a fairly good idea. Sam was in her position only six months ago.

"Good night," I say to her and drag Sam away from the door to have this conversation.

Once Delilah's back inside and I hear the lock engage, I turn to Sam.

"You're amazing. You know that?"

"I thought ... well, I thought you'd be mad that I'm sleeping in my car again."

"I am. But only because you could've come to me. You could've stayed with me and the kids. How long has she been here for?"

"On and off a couple of months? I met her when we first got together, but despite my warnings about her going back to her husband, she did, which only made this time so much worse. He tracked her down, and I was scared for her, and—"

I take him into my arms and hold him close. "You did nothing wrong. I just wish you'd trusted me enough to know I wouldn't have cared about you letting her stay with you."

"It wasn't only that I was worried you'd be mad," he says, his voice half muffled in my shoulder.

I pull back and look into his unsure blue eyes. "Then what was it?"

"I was scared that if you found out, you'd offer for me to stay with you like you literally just did, and what if you're not ready for that? I care about you so much, and I ... I, you know, don't want to scare you off with all the ... L ... l-lo—"

"I love you," I say. "I'm in love with you. I've almost said it so many times, but I've been scared it will change things."

As if a heavy weight has been lifted off Sam's shoulders, the tension leaves his whole body.

"I love you too. I've been holding on to that for a while."

I chuckle. "We're great at this relationship thing."

"We're both messes, and you know it."

"I do. And even if it's sooner than I thought it would be, I want you to move in with me and the kids. They love you. I think they love you more than they love me, really."

"It's because I can speak teenager to Trinny and gaming with Nick."

"Either way, this was probably going to happen sooner or later, right? So we should do it now. If it's too much, I'll buy you a new apartment to move into. I don't want you sleeping in your car anymore."

Sam nods. "I want to live with you. But you have to check with the kids first. Being their parent means respecting their space."

"That's how I know they'll be okay with it. Because you respect them."

"Check anyway."

"Fine." I reach into my pocket and pull out my phone, shooting off a text to Trinity, which she immediately responds to with an all-capitals *YES*. "See?" I show him.

"So, we're doing this? You're willingly moving in with a boyfriend who you only got used to saying the word *boyfriend* around recently? This isn't going to blow up in our faces?"

"Only if we let it." I close the small gap between us and press my lips to his.

When hooting and wolf whistling come from downstairs, I pull back.

"We should go tell them. They're probably wondering who the woman is."

"Why are they all here?" Sam looks out to where all of Mike Bravo team stands.

"They were here to defend my honor in case you were cheating on me."

Instead of laughing like I expect him to, he casts his eyes down. "I'm sorry I made you not trust me."

"Hopefully, it will mean next time I have a worry, I'll straight up ask you. And maybe next time you have something to hide, you might be quicker to share it?"

"It's still difficult for me—"

"I know," I whisper. "It's the same for me too. As long as we promise to keep trying."

"I never want to stop trying with you."

"Good. Because I don't want to stop either." I take his hand and lead him down to everyone else.

Everyone's waiting for an explanation, but I just wrap my arm around Sam's shoulder and go to say we're moving in together when I'm cut off.

"Saint and I are getting married!" Iris points at me. "Ha, I'm not stealing your thunder if I said it first."

"What are you talking about?" I ask.

"You very much looked like you agreed to get married up there. I just wanted to get in first."

Sam and I pull apart, both of us shaking our heads.

"Whoa, no," I say. "Not married. Nowhere near marriage." I turn to Sam. "I love you, but—"

"Hey, right there with you. Moving in with you is one thing, but marriage?"

"You're moving in together?" Iris coos. "That's so exciting! But not as exciting as Saint and me getting hitched." Iris holds up his left hand to show off a plain band on his finger.

Trav rubs his jaw. "Well, I wasn't going to say anything, but seeing as Iris tried to steal your thunder, I guess I should steal his. Rogue and I are getting married."

"Noooo," Iris calls out while everyone else mutters something like "about time."

I screw up my face. "Eww, marriage really is contagious. Atlas, I blame you. You started it." I turn to Sam. "Can we agree to never do that just to prove a point?"

"I'm totally fine with that. Marriage was originally about ownership, and after some of the toxic relationships I've had, I'd like to never be owned like that again."

"Hey, that's what I always say about marriage."

We really are perfect for each other.

"If I recall, you also said you'd never fall in love," Saint says.

"Iris, I don't like your fiancé. Shush him for me."

Only, I don't really care. Whatever the future holds, I'm no longer scared of change. Of growing or letting myself be the real me. I'm still a sarcastic jokester. I'll still race Iris to the front door of HQ and gloat about winning. I'll still be slutty, but only slutty with Sam. I'll also show the real me more often. The guy who cares about his niblings, who struggles to be responsible but is fucking good at it when I get it right. The person who resisted love in fear of ending up broken.

But Sam didn't break me.

He made me whole.

THANK YOU_

Thank you for reading *Mike Bravo Ops: Zeus.*

Did you know I have a Patreon? My "Hot Shot" and above tiers receive my solo release books before anyone else. Everyone receives quarterly merch, weekly updates, and access to my terrible (but amazing) drawings.
You can join my Patreon here: patreon.com/EdenFinley

To keep up to date with Eden Finley releases, news, and upcoming projects, join my reader group on Facebook here: https://www.facebook.com/groups/absolutelyeden

Alternatively, you can join my newsletter here: https://landing.mailerlite.com/webforms/landing/d4e2a5
I only send out newsletters when I have news, so there will be no spamming! Unsubscribe at anytime.

Eden Finley is an Amazon bestselling author who writes steamy MM contemporary romance.

As a socially awkward mess, she likes to lose herself in the written word, reading and writing for pure escapism. Her books aren't supposed to be taken too seriously, and while they sometimes touch on heavy subjects, she will always have a HEA. Because the world needs more of them.

You can follow Eden on any of the following platforms:
https://www.instagram.com/finley.eden/
https://www.facebook.com/EdenFinleyAuthor/
https://www.facebook.com/groups/absolutelyeden/
https://amzn.to/2zUlM16
https://www.edenfinley.com

ALSO BY EDEN FINLEY_

FAMOUS SERIES

Pop Star

Spotlight

Fandom

Encore

Novellas:

Rockstar Hearts

FAKE BOYFRIEND SERIES

Fake Out

Trick Play

Deke

Blindsided

Hat Trick

Novellas:

Fake Boyfriend Breakaways: A short story collection

Final Play

BOOKS COWRITTEN WITH SAXON JAMES

Power Plays & Straight A's

Face Offs & Cheap Shots

Goal Lines & First Times

Line Mates & Study Dates

Puck Drills & Quick Thrills

Egotistical Puckboy

Irresponsible Puckboy

Milton Keynes UK
Ingram Content Group UK Ltd.
UKHW011219280324
440101UK00005B/465